NANSHE CHRONICLES 1

GAMBIT

JESSIE KWAK

THERE'S MORE TO THE STORY!

... in *Artemis City Shuffle*.

Raj and Lasadi may both be down on their luck. But as a series of near misses and close calls spin their futures into a collision course, that's about to change.

Get the free Nanshe Chronicles prequel novella!
jessiekwak.com/nanshe

GHOST PIRATE GAMBIT

NANSHE CHRONICLES 1

But you, children of space, you restless in rest, you shall not be trapped nor tamed.

Your house shall be not an anchor but a mast.

KHALIL GIBRAN

CHAPTER 1
RAJ

RAJ CAN'T REMEMBER a time he felt so alive.

He's having trouble describing the sensation. It's like he hadn't realized the edges of the world had gone gray until someone flipped a switch, and suddenly? Color, sound, scents. Like he's been let out of a sensory deprivation chamber into a world of bright clothing, laughter, perfumes — all singing with possibility.

This is what he's been missing.

Not *this*, this. Not the party he's currently crashing, this soiree hosted by Parr Sumilang, Artemisian tech giant and two-martini lush. No. Raj has been missing a second chance at life, and this party is the perfect place to find it. He accepts a flute of sparkling wine from a passing server and pauses in the entryway, taking it all in.

Parr Sumilang's home is a vast waste of space — triple-height entryway with spiraling staircases, every surface done in holographic marble and neodymium glass and gold flake. The faux-marble floors are polished to gleaming and the walls draped with green-and-gold curtains. Staircases and a gilded lift lead to generously sized balconies that appear to float — a strange illusion on a planet whose scant gravity has been artificially enhanced.

It's an ostentatious display for a place like Artemis City, which is drilled deep into the heart of the dwarf planet Artemis. Raj doesn't know anyone rich enough to afford more than a pod in the city's deepest levels, let alone afford a view.

And what a view. Sumilang's townhouse is in Artemis City's Bell — the buzzy, neon, hundred-story open core — and the floor-to-ceiling windows overlook one of the Bell's more picturesque parts: the park platforms. The townhouse is about a third of the way down the Bell, and if Raj cranes his neck he can make out Artemis City's dome far above them, the lumbering ships docking in port beyond. The Bell's floor is too far down, and shrouded in interwoven platforms and the swirling lights of traffic, to be visible.

Everyone who's anyone on Artemis — and probably the rest of the chain of dwarf planets that constitute the Pearls in Durga's Belt — is here tonight, servers dancing through the throng with trays of food and drink. The energy reminds Raj of the parties his parents threw back home in Arquelle. The mood sizzles with ambition and possibility, guests prowling the crowd in designer labels, armed with fine-edged wit. Young ones looking to impress their way into a job or sink their claws into a mate. Old ones trading parries with business rivals or hunting for new blood.

Used to be Raj found the pulsing, raw ambition of these kinds of parties exhausting. But back then, he'd been trying to live up to his father's vision and follow in his footsteps: obedient son, model academy student, decorated officer in the Arquellian navy. Raj had almost managed to convince himself he wanted it, too — until his entire life washed out from beneath his feet like sand in the retreating surf.

Raj has spent the last three years tumbling in that surf,

scraping by in the Pearls, living life as a dead man, running out of places he can breathe free. But tonight the air's sparking electric with something more than second chances.

The feeling is *hope*.

Thanks in no small part to his business partner — sorry, *former* business partner — Ruby. Their last job went bad; he's willing to admit now that it was his fault. He'd been getting sloppy and, honestly, he'd stopped caring if he walked out alive. Only, his increasing recklessness hadn't just put himself in danger — it had endangered Ruby, too. He can hardly blame her for the "fuck off forever" note she sent him after. But he can thank her.

The message had been a wake-up call. It was time for a reset, to choose a new path. And this is the job that's going to give him the opportunity.

Ruby's still not returning his calls, but he managed to get himself a new identity and secure an invitation to this party even without her magic touch — there are other hackers and data techs in the system, even if Ruby's really *through* through working with him.

He'll make it up to her somehow. For now, he needs to get to work before he squanders this opportunity for his reset.

Raj spots Parr Sumilang on one of the balconies, unmissable in his gold jacquard suit, his round cheeks red with drink and mirth, his booming, barrel-chested laugh sounding through the crowd. Everyone's keeping an eye on him — he's the richest man in the Pearls — but he's not the only mark tonight.

Tonight, everyone's on the hunt. The man in the glossy suit, screwing up his courage at the bar. The cocktail server exchanging numbers with a woman whose face Raj recognizes from fashion advertisements. The woman in the blue evening gown, squaring her shoulders to approach a group of suits who hold themselves like investors.

Raj wishes them all luck. Combs a hand through his shoulder-length black hair, returns the coy smile of the woman who's been eyeing him from her date's arm, and heads straight for the person everyone's trying to get close to tonight.

As Raj approaches, a pair of muscled suits turn his way with pointed threat. Raj ignores them — and he ignores the fact Sumilang is already having a conversation. Just like his father would have.

Can't say Raj didn't learn anything from his old man.

"Mr. Sumilang," Raj says, dialing up his most charming smile. Sumilang's brows pull in slightly, eyes glassy with vodxx and — ah, there's the glint of a lens. Pulling in information about everyone at the party, recording it, processing it. A must-have networking tool. Raj holds out his hand. "Silvan Jordan. Thank you for having me."

Sumilang's expression flares bright at the name, the haze of vodxx burning away. "Mr. Jordan!" He pumps Raj's hand enthusiastically. "It's so good of you to come." He turns to the person beside him — Raj recognizes the face from studying Sumilang's company but can't pull up a name. "This is Seo-yeon, she leads our research team."

"It's a pleasure," Raj says. He's gotten used to toning down his Arquellian accent out here in the Pearls; now he lets the drawl through in all its pompous glory. Gives the vowels their breathing room, softens his consonants; it's like slipping into a comfortable sweater. He shakes Seo-yeon's hand smoothly, then leans in to Sumilang, all apologetic. "Mr. Sumilang, I'm sorry to rush the pleasantries, especially at such an excellent party. But as I said, my shuttle leaves in a few hours. Do you have somewhere quiet we can talk?"

"Of course, of course." Sumilang doesn't have to wave back the bodyguards, they sank into the background as soon as it became clear Sumilang was expecting Raj — or Mr. Jordan, at least. "I have just the quiet place."

Sumilang leads Raj out of the main room, angling towards a hall at the back of the townhouse. While the three-story entry is a semicircular bubble on the wall of the Bell, the rest of Sumilang's home digs into the stone heart of Artemis. There may be no views from these rooms, but no expense has been spared. And for Raj, who grew up on a planet with atmosphere and horizons and plenty of room to spread out, it's one of the first homes he's been in since his exile to the Pearls that doesn't feel subtly claustrophobic.

"This isn't the usual place I discuss business," Sumilang says with a sly smile. "But I think you'll appreciate it." He waves Raj through an open door draped with deep blue velvet curtains, watching Raj for his reaction.

A burst of professional pride warms Raj's chest: His story worked.

Sumilang has brought him to his private museum hall, which could be called understated only in comparison with the rest of the distressingly lavish mansion. It's at least ten times the size of the "luxury" one-room pod Raj is currently calling home on Dima, one rock over. The walls are hung with the same velvet curtains as the doorway, the floor interspersed with faux-marble columns in gold-shot white. Glass display cases on each column reverently display the objects within.

Sumilang waves Raj past him to admire the collection. "I heard you appreciate religious esoterica," he says, which means Sumilang did his due diligence and found exactly what Raj wanted him to find.

A few faked news reports here, a falsified profile there — it wouldn't have taken much digging for Sumilang to find that the mystery Arquellian investor who'd contacted him out of the blue was a collector. And given how much money Raj had hinted at investing, Sumilang would be dying to impress him. Seeding a backstory is the sort of thing Ruby normally handled for him, but he hadn't done a bad job himself. And writing the articles on religious esoterica had been simple. He just tapped into everything he'd learned talking with Vash and Gracie — his clients for this job — over the years.

Now all he has to do is convince Sumilang that Silvan Jordan's firm is about to invest a stomach-churning amount of money in the tech magnate's new venture, then send the man off to the bar for some more celebratory vodxx, leaving Raj alone in the museum hall for two minutes.

One problem.

Looks like the catering staff are using the museum as a shortcut to get to the kitchen; a woman with pale skin and dusky blond hair scraped back into a thick, utilitarian braid is passing through now with a tray full of empty glasses. There are other routes — Raj has studied them all — but this is the shortest, and of course the catering staff would cut through here and save a few steps.

Hadn't thought of that.

The woman's not hurrying, and Raj can't blame her. Sumilang's elite guest list is stacked with people who know how to dress, not how to treat the serving staff. Still, the staff using this hall as a shortcut will get in his way. He could call out the woman's presence. Make a cutting offhand comment about how in an Arquellian home, the servants would stay out of sight; goad Sumilang into ordering the catering staff to take an alternate route.

Like his father would have done.

Raj's stomach turns. He'll have to make this work without slamming a hullbreaker through some poor woman's night.

Raj steps to the closest plinth, studies a set of ornately carved prayer beads. "Cult of Saint Meiai, Bixian expansion period," he says; he's been paying attention to Gracie's lectures on art and religious history. "I've never seen one in person. People say you're a collector, but they're understating."

"A little hobby of mine," Sumilang says with faux humility. "Ah. Here's a piece of superstition that's closer to home. A mixla."

"Meeshla," Raj says. Correcting people's pronunciations is peak arrogant Arquellian.

"So you know these oddities? I hear they're quite rare outside of Coruscan homes."

"I had a Coruscan nanny." Raj bends to examine the little figurine; the part about the Coruscan nanny is true, but until now, hers is the lone Coruscan house god he's ever seen up close. Even before Indira's moon made a bloody bid for independence from the Alliance, Arquellians hadn't been welcome in most Coruscan homes.

This mixla is minimalist, a smooth figure that could nestle in the palm of a hand. It's carved of white marble with a bright streak of turquoise cutting diagonally through the figure like a sash. Even with the stylized features, Raj gets the sense the little god is winking at him.

Someone else is watching him, too.

The caterer with the blond braid. The glare in her smoky brown eyes cuts like a knife, though it disappears into a neutral customer service smile so quickly he's not sure he caught it right. Of course, the working class on Artemis probably hate the rich of Artemis City — and no one but rich tech giants likes Arquellians out here.

Raj gives her his most devastatingly entitled Arquellian grin and a wink; she snatches up the empty martini glass Sumilang left on top of a plinth and stalks towards the far entrance of the hall.

"Coruscans even travel with them," Sumilang is saying. "They feed these little bits of rock, like pets, and they won't make a damned decision without consulting them." Raj nods along, but he's watching the caterer's back. She's fit, with an athletic build and precise, controlled movements; her shoulders stiffen at Sumilang's comment.

"Ridiculous," Raj agrees. The caterer disappears around the corner. The way she carries herself says she doesn't take shit from anyone, and there was something of a predator in the set of her mouth. If she's really a caterer, she'll be climbing her way up the food chain into management in no time.

But he'd bet anything she's not. Whatever she's really here for, though, he'll let her have her game if she'll let him have his.

Raj straightens, begins to stroll the room; he needs to distract Sumilang from the item-by-item tour of the museum and get eyes on the object he's here for. "My firm is avidly searching for new connections with Artemis City," he says. "Strong, *successful* connections. Why don't you tell me more about your product?"

Sumilang smiles shrewdly and turns to another plinth, where a hardened leather pouch painted in geometric designs is slowly spinning. "A Teshan soul purse," Sumilang says. "Of course you know Teshans believed they could capture the souls of the dying in these purses and so prolong life. My product actually does that." He laughs. "Prolongs life, not captures souls."

"It's intriguing," Raj says. "Implants, is that right?"

"Brain implants that stimulate neural regrowth," Sumilang says. "Preliminary studies in patients with degenerative brain diseases have been promising."

Raj smiles politely and tunes him out, meandering through the display of rosaries and relics and charm coins. He skimmed the schematics and marketing blurbs

Sumilang's company puts out, but he hasn't retained much of it. Ruby would have understood it — and he needs to stop thinking about how she would have done things.

Where the hell is the totem?

"My partners will need proof, of course," Raj says when Sumilang pauses for breath. "What you sent over is impressive, but do you have a market? You're pretty far from — well. From people who can afford the treatment."

"From Arquelle, you mean." Sumilang doesn't seem offended.

Raj shrugs. "Of course."

"There's wealth in Durga's Belt," Sumilang says. "And you're wise to partner with a company in Artemis City. We Artemisians have an advantage. We can speak the cultured language of Arquelle, along with the language of the vast, untapped sleeper market of Durga's Belt."

Perhaps that's true, though Artemis City is nothing like the rest of the settlements out here in the black. The rest of the belt appreciates being far enough outside the gravity wells of Indira and New Sarjun to choose their own path. Artemis City is still trying to be Arquelle; even the streets are self-cleaning, with microbes and nanites disinfecting and removing every blemish, every hint of poverty or failure swept out with the trash.

Either way, marketing a brain-regenerating device is none of his concern. He's finally spotted what he came here for: a carved obsidian totem the length of his forearm, lying on a cream silk pillow.

Gotcha.

"Believe me," Raj says, turning away from the totem without seeming to notice it. "My partners and I understand what an advantage you have out here. Let's drink to new opportunities. Perhaps — "

"We must toast." Sumilang grabs Raj's arm and drags

him towards the door. "Come, Mr. Jordan. The relics can wait."

Raj curses and lets himself be swept out, leaving the totem — his second chance — behind him.

For the moment.

CHAPTER 2
LASADI

"You should start a restaurant, Las," says the voice in her ear. "Cazinho's: Service with a Snarl."

Lasadi Cazinho hurries through the pompous tech giant's posh hallway to the kitchen, her tray of empties getting heavier by the step.

"Not now, Jay."

But Jay Kamiya is on a roll, and after working together for so many years, Lasadi has learned to simply let him talk, the comfortable cadence of his voice in the background a soothing presence and constant companion.

Jay's got a touch more Coruscan lilt than she does, one of the indications of the class differences in their upbringing, where his family was solidly blue collar and hers played government roles. The lilt's cheerful, a little cocky, always joking until the real danger hits. Whether in dogfights together as pilot and mechanic during the Coruscan war for independence from Arquelle, or these last three years doing odd jobs for Nico Garnet since they washed up in the Pearls, Jay's voice has been her lifeline.

"I can see it already," he continues. "You'll have one of those port diners, where everyone's too disoriented and jetlagged to care what they're ordering, while you're at the register yelling at them to hurry the hell up if they don't know what they want the minute they walk in. I bet you take people's plate before they've had the last bite, too."

"Mmm-hmm."

Lasadi is only half listening; her attention is split, caught partly by the job at hand and partly by the Arquellian talking with Sumilang in the museum hall.

Something about him sticks like a barb in her mind.

He's eye-catching, and holds himself like he knows it. Wears that suit like he was born to it, his thick black hair curling loose around his ears to brush his shoulders. The casual way he'd run slender, tawny fingers through it, the way the flecks of gold embedded in his deep brown eyes caught the light. And, of course, the easy Arquellian grin that says he owns the world and has never had to worry about whether he's got enough food, water, air to survive until tomorrow.

Lasadi can appreciate a piece of candy without letting him go to her head — no matter how long it's been — but something happened when he caught her watching him. She can't say whether it was a flicker of an eyelash, a curve of his lips, a lift of his chin. But for a split second he'd dropped his mask, and there wasn't simply a live wire beneath the surface — a whole damned wild current of electricity had surged through her.

A fire like that could light you up like a torch. Or burn you to ash.

Danger. The man is pure danger. Maybe he really is an investor with ulterior motives he's keeping Sumilang in the dark about. Or maybe he's a grifter trying to get his hands in Sumilang's pockets. Lasadi doesn't care what game he's playing so long as he keeps Sumilang out of her hair long enough for her to finish this job.

And so long as she doesn't have to ever see him again.

Because he definitely saw straight through her, all the way to the core, and she can't afford to have that happen on such a critical job.

She rounds the hall to the kitchen, where the catering staff have set up for the evening. A kid in a busser's outfit is lounging outside the door, probably trying to avoid the explosive volcano in an apron who calls himself the head chef. Too bad.

"Here, I have to get back out there." She thrusts the tray of empties at the kid, who shoves his comm back in his pocket barely in time to catch it. She snatches Sumilang's glass back off the tray before the kid slinks away in resignation. "It's chipped," she says in explanation. "Go."

The busser — like all the catering staff — is wearing a pair of silver antimicrobial gloves. Lasadi is, too, but hers have been given an upgrade: a special coating Jay managed to procure from a friend, which he's reassured her will definitely, definitely work.

Here goes nothing.

Lasadi cups her right hand around Sumilang's martini glass, trying to mimic his grip and careful not to smudge the existing fingerprints. The faint flicker of a status bar pops up on her lens to tell her it's working, but she's not getting the full array of data Jay is back on the *Nanshe*.

"What do you see?" she asks Jay.

"I'd run Kamiya's Kitchen."

Voices from down the hall — a bartender and a cocktailer, bitching about some aristocrat in a blue jacket. Lasadi melts into a supply closet as they round the corner. She's got a cover story for if she gets caught lingering out here, of course, but she's not getting caught.

Not now, not ever.

"Jay?" she whispers.

"I'd run Kamiya's Kitchen," Jay says again. "Open up right next door, give you a run for your money."

"The glove, Jay."

"Throttle down, it's loading." He makes that clicking sound he always does with his tongue when he's thinking. "I'd serve barbecue like my grandma used to make."

"You've never made me barbecue," Lasadi says.

"I've made it for Chiara," Jay points out. "You never come over when I invite you. And the *Nanshe* doesn't have a proper kitchen."

Neither did the barracks of the Coruscan Liberation Army where they met, Lasadi supposes. Whether in the CLA or in their time on the run since the independence effort went up in flames, what she's known of Jay's cooking has been fast and utilitarian. Calories in to support calories out. Lasadi'd assumed that meant Jay was as uninterested as she is when it comes to domestic matters, but apparently he cooks for his girlfriend.

"I won't believe it until I taste it," Lasadi says. The voices have faded; the hallway's empty once more.

"Shift your grip," Jay orders. "Okay. Again."

"Is it loading?"

"What you should do is, you should talk Nico into some better kitchen gear on the *Nanshe*," Jay says. "After this job — "

"Jay."

"Sorry."

He clicks his tongue again in the silence, and Lasadi scans the hall. She doesn't own the *Nanshe*, Nico Garnet does. And "after this job" is not something she wants to think about, not if Jay's decided he no longer wants to work for Nico. This is Jay's last job, he's told her. He's got a girl, he wants to settle down. Hell, even in his job-banter fantasies he's talking about opening side-by-side restaurants.

And Lasadi?

Has no fucking clue what's next.

She shoves away the thought. Just enjoy working this last job with Jay, figure out what comes next after.

"Glove's ready," Jay says.

Lasadi takes a sharp breath of relief and glances at the silver glove, but she doesn't see any difference. "How do I know it's working?"

"You'll know when lasers don't shoot out of the base of the plinth and kneecap you."

"Very reassuring."

"Trust me, Las," Jay says. She can hear him typing. "This is good tech. I mean, I'm not — "

"You're not a hacker, I know." They've had this conversation a dozen times, about bringing in new blood. They'll need a few more people to complete the rest of this job, but Lasadi has put off looking. Maybe she can find someone decent once they get back to Ironfall, someone she won't hate working with — someone not like the stony mercenaries Nico Garnet normally assigns to jobs that require a few more bodies. Garnet's mercs are always competent, but soulless. And having them around always ends up reminding her of how good it used to be, back in the CLA, working with a group of people who believed in the same cause you did, and had your back no matter what.

Now Jay's the one person in this entire universe she trusts. He's had her back through the worst days of her life and beyond — and everyone else she used to trust is either dead or out of her reach.

"Plus," Jay continues. "I doubt you'll get kneecapped. Your reflexes are too good."

"Thank you."

"Not good enough to run the gauntlet you'll need to if you trip the security, though," he says, cheerful. "Sumilang hired almost every private security guard in Artemis and Dima for this event. So get moving, and — *DON'T!*"

Lasadi freezes with her right fingertips millimeters from

the handle of the supply closet door. "What is it?" she hisses.

"Don't touch anything else with that hand."

Lasadi snatches her hand back. "I thought the prints were set after the program ran."

"Nanites are shifty bastards and I don't want to take any chances. So don't mox them up by touching anything until you get back to the museum hall. Go, *gogo*."

"Sumilang?" she asks Jay.

"At the bar."

Which means the Arquellian asshole investor is probably there with him. Good. Las opens the supply closet with her left hand, then drops the martini glass in a nearby recycler chute, shoulders loosening and heart rate picking up in delicious anticipation. After the last few hours playing the role of catering staff, she's finally getting to the good part.

"Heya. Sweetheart."

Lasadi stiffens at the sound of the head chef's voice behind her.

"Deep breaths, Las," Jay murmurs in her ear. "Deep breaths."

Lasadi has never been one for keeping her feelings off her face, but she's practicing the finer art of acting lately, since more of these jobs seem to require it. She musters a patient smile as she turns to find the head chef looming in the doorway to the kitchen. The table beside the door is laden with food that needs to be run out to the party.

"Yeah?" She's trying for cheerful.

"I don't know where you servers all hide when I need you," the chef grumbles, jabbing a silver-gloved finger at a tray of puff pastry tartlets. "Take that out to the terrace, then."

"*Knee-capping lasers,*" Jay hisses in her ear.

"I'm going on break," Lasadi tries. She curls her right

hand protectively into a loose fist, harboring nightmares of smudging the shifty bastard nanites out of their new Parr Sumilang's fingerprint configuration. "But I can send someone back."

The head chef's cheeks flare even redder. "The nerve on you — there's no such thing as break," he scoffs. "Take the tray or I'll have security dump you out and you can forget about pay, can't you. The *help* you get these days." He's working himself into a roar; it's echoing down the hall. "People used to *work*, and now they expect *handouts*, to be *paid* for standing around smoking goddamned *moss* instead of doing the fucking jobs I hired them for."

He curls a lip at Lasadi. "Get on now, would you."

"Okay, okay." Lasadi reaches for the tray. "I got it."

"What you need to get is a *work ethic*," the chef growls. He starts to stalk back into the kitchen, then stops in the doorway as though thinking better of it and glares at her until she actually moves towards the tray.

"*Lasers*," Jay says.

"I know," she mutters. She manages to cradle the tray, awkward, using the side of her right hand to scoot the tray onto her left. The head chef shoots her one last disgusted look before finally turning his wrath back on the kitchen staff; still, Lasadi waits until she's turned the corner into the museum hall before ditching the tray. A long table has been set up on one side of the hall — maybe Sumilang thought they'd bring the party in here among his weird obsessive collection at some point and would need refreshments. If anyone asks, Las can claim that's what she's doing here with the tray of puff pastries.

For now, though, the coast is clear.

Finally.

Las cuts through the faux-marble plinths, attention on her objective — and feet slowing of their own accord as she passes the mixla Sumilang and that Arquellian bastard were making fun of. She frowns at it, annoyed at herself for pausing but curious nonetheless.

It's much smaller than the one her grandmother has set up in her kitchen, and a completely different stone and carving style, but the sight of it unseals a store of memories from home. The scent of lavender tea in the morning; Grandma sharing her cup with the mixla, pouring the hot liquid into a thimble-sized bowl with a prayer. The perfume of roses at new year; the shrine covered in petals and Lasadi's hands bleach-rough from scrubbing the house clean. Crumbs of cake and precious coffee beans set out on ancestors' birthdays. A smear of blood from her little brother's first lost tooth — Lasadi had yelled at him to wash it off first but Grandma had said the mixla wouldn't mind.

And, of course, the silver necklace she'd left on the altar when she left home against her grandmother's wishes to join the liberation movement.

Sumilang had called the mixla superstition, but it's more than that. Her grandmother was a Coruscan senator, and the most rational person Las knew.

Knows.

Her grandmother's still alive, of course. It's Lasadi who's technically dead — or worse. Her family had held banishing on hearing of her death; Anton told her. Her grandmother, her sister, her brother, her cousins — they'd ensured her name will go unspoken and her memory unshared because of the things she was responsible for in the war. No one is leaving offerings at Grandma's shrine for Lasadi's memory. She might as well have never existed.

"Las."

She blinks the memories aside, clears her head with a sharp shake. "I'm on it."

She scans the room once more to make sure she's still alone, then stops in front of the plinth that holds the obsidian totem. She tries not to think of kneecapping lasers, a hand's span away from her shins, as she slowly settles her hand on the bioscanner.

"This better work," she mutters.

"Trust me."

"You know I do."

Yet when the bioscanner pulses red three times under her silver-gloved fingertips, each pulse spikes Lasadi's adrenaline through the roof.

She smudged the fingerprints, she thinks.

She didn't get a good enough grip on the martini glass.

Jay's hacker set them up to fail.

Nico set them up to fail.

"Is that normal?" she hisses; Jay clicks his tongue. That's an *I don't know.*

Her muscles tense, ready to leap back from the plinth — and she freezes.

Behind her, someone clears their throat.

"So." The elongated vowel holds an unmistakable Arquellian drawl; Lasadi spins to meet those familiar dark eyes, light catching in the gold flecks of his irises like a warning. The mask the Arquellian asshole wore for Sumilang is gone entirely, and the way his gaze bores through her sets every fiber of her being on fire.

Danger.

CHAPTER 3
RAJ

THE WOMAN with the blond braid has dropped the service industry facade, but she doesn't seem worried at being caught red-handed in theft. There's a sort of feral grace in the way she tensed at his voice; she holds herself like a fighter. Something tells him she'll struggle almost to the death before accepting captivity — and that she's done it before.

Her gaze rakes down his body, evaluating; the calculating glint in her smoky brown eyes tells Raj she's no stranger to getting herself out of a tricky situation.

Oh. And that she'll write him off as collateral damage in a heartbeat.

She definitely isn't a member of the catering team. Raj likes being right more when it doesn't mean a major kink in his plans.

"Stay back," she hisses. Her fingertips are on the plinth's control panel, her hand clad in one of those shimmering silver antimicrobial gloves all the catering staff are wearing. "You'll get us both killed."

Raj freezes.

"Lasers," the woman says in explanation. She waves her

free hand at the base of the plinth. "They'll kneecap us both if I screw this up."

"I knew you weren't a caterer," Raj says.

"And I knew you weren't an investor," she answers. The bioscanner under her fingertips shifts from threatening red to a soothing green, pulses green a second time, then stays that way. A faint click sounds from the control panel and the forcefield around the obsidian totem dissolves with a sigh. The woman's shoulders loosen imperceptibly. "But you didn't turn me in to Sumilang."

"It wouldn't have been polite."

"Polite? It'd fit perfect with the asshole Arquellian act." She tilts her chin to study him. "Unless it's not an act."

And at that he places her accent: Corusca.

Ah. Could be another problem.

Indira's moon is the newest member of the Indiran Alliance, which includes Arquelle. Only Arquelle is a founding member — and perhaps a touch aggressive when it comes to bringing new countries into the fold. Corusca's citizens had been split on joining, and Arquelle had pushed, coercing an unpopular decision through the Senate. Frustrations in Corusca led to an Alliance occupation, which led to a viciously effective insurgency, which led to a retaliatory "peace" effort. Which led to Raj's first command post.

Tensions had spread on both sides, until the deaths of seven hundred and twelve souls aboard a neutral New Manilan medical transport poured fuel on the flames. The resulting Battle of Tannis had been disastrous for everyone involved — but far, far worse for Coruscans.

"Let's talk this through," Raj says.

"Nothing to talk about," the Coruscan woman says. "You walk back out of this room and I won't tell Sumilang about your grift. We both get what we want."

"One problem," says Raj. He may feel bad about the

war, but he's got a job to do. He lifts his chin to the obsidian totem behind her. "I'm here for that."

She blinks in surprise, but her hesitation doesn't last long. A flash of decision in her eyes; he tries to move before she does, but she's too quick. She ducks his arm, snatching the totem as she pivots, an elbow to his ribs as she whirls past.

Raj muffles a groan at the burst of pain in his side, bites back a curse as he lunges after her, acutely aware of the slightest sounds of their scuffle. The party outside the museum hall is loud, but not loud enough.

He catches her arm and spins her off her footing; she nearly drops the totem, but as he lunges for it, she tightens her grip once more and swings it at his head. He ducks, just in time. The breeze it makes passing over his head sets his hair on end.

She wasn't expecting to miss, and she put a touch too much force into the swing. Just enough that Raj can use her momentum to push her off her footing. She pivots at the last second to avoid hitting another golden plinth — this one topped with a saint's altar — and Raj tackles her before she can take off running again.

They roll to the floor, barely missing the tray of puff pastries she'd left on the table against the wall, Raj cushioning their fall to keep from making too much noise. She's wiry, but he's stronger, and he's gaining the upper hand. He catches her wrist above her head when she tries to swing the totem at him again, frees the electric barb from his belt with his other hand, and jams it against her temple.

She goes still, chest heaving with breath. Every muscle in her body is tense; he can feel her taut strength pressed against his own. She smells like vetiver, with heady undertones of sweet caramel and brush fire.

Focus, Raj.

"I think I win," Raj says.

In response, the woman ghosts him a smile and glances down. When he tries to follow her gaze, the cold point of a blade pricks below his chin. The corner of her mouth curls up.

"Try it," she says.

The electric barb won't kill her, but if he discharges it into her temple it could do some gnarly things to her wiring. Course, he won't get far at all if she bites that blade into his jugular. He's not interested in leaving any bodies behind on this job, but he's pretty sure she doesn't have that same hang-up — especially about an Arquellian. Either way, she's faster than him. Even if he was willing to pull the trigger, she could slit his throat before the jolt knocked her cold.

She's watching him make his decision, a hint of amusement on her lips. Like she's already solved this particular puzzle and she's waiting for him to catch on.

Her lips part as though she's about to speak, then she glances up, eyelashes sweeping wide.

He hears it, too: voices heading towards them.

Raj acts before he can second-guess himself, rolling them both out of sight under the hem of the tablecloth. He keeps his grip on her wrist, the electric barb against her temple. He can still feel the edge of her blade against his throat — only now their positions are reversed and she's straddling his chest.

The woman gives a startled laugh, then presses her lips shut tight and holds as still as he, waiting for the scuffing heels and muttered complaints of the caterers to pass by. Her professional mask has melted into something more playful, and he revises her age downwards. She can't be any older than him, despite the experienced way she carries herself.

"What's your name?" Raj whispers when the caterers

have passed. One of the woman's eyebrows lift, but she doesn't move the knife from his throat. "I'm Raj."

"Hi, Raj. I know you're not going to pull that trigger."

"And you're not going to slit my throat."

"I'm not?"

"You've got a buyer for this thing?"

"None of your business."

"Mine pays top dollar. Tell you what. We work together to get out of this and I'll make sure you get your share. Fifty-fifty."

"I kill you, I get one hundred percent."

"You don't know how good my buyer's rates can be. What's your name?"

The woman snorts a laugh and moves without warning, rolling off him and out from under the table, disappearing in a rustle of tablecloth.

Raj hisses out a curse and scrambles out after her, but the woman's halfway across the hall by the time he gets to his feet. And — how the hell? — she stole his electric barb.

She glances back to gauge her lead, and that's why she doesn't notice him: the burly wall of a security guard stepping around the corner. She runs smack into the guard's chest and the big man's hands close around her shoulders like vise grips.

And there's that animal desperation flashing over her face once more — the wild fear of the trap, the feral instinct to fight her way out even if it kills her.

"Hey, I'm so sorry," Raj calls. He lets his voice slur, lets his asshole Arquellian drawl lengthen, puts a wobble in his step as he catches up to the woman and the guard. "I wasn't trying to upset you, I completely misread the sitsh — the situation." He straightens his tie and shines chagrin at the security guard before turning back to the woman. "I'm an idiot. I'm sorry."

The fear in her eyes drains away as she realizes his

charade; a mask of faux fury slips into its place. She shrugs her arm free from the security guard and slaps Raj across the face.

"Shit, woman." Raj massages his jaw and stares at her in unfeigned surprise.

"I have to get back to work," she announces haughtily. She jabs a finger at Raj's chest. "And you're cut off." She pins the security guard with her glare; he flinches back out of reflex. "He's cut off."

"Yes, ma'am," the security guard says, stepping out of her way.

"Wait," Raj calls to her retreating back. The security guard's subtle shift in stance says the big man isn't going to let Raj go after her. "What's your name?"

She's not going to tell him, he knows that. But it's one last reminder he's the reason neither of them got caught, and all she's leaving him with is a stinging cheek and empty pockets. The woman glances over her shoulder. Her face is angled away from the security guard, her hand is not — even so, the wink and the rude gesture are a perfectly matched set.

"Looks like your party's over, sir," the security guard tells him.

Raj clenches his jaw in frustration. He has to get that totem. He has to get outside and figure out where she'll go — maybe he can go back to the hacker he bought tonight's identity from, ask for help with the security footage, track her down before she disappears for good.

He keeps his shoulders loose and grins sheepishly at the guard. "Sorry about that, man," he says.

"I'll call you a ride," the security guard says. "What's your name?"

Raj opens his mouth to spit out his alias, but he's too slow. "Silv— "

"Raj Demetriou," says a voice behind him.

Ice pours down Raj's spine and he turns slowly to come face-to-face with Parr Sumilang and three of the biggest guards he's ever seen. Sumilang's cheeks are still flushed, but now the heat of the vodxx is joined by fury. He lifts a finger, jabbing it at Raj's chest.

"Artemis City security is on their way," he says to Raj. "And it seems you've developed a reputation. I think they'll be *very* happy to get their hands on you."

CHAPTER 4
LASADI

SHE'S HOME FREE. She can feel it in her bones, the moment in every job when the dubious variables click into place and the forever-branching uncertainties resolve into a single, well-lit path. The obsidian totem is secured, she hasn't been made, and the olds have gifted her a distraction on a golden platter. Now she just has to head through the kitchen, down the service stairs, and out the back — leaving the caterer's jacket in a bin and letting loose her braid. From there it's one block to the tram station where she'll disappear in the crowds. Final stop: the *Nanshe* and home.

Only one thing.

"Don't you even think about it, Las," Jay mutters in her ear.

The Arquellian asshole, Raj — he's moxed, his cover's blown. It's not her fault, and it's definitely not her responsibility. Just like him unsnarling her mess with the security guard wasn't *his* responsibility.

He could have turned her in, but instead he was about to let her walk away with the goods. Maybe it was part self-preservation — she could have taken him down with her.

But she senses something deeper. Raj, whoever he is, doesn't entirely belong in this world of backstabbing criminals Lasadi has grown accustomed to.

Doesn't mean you have to catch the flak for him.

After all, she's learned better, hasn't she? After the disaster at the end of the war, well. If she's learned anything in the past three years, it's that Jay's the only one she can trust. After Anton —

And you're going to keep letting Anton define you?

Olds be damned. Lasadi takes a sharp, annoyed breath and melts into an alcove where she can watch the scene play out.

"Las!"

"I'm thinking."

Three years ago, she wouldn't have had to think. Old Lasadi would have gone with her gut, gone out on a limb for the charismatic stranger in a heartbeat, given him the benefit of the doubt. Old Lasadi still believed in the innate goodness of people.

Walk away, Las.

She stays welded to the spot.

Sumilang's cheeks are red with drink and anger, but the glassiness in his eyes is all top-shelf vodxx; he's been downing martinis all evening. He stretches up to his full height — though it's hardly impressive when surrounded by burly mercs — and jabs a finger at Raj's chest.

"Your cover is blown, Demetriou," Sumilang slurs. "You got your false identity from a hacker who owes me, and he sent me a warning. Search him."

The security guard who'd caught Lasadi digs his meaty fingers into Raj's biceps, holding him still while one of the others pats him down. They won't find the totem, and apparently Raj wasn't carrying another weapon besides the electric barb Las stole, because the guard steps back empty handed.

"He's clean," the guard says, puzzled.

"Because I'm not a thief," says Raj. He brushes off the security guard's grip and lifts his chin to Sumilang. "You're right, I'm not who I said I was, and I apologize for the ruse. But an antiquities thief who is wanted by the Alliance has taken refuge in Artemis City, and my mission is to apprehend him. I've been building trust with your local lowlifes as part of my investigation, which is where I met your hacker. I thought using his services would help build trust and ingratiate me further into the criminal community."

Sumilang frowns at him. "You're a — "

"I'm a special agent with the Indiran Alliance."

"Bullshit," says Sumilang, but he sounds uncertain. A savvy businessman like him wouldn't want to risk the wrath of the Alliance, if it turns out he's wrong.

Lasadi drums her fingers against her thigh. Maybe this guy will manage to talk his way out of the situation after all. Of course, if he does, it's another sign that he's a silver-tongued grifter and she should set a course far clear of him.

"You heard him," Jay says in her ear. "He's Alliance. Get out of there, Las."

"Hold on."

There's a chance he's actually telling the truth. Lasadi hasn't heard of Alliance special agents operating out in Durga's Belt, this far away from Indira. But the Alliance did get stronger when it crushed the insurgence on Corusca, and this man does have an air of military training.

"Let me tell you what," Raj is saying. "I'll give my supervisor a call. She'll be more than thrilled to have your help on this case, Mr. Sumilang. This could lead to some very good connections with Alliance corporations."

Sumilang nods unconsciously along with Raj, the new piece of information sifting slow through his mind and searching for a place to stick. "Why don't you call her," he says after a moment. "We can head back to my office, and — "

Sumilang's gaze shifts past Raj to the museum hall, where the plinth that used to hold the totem is empty. His cheeks blaze, frantic.

"Where's the totem?"

Raj holds up his hands. "As I said, the thief I've been — "

"You're a spy," Sumilang snarls. "Which corp do you work for?"

"I'm an Indiran Alliance special agent, Mr. Sumilang. I don't work for a corp."

"I don't care who you say you are. You're not on Indira, Mr. Demetriou. And you're about to find out how we deal with corporate espionage in the Pearls."

A pair of guards clamp their hands on Raj's shoulders.

"I don't know anything about corporate espionage," Raj says; the faintest note of desperation has crept into his voice. "An antiquities thief — "

"There are far more valuable antiquities in this museum," says Sumilang. "And only one reason you would have stolen that particular totem." He waves a hand at the guards. "Take him."

"Jay," Lasadi whispers. "I need some friends."

"You're wasting a perfect exit plan on an Arquellian," Jay grumbles.

"I owe you."

"Yeah you do." He sighs. "Demon army's good to go when you are."

Lasadi fishes a ten-sided silver Devilier die out of her pocket and taps the sequence to arm it, then counts to three and rolls it down the hallway. The sound of it striking the faux-marble floors can't be heard above the scuffle of Raj's futile struggle against the guards.

The die comes to a rest at the toe of Sumilang's gold

dress boot. Lasadi drums her fingers against the wall, silently counting. Alliance special agent, Arquellian investor, Pearls grifter lowlife? Whoever this guy is, Lasadi's about to find out what he's made of.

The hallway erupts — voices echoing off the walls, the sound of bullets ricocheting overhead. A full, 360-degree immersive auditory experience designed to cause maximum chaos and confusion.

It's immediately clear which of the guards have actual military training and which took the bar-brawler path to their career in private security. Sumilang cries out as two of his more levelheaded guards get him to cover; the other two are swinging their guns wild, too shocked to go for decent cover or secure their boss.

And Raj Demetriou reacts like he's been here before.

He breaks free of the one security guard who's still halfway holding him and pivots away, decking the guy across the face and sprinting down the hall towards Lasadi. Good instinct, but the security guards on the main floor are going to be running this way to check on the noise. He'll run straight into a swarm of them if he continues.

"Hey!" she barks from her alcove, and he slows; he doesn't seem surprised to see her. "Follow me."

She darts past him, leading him down the side hallway and back into the kitchen, where the sounds of "gunfire" are fainter and the staff are more confused than frightened.

"What's going on out there?" roars the head chef.

Lasadi rolls her eyes. "These people can't hold their liquor," she says. She pushes past him, fingertips dipping into his jacket pocket to close around his keycard. "I'm going to grab the mop."

No one stops them until they're at the staff entrance, where the guard in the loading dock has obviously been alerted to the chaos inside. He straightens, pulling out his stun carbine and shouting a warning.

"They're in the kitchen!" Raj yells at him. "Go!"

The security guard's head swivels between Lasadi and Raj and the shouts following them out the door; he scowls as he decides he's been tricked, but Raj had bought them enough time to cross the loading dock without the guard firing on them.

Lasadi dives for one of the refrigerated delivery pods emblazoned with the catering company's logo, throwing herself in the driver's seat. Raj doesn't wait for an invitation to pull himself into the passenger seat beside her. She jams the head chef's keycard into the dashboard and grinds the little pod into gear.

An energy blast from the security guard's carbine ripples over the insulated body of the pod as she slams her way through the security grate and skids into Artemis City's transit channels.

"Locking in," the little pod chirps.

Lasadi jabs at the override button to keep the steering manual and swerves through oncoming traffic to take a surprise left into a crosschannel. She overrides the pod's lock-in request once more — it sounds a bit more peevish this time — and wrenches the controls sharp to the right, straightening out the fishtail at the last second to dock perfectly in a station out front of a nightclub. A sea of neon hands flashes eerie above the club's entrance.

Raj is clinging white-knuckled to the door handle. "Thanks," he says.

"No problem." Lasadi kicks open the driver's side door. "You're on your own from here. Pod's too noticeable."

She tosses her caterer's jacket on the seat, then sets out at a pace designed to get her out of the area quick without attracting attention.

"Nice driving," Raj says over her shoulder.

She glances back; he's keeping up. "I'm not a bad pilot, either."

"Where are you going?"

"None of your business."

"My way off Artemis is compromised. I assume you're not staying here."

Lasadi hesitates; Jay clears his throat in her ear.

"You're not bringing an Alliance agent on this ship," Jay says.

"He's not an agent," Lasadi mutters, turning her back on Raj. "And it's not your ship."

"It's not yours either," Jay points out. "And if he *is* Alliance? Nico's going to blow a gasket."

That does give her pause. "He could be playing a line," she says. "And either way he saved my ass back there."

"He was just covering his own," Jay points out.

Las checks over her shoulder, but Raj doesn't seem to be listening to her. "Fire up the engines," she says to Jay. She turns back to Raj. "Come on."

They're not far from the docks by transit tube, and as Lasadi wordlessly changes up her appearance, so does Raj. Tying his shoulder-length black hair back under a hat, donning a pair of gold-tinted glasses he'd had hidden away somewhere. Shirt untucked and clever jacket turned inside out to go from evening wear to street style, he lounges in his seat with a simple bangle on his wrist his sole piece of jewelry. The look is as good on him as the aristocratic gentleman one was.

The corner of his mouth tugs into a smile when he notices her attention; Lasadi turns away to stare out the window with heat flaring in her cheeks. *You're on a job, Las, not picking up a toy for the night.*

She can still smell his cologne on her from their fight, and her body blazes with memory. As though she can still feel his weight. She tells herself it's old scars acting up. Jay would tell her it's pent-up frustration and she needs a good night out on the town, and he'd probably be right. After the crush of family in her grandmother's home, then the chaos of the CLA barracks, Lasadi's grown accustomed to solitude. But besides the doctors that pieced her back together after the Battle of Tannis, no one has touched her in three years. It's clouding her judgement.

Sure, he's charming. Playful, when they tussled in the museum hall; precise and practiced with his movements. He's smart, he keeps making her laugh. But he's Arquellian — or is he? She's seen a half-dozen faces of Raj Demetriou in the past thirty minutes, and the only thing she knows for certain is he's a smooth liar.

Slow certainty dawns on her: She's letting another grifter blind her. First Anton, now this Arquellian — her grandmother's words echo in her head: "Think with your brain, not with your heart, Lala. That's what it's there for." She hasn't slipped up once in three years. Until today, when she threw her mission out the window and endangered Jay by going back for an Arquellian with a captivating smile.

When she meets Raj's gaze again she's got her emotions under control. He's nice to look at, sure. He kept her out of enemy sights, and she repaid the debt. When he smiles, she returns it — and tells herself she feels nothing.

No one bothers them through dock security, and Las breathes easier when the *Nanshe* is in sight, cargo ramp lowered for them.

Jay's got one shoulder propped in the cargo bay door, waiting for them. He greets Lasadi with a jerk of his chin, but he steps out to block Raj's path as soon as she's past him. His rifle kicks up, aimed square at Raj's chest.

"Got some questions for you first, man."

CHAPTER 5
RAJ

Raj lifts his hands, going still with one foot on the cargo ramp, the other on the dock.

The man standing beside his mystery rescuer is skinny but strong, the lean, hard muscles of his bare brown arms tensed as he aims the rifle, a shock of black hair falling over his eye as he aims down the sight. He's dressed like a cross between a ship's mechanic and a backup dancer from your kid's favorite new kafusa group, wearing frayed work trousers slung low over his hips and a band promo tee with the sleeves and neckband cut out. Silver spike studs jut from his ears; his fingernails are caked black with grease.

And he's definitely not a fan of Raj.

The mechanic narrows his dark eyes. "Accent's fake, right?" he asks Raj. "Tell me it's fake."

His lilt's Coruscan, like the woman's, but with a harder, working-class edge. Raj glances between the pair, trying to judge the threat. She doesn't seem concerned — either for her own safety or for Raj's. There's a chance she led him here as a trap, but it's a weird route to go. If she wanted him gone she could've let Sumilang's guards beat him to death. Dragging him here for her buddy to shoot him in the middle of the docks is a little personal.

That war between Corusca and the Alliance went down bad, though. Some people hold grudges in unusual ways.

Raj could lie. He's always been good with accents, ever since he was a kid. He could go pure Ironfall, or Teguçan patois. He could fake a Coruscan lilt like these two, so good even the natives wouldn't second-guess him.

He can be anyone he wants to be, that's the blessing and the curse.

The woman is watching him impassively; the mechanic's finger tightens on the trigger.

"It's real," Raj says. "I'm Arquellian born and raised."

The pair share a look. The mechanic's says, *I told you so.*

"Tell me at least you were lying to Sumilang about being an Alliance agent."

"I'm not an Alliance agent, just a drifter living in Ironfall for the moment." A muscle twitches in the woman's cheek; she's searching for the lie, and the shrewdness in her eyes tells him she'll find it. "I was an officer in the Arquellian navy," Raj says. "Long time ago."

That doesn't make the mechanic lower his rifle, but Raj didn't expect it to.

"You fight against Corusca?" the mechanic asks, and Raj swallows. If he tells the truth to this question, there's a good chance he dies with a bullet in his chest in the middle of Artemis City's docks. But this woman came back for him. She risked her life; he's not going to repay her with lies. Raj clears his throat, the word *Yes* on the tip of his tongue.

"Let him in, Jay," the woman says, before Raj can speak. "We don't have time for this."

The mechanic — Jay — doesn't lower his rifle, so Raj doesn't move either. "It's fine," Raj says. "I'll go."

"I offered you a ride and I'm giving you one," she says.

She turns her back on them both, disappearing into the cargo bay. "Come on," she calls back. "Both of you."

Jay lowers his rifle, keeps his scowl in place; Raj takes a deep breath.

Maybe she didn't let Raj answer because she's impatient to get going. Maybe she's already made her decision to help and she doesn't want to hear the thing that'll make her regret it. Maybe she can see the truth on his face and is planning on sending him out an airlock once they've left Artemis City.

Maybe getting on this ship with a pair of Coruscans is an incredibly bad plan, but staying in Artemis City with a blown cover and no ride off is a worse one.

Raj takes slow steps up the cargo ramp, giving the mechanic a smile the other man doesn't return. "I appreciate the ride," Raj says. Jay ignores him, slipping the safety on and slinging the rifle over one muscled shoulder. He turns to punch buttons on the control panel, keeping one eye on Raj as he walks by.

The ship's a boxy cargo hauler, a Mapalad Lowboy similar to one Vash and Gracie have junked out on their asteroid; he has a vague memory of Vash waxing rhapsodic about how reliable the model is. The name *Nanshe* was emblazoned on the hull.

"Where do you want me?" he asks Jay.

Jay sighs. "Where do you want the Arquellian," he asks over the comms. His lips press together in annoyance while he waits for a response, then he jerks his chin at the ladder. "Las says bridge. Don't touch anything."

"Thanks," Raj calls at the other man's back as he stalks past him to the engine room.

Raj hasn't been inside Vash and Gracie's decrepit Lowboy, but this one has a pretty standard scrapper layout, with a belly full of cargo bay that doubles as auxiliary living area during the long-haul runs. Crew cabins and galley are on the upper deck, with the bridge at the top. The Coruscan woman is strapped into the pilot's chair; she spares him the briefest glance before going back to her checklist.

Normally he'd offer to help, but right now seems like keeping a low profile is the way to go if he doesn't want to ruin his tenuous welcome. Besides, these two are old pros at this, rapid-fire commands and checklists back and forth from the bridge to the engine room until finally they break away from the Artemis City docks with a gut-churning lurch and shoot out into the black.

Raj waits until the ship's on autopilot before he interrupts.

"Big ship for a crew of two," he says. It's strikingly clean, too, at least the bit he's seen. No sign they've got any attachment to it beyond a place to crash between jobs.

The woman spins her chair, tilting her chin as she studies him. She ditched the severe braid on the transit tube, and now her dusky blond hair is back in a loose ponytail, strands of it floating around her face. Her pale skin is ghostly in the blue lights of the dash, her eyes hard, and he can't tell if it's the lighting or the fact that he revealed he was an Arquellian officer that extinguished the vibrant flame of soul he'd seen back in Sumilang's mansion.

Raj fights the urge to crack a joke, to excuse himself, to come up with a story to get away from that searching gaze.

Growing up, his parents had seen only the child they'd wanted to see, and he'd shaped himself as best he could to fit that mold. He'd followed the same path his father had, wearing the right mask every step of the way: the model student at the naval academy, the promising young officer moving up the ranks, the eager new captain ready to earn his stripes in glorious battle and finally win the respect of his father, the admiral.

Then his life had been smashed to pieces and he'd been

swept out to sea. He'd washed up in the Pearls with a whole new set of masks to wear: hardened criminal, wise-cracking grifter, carefree thief. In all his life, no one's ever looked at him as clearly as this woman is studying him now.

Well, no one but Ruby — and his once business partner has washed her hands of him. There's a reason Raj keeps the mask on tight.

Whatever this woman sees, though, she doesn't call Jay to haul him out the airlock. Instead, she pulls the totem out of her jacket and releases it from her fingertips, letting it spin gently in front of her.

"You were telling the truth to Sumilang, weren't you?" she asks. "You don't work for a corp. You have no idea what you were trying to steal."

Raj can't help the surprised laugh. This wasn't where he was expecting the conversation to go.

"Art history may not be my area of expertise, but I do my research," he says. "It's a sacred object from the Tisare cult, believed to be around two centuries old, found about thirty years ago in an excavation of the cult's last known settlement on asteroid N49-B1008. Obsidian and leather of an unknown origin. Scholars believe the carving is supposed to depict a heron or an ibis — which is a bit unusual for a cult based around the concept of never setting foot on a planet that has atmosphere. It was thought to be used in Tisare birthing rituals."

The woman blinks at him, then takes the totem gently in her fingertips. She tilts her head, studying it. "I could maybe see a heron," she says finally. "Who's your buyer?"

"Antiquities dealer who specializes in this sort of thing."

"You're serious." When Raj doesn't answer, her eyebrows shoot up. "Oh."

He's obviously missing something. "Who's *your* buyer?"

"Not buyer, client. Of sorts." She pulls out a utility knife, flipping it open. "He's definitely not into Tisare sacred objects."

Raj holds out a hand. "Hey. Careful with that."

"Relax."

She spins the totem on her palm, then eases the edge of the blade into a barely visible seam on the back. A panel clicks open, and a slender data chip floats free. She takes it reverently in the tips of her pale fingers, then shifts her gaze past Raj to the ladder that leads down to the rest of the ship; Jay has floated up to join them. She flips the data chip to him, and the mechanic slots it into his cuff and slips a heads-up display down his forehead.

"Looks legit," he says after a moment. "Plenty locked down, but I'd say we got what we came for."

"What's on the chip?" Raj asks.

"I didn't ask," the woman says. "But I'd guess it has something to do with Sumilang's latest research."

"The implants that stimulate neural regrowth — which is why he accused me of corporate espionage." Raj had thought it was the ramblings of an egotistical angry drunk, to be honest. "That's not really my thing. Or, at least, no one's paid me to do it yet."

"You freelance?"

"Yeah."

"Catch." The woman flips her utility knife shut and snaps the compartment on the totem closed, then tosses it to Raj. "Guess we both get our paydays. Unless your buyer was bullshitting you about just wanting the artifact."

"They weren't," Raj says. Vash and Gracie couldn't care less about some software, not when they'd have a new piece for their weird collection.

The carved obsidian is cool in his palm — Raj turns the totem over to view the strange stylized carving. A bird, maybe, the wings stretched overhead, spiraling upwards. If he didn't know to look, he'd never notice the hairline where the panel joins the body of the totem. It doesn't seem damaged.

The woman is watching him speculatively when he glances back up.

"You can fight," she says. "And you must be a pretty good grifter when you're not being betrayed by the people you hired."

Jay shoves the heads-up display back up. "Not a good idea, Las," he says to her. "He's Arquellian military. How do you think that's going to play?"

"Nico will hate it. But Tora won't care, and she's the one who said we had to hire a full crew for this next job." She turns back to Raj. "You looking for work?"

"Depends," says Raj. "On if you're ever going to tell me your name."

There's that smile, ever so faint in the curve of her lips.

"Lasadi Cazinho," she says finally. "He's Jay Kamiya. Welcome aboard the *Nanshe*."

"Raj Demetriou," says Raj. He can't remember the last time he introduced himself with his real name. It feels good. *Don't get used to it.* "Nice to meet you both. What's the job?"

"Retrieval a few day's ride from the Pearls."

"And who's the client?"

Lasadi's lips press together; for a moment he thinks she won't tell him. Then, "Nico Garnet," she says.

Raj's blood runs cold.

CHAPTER 6
RAJ

"A few things you need to know about Nico Garnet," Lasadi says.

They've landed at Ironfall, docked the *Nanshe*, and navigated the link system to Xiè's Luck, one of Ironfall's handful of hub neighborhoods. It's been hours since she offered him this job, and Raj still hasn't been able to wrap his head around the fact that these two Coruscans work for one of the most reclusive crime lords in Ironfall. Raj has been racking his brain to remember if he's taken any jobs that would put him on the Garnets' shit list, and he's coming up blank. A good sign, maybe? But that's the thing with Nico Garnet. His organization is secretive. You don't know if you've pissed him off until it's too late.

Artemis City and Ironfall — the main settlement on the Pearls' second-largest planet, Dima — embody the tech sector and the manufacturing industry respectively, the twin powerhouses that turned the Pearls from scrappy mining colonies to international players. The two cities share governing duties over the rest of the settlements in the Pearls, but that's about all they have in common. Artemis City, the executive capital, is all glitter and show;

Ironfall, the constitutional capital, is stodgy and unassuming.

Most would call Ironfall ugly, especially when compared to its neon-and-glass-clad sibling. But there's a brutal grace to Ironfall's relentless corridors of stone and cement and ceramic, and Raj has been calling the city home long enough to feel oddly protective. Raj likes Ironfall — he had his fill of pretentious, cutthroat social scenes growing up in Arquelle, and he appreciates the slower pace of life here. People respect each other's privacy. Everyone's got enough of their own past to keep their nose out of everyone else's.

Plus, Ironfall has something Artemis City doesn't have: the hubs.

Ironfall's hubs are pockets of life: clutches of services and residences carved into caverns, each named for the fortunes — or misfortunes — of the prospectors who'd originally staked claims there. Xiè's is one of the nicer ones. It's about half a kilometer across, with its rocky ceiling domed at least fifty meters overhead. The link line put them out in the center of the hub's busy open common space, which is ringed by shop and restaurant pods. Residential pods are stacked up the walls in an orderly fashion; most are just a place to sleep, with meals taken in joint kitchens and eateries, the central plaza the shared living room.

In Xiè's, services are reliable, the air supply is fresh, the water recyclers and electric never brown out. Crime is almost nonexistent, and the streets are clean.

Everyone knows why.

The hubs may technically be run by Ironfall's municipal commission, but certain ones carry the fingerprints of their most influential residents. Grenala's Windfall is essentially a corporate town, run by a mining co-op. Trin's Bad Bet is completely overrun by the local gang and closed to outsiders.

And Xiè's belongs to Nico Garnet.

"First thing you need to know is Nico's fair," Lasadi is saying. "Which means he treats you with respect if you do the same. Don't bullshit him."

"Got it."

"Second is that he pays extremely well, and he expects to get his money's worth."

"Understood."

"And three." Lasadi shoots Raj a look. "He supported Corusca in the war."

Raj blinks at her. "Oh." Explains why two Coruscans are out in the Pearls working for Garnet, at least.

"Doesn't mean he'll space you out of hand," Lasadi says; Raj can't tell if it's meant to be a joke. "Just don't needle him."

"Maybe go easy on the accent," Jay says.

"We're good," Raj says, all traces of Arquelle gone. "You don't have to worry about me. How long've you worked for Garnet?"

"Long enough."

Lasadi turns, but not before he catches the muscle jumping in her jaw. Raj glances at Jay to see if he'll get an answer there; the other man gestures him ahead with a jerk of his chin. Jay's still keeping up a front, but he doesn't strike Raj as the kind of guy who's good at holding grudges. Even in the few hours since they left Artemis City, Jay's been letting his gruff mask slip, laughing at Raj's jokes and throwing him tidbits of information. Lasadi's the one who's stayed effortlessly cool, despite Raj's best efforts to uncover the warmth he'd sensed earlier.

Their destination is a pierogi shop on the south end of the hub, unobtrusively tucked between a cleaning service and a repair pod. Raj's stomach rumbles at the delicious smells wafting out when Lasadi opens the door. The finger foods he'd snacked on at Sumilang's party were far too long ago.

The woman behind the counter raises a hand to greet Lasadi and Jay, then gives Raj a second look. Her right eye has an implant, cloudy mercury silver that flashes poison green for a second while she scans him. The hairs on the back of his neck rise, but she just blinks her lens clear and nods.

"She's waiting in the white room," the woman says.

"Thank you." Lasadi pushes through a beaded curtain in the back of the shop, which leads to a large supply closet with an insulated door at the back. She presses her palm into the biolock beside the door and it pulses green, then hisses open.

The hallway beyond is a stark, soulless contrast to the pleasant charm of the rest of Xiè's Luck. Though the converted mining tunnels have the familiar trapezoidal shape common to many of the tunnels boring through Dima, here the bare stone has been plastered with polished concrete that looks like it was advertised as being easy to clean blood off of. Strips of blue-white lights set low along the ground gleam off the satiny gray surface. No doors along the walls, though Raj spots camera eyes and, set at regular intervals, metal panels that probably house defensive weapons.

Breach the front door? Welcome to the murder chute.

Lasadi palms open another door at the far end, which opens to a large room featuring more polished concrete. Strips of white lights slash across the wall at an angle, casting a cool glow. Four doors lead out of the room, each unmarked, each secured with its own biolock.

A woman is sitting at the only furnishing in the entire room: a frosted white conference table in the direct center. Her black hair is cut into an asymmetrical bob, and her eyelids and full lips shimmer with gold. She's wearing a smart gray suit, a gold cuff, and gold pumps polished to gleaming. The tips flash in the light as she stands and crosses towards them.

"Tora," Lasadi says. "This is Raj Demetriou. Raj, meet Tora Garnet. Nico's daughter."

Tora's hand is as cold as the room, and equally smooth. Not a single gold nail is chipped.

"A pleasure," she says. "Have a seat then, and I'll begin the briefing."

Raj glances back and forth between the two women. "Briefing? I thought this was an interview."

"It's a job offer," Tora says. "We've already done our research on you, Captain Demetriou." She tilts her chin, waiting for his reaction. Raj gives her an easy smile.

"Raj is fine."

"Of course." The corner of Tora's mouth turns up. "I don't imagine the Arquellian navy allows deserters to keep their rank."

"That a problem?"

The word *deserter* caught Lasadi's attention, Raj notes. Whatever info Tora dredged up on him, she'd decided not to alert Lasadi and Jay before the meeting.

Whether or not Raj gets to walk out of here depends on what she found. His public record is bad: Captain of the *Lisaro Chaves Symes* cracks under pressure and leaves his post during the Battle of Tannis, disgracing his admiral father and disappearing into the black. But his private record is a death sentence if the wrong people find it. And if Nico Garnet supported Corusca in the war, he's definitely the wrong person to find it.

Tora seems to be waiting for a response, though he's the one who asked the question. Lasadi's watching him curiously; Jay is lounging, arms crossed, against the conference table.

"I don't need to tell you the Alliance asked us to do

some shitty things," Raj says finally. "Couldn't stomach the orders anymore, so I stole a fighter, skipped out, and got as far from Indira as I could. Never looked back." There's more to the story, of course, but Raj would need to be well into a bottle of whiskey before he'd be willing to tear those wounds back open. So he grins. "You got all night, I can bore you with my thoughts on war and ethics."

That gets a faint smile from Tora. "Another time, maybe," she says. "Are you a pacifist then, Mr. Demetriou?"

"No, ma'am." He meets Lasadi's gaze. "I just make sure I'm more informed about what I'm fighting for before I go in, these days."

A flicker of emotion dances through Lasadi's eyes and vanishes once more. When Raj turns back to Tora, though, she's not looking at him. She's watching Lasadi.

Raj isn't the only one Tora's putting through some sort of test.

"If the history lesson's over," Lasadi says, "let's get to business." She pulls Sumilang's data chip out of her pocket and tosses it across the table to Tora. The other woman slots it into her gold cuff, then blinks as the information loads on her lens. The corner of her mouth turns up.

"Good work, thank you." Tora blinks her lens clear and secrets the chip away. "We appreciate the last-minute pickup, especially as we're on a timeline for the next."

"Which is all we know," Lasadi points out.

"You'll understand the secrecy in a moment," Tora says. And apparently both Raj and Lasadi have passed their tests, because Tora waves a gold-manicured hand at the conference table. "Sit, everyone."

Raj lets the others take what seem like their usual places at the conference table before he pulls out an empty chair across from Jay.

This meeting may not have been a trap, but he's getting

less and less certain about taking whatever job Tora Garnet wants to offer him. There's a deadly undercurrent in the room, something thrumming below the surface and out of sight. The tension between Tora and Lasadi is sucking the air out of the room, and Jay plainly doesn't like Tora. The other man's turned his chair around, sits with his arms crossed over the back. There are half-moons of black under every fingernail, a smudge of grease on his slim wrist. The idle interest in Jay's dark eyes reminds Raj of a not-quite-hungry panther watching a prey animal who's on the verge of becoming annoying. One lazy swipe of claws across the throat and the panther can go back to napping in the sun.

A few days ago, Raj would have taken this job in a heartbeat, walked past all the red flags in his subconscious search for a blaze of glory, death, and the bliss of oblivion. He would've told himself the risk, that's his odds in life. That he'd been dealt a shitty hand, and pretty soon — this job, the next job — his luck was going to run out and the short and ignominious saga of Raj Demetriou would finally be put to an end.

Then Ruby left, and he took one last job that should have ended with him in the crematorium, nothing but ash glittering out among the stars. But life had dealt him one more reset, and Ruby's "fuck off" letter had been the push for him to actually take it.

Raj doesn't need this job. He has the totem for Vash and Gracie, and a decent bank account from surviving the job that gave him the wake-up call. He can sit through this meeting, then politely decline and charter a seat on the Loop out to the asteroid Vash and Gracie call home. Drop off the totem and enjoy their hospitality. Spend some time thinking through his next steps.

Vash and Gracie can put in a good word for him to Ruby, too. He'll convince her he's changed, promise her he'll start being more choosy about jobs if she works with him again. None of this complicated bullshit for underworld crime lords — they'll take gigs he and Ruby can both feel good about.

He likes this plan; the worry twisting his gut unkinks a notch.

Until, that is, Tora swipes files from her cuff onto the conference table and a schematic rises from the table. "May I present Auburn Station," she says.

The words drop like a sonic detonator; shocked silence follows.

Raj glances around the table to see if he's missing part of the joke, but Jay's eyes are wide. He can't tell from Lasadi's expression if she knew what was coming.

Raj finally clears his throat. "*Auburn* Station?"

"Shit's haunted," Jay says.

Raj cocks a thumb at him. "What he said."

"You heard those recordings?" Jay asks him.

"Of the children singing," Raj confirms. Ships that fly too close to the abandoned station get a distress signal, but when they answer it, all they hear is nonsense or nursery rhymes. "Creepy as fuck."

Jay nods. "And there was that girl a few years back, remember?"

"The rockhopper family. That's what you're talking about?"

"Right. Stopped to scavenge fuel to make it back to Ironfall, but only the teen daughter made it out."

"Wasn't she picked up by an ice freighter?" Raj asks. "And she told them ghosts on Auburn Station had murdered the rest of her family."

"Gentlemen." Lasadi spears them both with a look, but he catches a ray of amusement before she slams her guard shut once more. "Glad you two finally agree on something. But we're here to talk about the job."

Jay gives Raj an eyebrow like *Can you believe this shit?*,

then turns his attention to the schematic in the middle of the conference table.

Auburn Station floats in glowing pale blue between them. A trio of habitable rings form a protective sphere around the knot of chambers and corridors in the station's heart; hundreds had lived there during the station's heyday, and given its size, it could have housed even more. Now one of the rings is cracked in half, scorch marks and pockmarked craters marring the surface. Raj has seen pictures, of course. And the station's developed an almost mythical bragging status over the past decade among the sort of adventurers Raj tends to keep company with these days. Everyone claims they've been; no one believes them.

Despite the rumors, Raj's curiosity is piqued. Who wouldn't jump at a chance to actually explore the place for themselves? Even Ruby —

He straightens, pieces of the puzzle he's been worrying at for days snapping into place. *Ruby.*

He hadn't planned on taking this job for himself. But could he take it for her?

"It seems you all are aware of Auburn Station's reputation, so I won't cover that," Tora says. "But a bit of historical context without the mythologizing." She swipes a gold-tipped finger over the station schematic and it begins to slowly rotate in front of them. "Over half a century ago, Auburn Station was the base of operations for pirate queen Rasheda Auburn. She was the scourge of the shipping lanes up until her crew mutinied and killed her — but after the mutiny, the crew didn't hold together long. They abandoned the station within a few months, claiming Rasheda had cursed them. It's been abandoned ever since."

"By abandoned, you mean no one's willing to go near it," Jay points out. "What with the curse."

"Drifter gossip only," Tora says. "Station's been

purchased by SymTex, and they'll begin scrapping it in a month's time. We need something off that station first."

"Not a problem," says Lasadi. Jay shoots Lasadi a look, rakes his unruly hair back from his forehead, but doesn't speak. She ignores him, turns to Raj. "Are you in?"

"If the money's right," Raj says, because that's what he's supposed to say. He's absolutely in — for Ruby. Vash and Gracie will have to wait for the delivery of their trinket, but they'll understand. And maybe he can bring the couple a fun souvenir from the ghost station.

"Does this seem right?" Tora asks, and flicks a message across the table. His comm chimes and he checks his cuff.

Well. That's a number with a proper amount of zeros behind it.

"Fine by me."

"Good." Tora turns back to Lasadi. "I have no concerns about you getting through the station's physical security, but the network could be a problem. You need a hacker."

"Jay can do it," Lasadi says.

"I'm not a fucking hacker, Las." Jay shakes his head; by his tone, this is an old argument. "Have you called Jarret?"

"He's away at the moment," Tora says.

"Garcia?"

"Got picked up by the Alliance a few weeks back."

"There's no way in hell I'm working with one of the DarkStar contractors again." Lasadi sighs. "I'd suggest a recruiting run to Artemis City, but I may need to keep a low profile there for a bit."

Raj clears his throat. "Lucky for you, one of the best hackers in Artemis City lives in Ironfall." And she'll be dying to take this gig, once he tells her what the target is. No matter she swore she'd never work with him again.

Tora tilts her head. "Ruby Quiñones?"

Raj opens his mouth, closes it again without a word.

"I told you I did my research on you," Tora says, a smile

ghosting over her golden lips. "And your partner's reputation precedes her."

"I've never heard of her," Lasadi says.

"Few have," Tora answers. She gets to her feet and the others follow. "Set up a meeting with your partner and Lasadi," she tells Raj. "Tell her we'll pay her the same fee I offered you." She turns to Lasadi. "Dad would like to speak with you." The worry in Lasadi's eyes is there and gone so quickly Raj isn't sure he sees it. But he doesn't miss the look she shares with Jay.

Jay clears his throat. "Do you want me to wait?"

"I'll meet you back at the *Nanshe*," Lasadi says, then turns to Raj. "Let me know when you've set up a meeting with the hacker. We ship out tomorrow night."

"Understood, Captain."

The title seems to catch Lasadi off guard; her hand stills on the table, and that muscle in her cheek jumps again. Then she straightens her shoulders, expression blank as stone once more.

"Let's go," she says to Tora.

CHAPTER 7
LASADI

THE *CLICK-CLICK-CLICK* of Tora's sharp gold heels echoes through the polished hallways of Nico Garnet's lair, a mirror of the recriminating thoughts echoing through Lasadi's mind: bringing Raj in on this job was a mistake.

Not because he won't perform. He seems competent enough, and he passed Tora's background checks, which are always thorough. Not even because he's Arquellian, or that he fought for the Alliance. Lasadi's learned you don't end up in the Pearls without a good reason to sever ties with your past. She got her fresh start, and she'd be a hypocrite not to give someone else — Arquellian or not — theirs.

No, his ability to slip through her defenses is why hiring him was a mistake.

On the transit tube, she'd written him off as a common liar, but despite the fact that he's an obvious chameleon, the charm he's pouring on right now seems genuine. He's hasn't tried to bullshit her or Jay. Yet.

She can't figure out what his game is. She's here for business, and here he is joking with Jay, trying to make her smile, worming his way into her thoughts with the way he caught her eye and smiled, running a hand through his dark hair. That same hair she's dying to run her own fingers through.

That same hand she can still feel pinning her wrist above her head while the length of his body presses hers down. That same curve of smile as when he'd realized she had a knife to his throat. She flushes, suddenly way too hot in this icy tunnel.

Dammit, Las.

It's been three years since Anton shut her out and turned his back on her, and this new and improved Lasadi isn't supposed to get distracted by attractive, charismatic men anymore. She isn't supposed to let her feelings dictate her actions.

That's how she gets people killed.

"Lasadi."

Tora's been talking, and Las has no idea what about. Her attention's gone off like a torpedo, locked on an unavailable target.

"Sorry."

"I asked what your impression is of the new one."

He's gorgeous. He's dangerous. He smells like sea salt and citrus and I want to know how he tastes.

Lasadi clears her throat, banishing the thoughts with a vicious, silent curse. "He's a quick thinker and even faster on his feet. Very cool under pressure. A good grifter if he got into Sumilang's confidence so fast — I saw them together, Sumilang was practically eating out of Raj's hand."

"Could be useful."

"You have to keep an eye on grifters."

"Then keep him on a short leash," Tora says, and heat flares in Lasadi's cheeks once more. She pretends to check her comm to hide her face, and almost bumps into Tora when she stops in front of a door. "He's Alliance."

"*Was*, you said. He deserted." It's what Tora had claimed, and Raj had admitted it free, but Lasadi doesn't miss that flutter of gold lashes when Tora blinks now; she's not telling Lasadi everything she knows. It might not mean anything; Tora always did keep her information close. With Tora, Lasadi knows to do her own research. "Anyway, we're all drifting with no past out here, right?"

The corners of Tora's gold lips tighten, just for a second. The color is perfect for her — rich and cold and untouchable.

"Then Dad doesn't have to know, does he." She turns to the door of her father's suite, doesn't reach to open it. Lasadi can't quite decipher the mixture of worry and determination on the other woman's face.

"How is he?" she asks, to break the silence.

Tora glances over her shoulder. The blue strip lights dull her coppery skin. "He's a fighter," she says after a moment of deliberation. She takes a deep breath and presses her palm to the biolock. It hisses open. "And he's fighting. Come in."

Lasadi has no idea how extensive Nico Garnet's network of tunnels is, since she's never been beyond the big conference room, Nico's room, and, of course, the medical suite. When she had first recovered enough to live on her own, Nico offered her a suite in the compound, but she'd found it more comfortable to stay on board the *Nanshe* rather than remain on as Nico's guest, or rent a pod like Jay's.

She tells herself there's something comforting about her ability to lift off and fly should something go wrong. But in truth the sterile hallways always have a slight medicinal smell — her imagination or not — and being here chills her to the bone in more ways than one. Lasadi rubs a thumb over the ridge of scar tissue in the hollow of her abdomen, chasing away the phantom ache.

Physically, she's healed. She may never wear a revealing dress again, but she'll leave fashion to Tora. She's been telling herself she's fine mentally, yet every step into Nico's lair feels like a step backwards. Jay's told her he's done working for the Garnets after this job, and it's past time for Lasadi to be done working for him, too. To release herself from the hold that Nico, the Battle of Tannis, Anton — all of it — has had on her the past three years.

It's time to move on.

If she can figure out how.

The sickly sweet hospital scent hits Lasadi as soon as she enters Nico's suite; she keeps her expression carefully neutral. The sitting room is comfortably furnished, always a surprising contrast to the soulless polished concrete outside. Warm reds and oranges, plush carpets, paintings of surreal, silvery Coruscan landscapes decorating the walls. A door in the far wall reveals a sliver of bedroom; Lasadi can make out the hum of medical equipment beyond. A cloying cloud of incense tries and fails to mask the stench of sickness.

Nico always used to do business out in the open, in his favorite restaurants or while strolling around the central plaza of Xiè's Luck. Since his illness, though, he's withdrawn. Now he's seated on an ornate armchair like it's a throne, with a pair of velvet-cushioned chairs in front of him for an audience. Lasadi follows Tora's lead and sits.

He's dressed to greet her in an impeccable plum suit. Rings on every finger, gold collar circling his throat. His hair is still thick and darkened with dye, his skin taut over rounded cheekbones, his back still straight even if it seems to cause him pain. Lasadi had always speculated that Nico'd had his fair share of surgeries to keep himself looking so youthful — since his health started failing, though, the faint scars of nips and tucks stand out against jaundiced skin.

The last time Las saw Nico, she'd been shocked at how much weight he'd lost. Now he's almost skeletal.

Nico smiles, gentle. "Lasadi," he murmurs. "It's good to see you."

"It's good to see you too, Nico."

"I trust you've been well?"

"Tora's kept us busy."

Nico coughs, then dabs at his lips with a handkerchief; Lasadi pretends not to notice how bad his hand shakes.

"Tora briefed you on the next job?" Nico asks. "Good. I hope you don't believe in ghosts."

"Of course not," Lasadi says. "I believe in squatters and pirates preying on people's fear, not ghosts."

"You might reconsider," Nico says. "Once you've visited Auburn Station."

Lasadi laughs and turns to Tora, expecting to share the joke — especially after how the other woman shut down Jay and Raj's speculation. But Tora is deadly serious.

Lasadi lets her smile fade. "What do you mean?"

"Let me tell you a story about the pirate queen Rasheda Auburn," Nico says.

"I've heard about her."

"You haven't heard this." Nico coughs again, daubs at his lips again. Lasadi wants to stop him — let Tora do the briefing. But Nico settles into his chair and lifts a hand. "Before Rasheda was a queen, she was a common pest," he says, and his voice strengthens as he warms to his story.

"She started out working the trade routes between the Pearls and Bixia Yuanjin's moons," Nico says. "Until she and her crew killed the wrong person."

"I've heard this part," Lasadi says. "She thought she was cursed."

Nico winks. "That's it. Rasheda and her crew came upon an elderly prospector traveling with her granddaughter. The girl was killed as they boarded the ship, and the prospector cursed them, saying their lives would be cut short by the same horror and grief they sowed, as soon as they found their own home. Rasheda laughed it off for years while she and her original crew prospered. Eventually, though, she decided she needed a base of operations."

"Auburn Station."

"Exactly. As each piece of the station came together, Rasheda felt more physically secure," Nico says. "But she remembered the prospector's curse, and her paranoia grew. The year she finished building Auburn Station, the original crew who'd been with her on that raid began to die. One by one, in freak accidents, until she was the only one left.

"The old prospector had said the curse would come true when the pirates found a home, so Rasheda thought she could skirt the letter of the curse by never finishing her own quarters in the heart of the station. She built constantly, tearing down modules and rebuilding corridors, with workers in shifts at all hours. As though the spark of the welder in the black of space was a talisman to keep the curse from finding her."

Nico pauses, fumbling for the water glass at his side. Tora tenses like she's about to help; maybe if they'd been alone she would have. Lasadi pretends not to notice how hard it is for him to drink.

"It obviously didn't work," Lasadi says. "She died fifty-some years ago."

"She did," Nico says. "But Rasheda wasn't just fighting the curse with semantics. She also turned to technology. She had the money and the means to work with some of the best scientific minds in the system to try to accomplish the impossible." Nico's smile sharpens. "She wanted to live forever."

Lasadi stills, the puzzle pieces finally starting to click into place. Nico's dark, bloodshot eyes gleam. Lasadi steals a glance at Tora, who's watching her father with an expression Lasadi can't quite make out. A hint of worry, a touch of skepticism, resignation.

"So, genetic technology? Like the sort of thing Sumilang is working on."

"Something more — Rasheda didn't simply want to replicate herself, she wanted to transfer her consciousness into a body that couldn't be destroyed."

Nico smiles, waiting to see if she's gotten it.

"She wanted to replicate herself with an AI?" Lasadi guesses. Tora's lips thin, but she doesn't speak. "It didn't work, right? Auburn's dead, her crew mutinied and saw to that."

Nico nods slowly. "She's dead. But I believe she was on the verge of succeeding."

"And you want us to . . ."

Tora clears her throat and leans forward, placing a sleek holoprojector on the coffee table between them and calling up the schematic from her cuff once more.

"You have no idea how much it cost to acquire these," she says. "Finding someone who's been inside Auburn's inner sanctum is difficult — finding someone who's been there and isn't currently locked up speaking in tongues is almost impossible."

She spreads her fingers, zooming in on the knot of corridors and modules at the heart of the station. At her touch, a small chamber near the core begins to glow.

"We believe Auburn did most of her experimentation in this chamber," Tora says. "Your job is to retrieve the records locked inside."

"Just the records?"

"We believe we can re-create everything she was working on here," says Tora. "We only need the data."

"Gotcha."

"Tora says you haven't had trouble assembling a team," Nico says; beside him, Tora's dark eyes flicker with warning. Tora doesn't have anything to worry about, though. Lasadi won't mention they'll be shipping with an Arquellian — an ex-Alliance officer, at that. Nico looks like a bad shock might kill him.

"No, sir."

"Good. I know you prefer to work alone, but you'll need all the help you can get this time. There may not be ghosts, but there will be complications."

"Understood." Lasadi sighs. "I'll get my team prepared."

"Thank you," Nico says, and the effort of holding himself straight begins to show; he wilts into his chair. "Now go. And may the old ones illuminate your path."

"And yours," Lasadi says. The old Coruscan superstition sits sour on her tongue, but if it makes Nico feel at peace, she can parrot the words her grandmother taught her.

"You can find your way back?" Tora asks, and Lasadi nods.

Lasadi lets herself out with a glimpse of Tora bending over her father, who's beginning to look like a ghost himself.

What the hell has she gotten herself — and Jay — into?

CHAPTER 8
RAJ

THE ICY CHILL of Nico Garnet's lair lingers with Raj even as he and Jay reenter the embrace of the pierogi shop's warm steam and rich aromas.

"She okay in there?" Raj asks Jay quietly; the other man's lips thin.

"Not your concern."

That lazy panther's stare is back, but Raj got a glimpse of camaraderie back there, a bit of bonding over the ghosts of Auburn Station. Jay strikes him as fundamentally easy-going. If they're going to be flying a job together, Raj needs to know how committed Jay is to hating him. Good thing Raj is starving; a shared meal's always a good way to knock a few bricks out of someone's wall.

"You hungry?" Raj asks, stepping up to the counter.

Jay narrows his eyes, arms crossed over his chest, shoulder propped against the wall.

"I'm buying," Raj says.

The woman behind the counter is watching them both; Jay finally lifts his chin to her. "The usual."

Raj studies the case a moment. "And a half-dozen of the potato cheddar. To go."

He turns back to Jay while the woman reheats their orders. "What's your impression?" he says. "You didn't say much in there."

Jay lifts an eyebrow. "Not gonna say much out here, either."

But this, at least, isn't a shutdown. Jay's gaze flicks past him to the woman behind the counter. The message is clear: this isn't the smartest space to chat.

Raj studies the art on the pierogi shop's walls — mostly humorous paintings of dogs — until the woman at the counter calls out their order. He thanks her and hands one of the takeaway bags to Jay.

"Walk and talk?" he asks.

"I've got some errands to run," Jay says, accepting the bag with a wave of thanks to the shopkeeper. But, again, it's not a shutdown. Raj follows the other man's lead to a bench across the street from the shop, at the edge of the park that fills the center of Xiè's Luck. Around them, a classroom must be breaking for the day — children stream out of a nearby building and into the park, shrieking and running. A few shout out to Jay, who grins and waves.

Raj waits until Jay digs into his bag and fishes out a dumpling before sending out his first probe. "Is this the usual sort of thing you and Lasadi get into?"

"No usual sort of thing," Jay says noncommittally.

"You seemed surprised, is all."

"Location's new."

"Just the location got you worried?"

Jay stares at him flatly.

"Look," Raj says. "This hacker I'm supposed to call? She's a friend of mine. I may gamble on saying yes to a gig with a couple of cantankerous Coruscans I just met, but I'm not going to ask a friend to get tangled in the same trouble if it's a bad bet."

"You can always back out."

"C'mon, man. If we're gonna work together, you've got to trust me at least this far," Raj says. "I'm not asking you to make me your kid's godfather."

The corner of Jay's mouth finally turns up. "I'll cancel the naming day shindig."

"Good," Raj says. "You got something to say to me, time to get it off your chest."

Jay pops the rest of a dumpling in his mouth and chews thoughtfully. "You fight against Corusca?"

"I did."

"And deserted."

"My record's public, you can find it easy," Raj says. An hour ago he wouldn't have suggested Jay go searching, but after realizing Tora had only found the public part of his record, he's more confident that the worst has been hidden. His father would have made sure of that; bad enough having a son labeled a deserter. For once, Raj can be grateful for his father's pride — if the classified part of his record ever got out here to the Pearls, it would be a death sentence.

"I was captain of the *Lisaro Chaves Symes*," Raj says. "We were called in for the blockade against Corusca. I didn't like what I saw. I resigned in protest."

"Resigned isn't deserted."

"They don't just let you take a shuttle back home if you change your mind," Raj says. "They threw me in the brig, and some friends got word I wasn't going to make it through the night. They got me out." Lying with the truth is the most convincing, he's learned. Raj fishes out a second dumpling and takes a bite. "That's not quite what you'll see in the public record. They got some doctor to testify I cracked and ran — looks a lot better than 'captain resigns in protest against atrocities.'"

"When'd you leave?"

"Right before the Battle of Tannis."

Jay stills a fraction of a second before he catches himself. "Took your sweet time developing a conscience, then."

"Yeah, I did." Raj clears his throat. "I'd do a lot of things different if I had the chance." Around them, the residents of Xiè's Luck break and swirl in eddies of domestic traffic, and Raj decides to float a theory. "You two fought together?"

It's the vibe he's getting: former comrades in arms, closing ranks together in the strange new world of the Pearls. He's trying to figure out if there's something beyond that, though. Maybe the flirtation Lasadi had shown him in Sumilang's mansion was an act, maybe not. Either way, he wants to make sure he's not stepping on any toes, on the off chance she warms to him again.

"CLA." Jay says it like he's expecting Raj to be shocked, but he's confirming what Raj suspected. Coruscan Liberation Army. Terrorists — or, freedom fighters, they probably called themselves. The crew Raj fought with may have been sanctioned by the Alliance, but no one fighting in that conflict had been above reproach.

"Did you fight at Tannis?" Raj asks.

"Yeah," Jay says. "Las almost died there." A muscle jumps in his jaw; that's a story he doesn't like telling. And one Raj isn't sure he wants to hear. Too many people died — or almost died — because he'd failed to stop that tragedy.

"She was a pilot?" Given the way Jay tensed at Raj's last question, he doesn't expect the other man to say more.

But, "Captain. Mercury Squadron."

There's a hint of challenge in his voice, and Raj straightens, impressed. Probably not a lot of people out on this rock know much about the Coruscan conflict, but everyone in the Durga System has heard of Mercury Squadron. About their flashy, unusual tactics, the liquid formations none of the Alliance's fighters could match, sure; but most people remember them — truth or lie — for the destruction of the

New Manilan medical transport that sparked the brutal Battle of Tannis. Raj knows better than anyone that those charges against them are propaganda — and that every rumor about their fearless, anonymous captain is true.

Lasadi Cazinho was that captain?

"I remember Mercury Squadron gave Alliance command more than one sleepless night," is all Raj says. "You fly with them, too?"

"With her."

Raj waits, but that's it. "Corusca deserved better," Raj finally says.

"Fuck yes it did." But Jay's posturing has melted away, and there's no venom in those words. Now they're just two co-conspirators eating dinner on a park bench while the busy traffic of Xiè's Luck eddies around them.

After a moment of silence, Jay turns his dark gaze on Raj; there's a faint ring of bronze set in the dark brown of his irises, around the pupil. "Listen, Las doesn't much know how to trust strangers, and she needs a second opinion who's not afraid to shoot. If Las calls you good, you're fine by me. But if I find out you're bullshitting us?"

"Understood." Raj fishes another pierogi out of the bag. "Did you meet Garnet during the war?" It's Raj's current theory; Lasadi had said the crime lord had supported the Coruscan freedom efforts.

"Not until after. He came from there when he was a kid, and he helped the CLA with some funding — and an escape plan when shit hit the fan. We've been here since after the Battle of Tannis."

So, three years. Same as him.

"You trust him?"

"Yeah."

"But you don't like him."

Jay laughs. "Don't like you, either."

Raj shares his smile. "I'm starting to like you, though."

He winks at Jay's startled expression and gets to his feet, suddenly bone-tired. Given the party and the time distance, he's been up for more than an Ironfall day. "Thanks for the intel, man. I'll see you tomorrow."

He polishes off the rest of the pierogis on the link back home to Nestor's Folly. Nestor's, like Xiè's Luck, is one of the early caverns-turned-settlements-turned-neighborhood-hubs. But unlike Xiè's, Nestor's is more disorderly. Pods are stacked haphazardly up the walls and layered over the common area to make a tangled warren of homes and balconies. The residents put up with fewer amenities and the occasional brownout in exchange for more affordable rooms; the north wall, where Raj rents a pod, is billed as "luxury" because the infrastructure isn't at least a century old and he doesn't have to share a bathroom.

Nestor's may not be Nico Garnet impeccable, but it's much more Raj's style. Garnet's lair had given him flash-backs of childhood: *Don't touch anything, don't break that, don't leave fingerprints, is that a water ring on the countertop?* The shift from the Demetriou household to the regimen of the military had hardly been noticeable, and the relaxed chaos of Nestor's Folly feels like home in a way he's never actually known.

The other reason he likes Nestor's is because it's tight-knit. Street vendors, security guards, neighbors all know each other at least by sight, and the working-class families and retirees don't invite much excitement. Nobody has a reason to come to Nestor's unless they live here. Which is why the man in the drifter's flight jacket, work boots, and assassin's gloves waiting by the exit to the link station stands out.

The drifter is pretending to study a safety poster, but he's definitely scanning the crowd. And — yep.

He's definitely here for Raj.

Raj keeps walking even as the drifter slips into the

crowd behind him; he pauses at a recycler to toss his empty takeaway packet and check to make sure he's not mistaken. He's not. The man's following him, fingers twitching towards whatever's hidden under his flight jacket.

Dammit.

Raj stays with the crowd, stooping to help an elderly man carry his cart of — what is this, cement bags? — up the short flight of stairs. He doesn't let on that he notices, but the drifter man's not alone. A woman's lounging at the top of the stairs, and she's also got an eye out for Raj.

Raj helps the old man set his cart back down at the top of the stairs and turns away, whistling. In the window of a snack pod he catches a glimpse of the woman breaking off from her post to follow him. She's flanking left, the man in the flight jacket heads right.

Raj doesn't see anyone else with them, but he doesn't expect to. Headhunters work alone or in pairs; Raj knows this all too well by now.

Time to get these two off his tail without shooting up the neighborhood. People like him here in Nestor's, and he likes them. Last thing he wants is to make a name for himself in a bad way in his own hub — Ironfall's getting small enough already.

He ducks under a swath of prayer flags and into an alley formed between the rear of a row of restaurant pods and the area's main recycler chutes. Crates of empty produce bags and cooking fuel are stacked haphazardly; a burst of steam erupts from the vent of a bakery unit.

Raj scrambles up a pallet of bagged rice and vaults on top of the third pod down from the alley's entrance, coughing into his sleeve against the steam. Two people are arguing further down the alley and one of the pods is cranking out New Manilan ballads, but he keeps his movements muffled as he creeps back towards the entrance to the alley.

The drifter man enters first, his pistol drawn and gleaming in his hand. The woman's right behind him, swatting away the low-hanging prayer flags.

Raj flattens himself against the top of the pod and gives them a five-count.

And drops.

He catches the woman around the throat, heel to the back of her knee as they hit the ground. Electric barb at the nape of her neck and she goes limp with a strangled cry.

Her partner whirls on Raj, firing off a shot that ricochets terrifyingly close to his head — this contract must have dispensed with the usual "must be brought in alive" clause.

Raj rolls to his feet, springing up under the drifter's gun arm and wrapping it in a lock of his own. A jab back with his left elbow into the man's sternum, then a straight chop down that has the man groaning and watery at the knees.

Raj lets him fall, stripping the pistol as he steps back.

The drifter rolls into a ball, moaning.

Up and down the alley, heads are poking out of the backs of restaurant pods to see what the fuss is about. Good thing about being a local, though — Raj's eaten at every one of these pods at least once, and he likes to make conversation and tip well. The chef of a curried noodle joint lifts her chin at him.

"Heya, man," she calls. "You okay then?"

"Call this in?" he asks. "Got a couple of drifters tried to mug me."

"You bet."

Raj thumbs on the safety and tucks the pistol into his own waistband, then bends over the drifter, finding a pair of disposable cuffs at his belt. He cuffs the man's unbroken left wrist to a nearby pipe, then turns to the woman. He disarms her, cuffing her arms to a crate as she begins to mumble herself awake.

He nods to a waiter. "Keep an eye on them?"

"Fucking drifters," says the waiter. "Nestor's needs a security checkpoint, doesn't it. Keep them in the upper hubs."

"Exactly."

It's one of Raj's favorite things about living in Nestor's: The people here are paranoid as hell. Raj had gotten the exact same critical suspicion when he'd first moved into the hub, but he's a known quantity now. Which means no one here's going to remember seeing a thing go down in this alley, and the police definitely won't believe whatever bullshit story the headhunters make up to cover the fact that they were illegally pursuing a contract in an Ironfall hub.

If it'd been the docks, Ironfall's security might've looked the other way. But Ironfall's home to far too many political refugees, deserters, indenture-skippers, and other riffraff from around the system. The municipal council needs to keep up Ironfall's reputation as the sort of place you can make a new life — and pay taxes — in peace.

Still, Raj navigates the final lattice of ladders, elevators, and balconies to his pod with the itch of crosshairs between his shoulder blades. It's around dinner time, so the routes are busy. Front doors open to the balconies, the smell of food wafting out, kids and pets playing outside, second-shifters heading home and third-shifters heading out. Raj presses against the wall, two pods down from his, as an elderly woman with a cane shuffles by on her way to the elevator.

"Nice weather," she says to him, like she always does.

"It's a gorgeous day," he replies. Sometimes when she's chatty she'll keep him for an hour, trading stories of lovely days she'd known from her girlhood in New Manila: sunny days, rainy ones, thunderstorms, snow — all in her memory.

Today she pats him on the arm and keeps walking.

Raj's hole in the wall has enough room to unfold his bed

and dining table at the same time — the perks of a "luxury" model. The security system's broken, but he doesn't keep anything valuable here anyway. He has few possessions, and only one he'd be pained to lose: a cittern hanging on the wall. Of course, it's gathering dust. It was an impulse purchase when he first landed here in Ironfall, and he'd found his fingers still remembered the chords even if his callouses were long gone. He entertained his neighbors for a few months before breaking a string. He's been meaning to buy a new set for years, but somehow he's never found the time.

Always another job right after this one.

And another one, and another one, he hopes, each one peeling back another layer of Lasadi Cazinho until he can figure her out. Seeing what it takes to uncover that bright flame she'd been in Sumilang's mansion, the bright flame she must have been as captain of Mercury Squadron. Learning how to make her trust him.

Raj shakes off the runaway train of thought. *Whoa there, cowboy.* All this fantasy about Lasadi opening up to him? A woman like her, she can see straight through to a person's core. Only a matter of time before she'd realize what little there is at Raj's. And then there's the matter of his private record — she'd never trust him if she knew.

No, best to make the most of this job and move on.

Raj collapses on his bed, pulls out his comm, and sends up a sincere prayer to anyone in the universe that might be listening that Ruby Quiñones picks up the other end of the line.

The chiming stops; music thrums, tinny and distant. He hears her take a breath.

"Hey, Ruby," he says before she can speak, trying not to sound surprised she answered. It sounds like she's in a nightclub, voices calling to each other in the background.

"Heya, Raj." Her tone is clipped, business-like. "You got

headhunters on your ass again? Or why are you calling me after I said we were through."

"Actually, I got us a gig. Travel's involved, but it pays well."

On the other end of the line, Ruby barks a surprised laugh. "We're done, Raj, aren't we. Over. Partnership terminated."

"Yeah, I know," Raj says. "But you're gonna like this gig. New client, definitely won't stiff us this time."

"Fuck off, Raj."

"Ruby." He can already hear her getting distant. "It's Auburn Station."

There's a breath on the other end of the line, a woman cooing Ruby's name over the backdrop of club music.

Raj waits. He's known Ruby almost as long as he's been in the Pearls, and she's always been cagey about her past. But her little brother, Alex, is chatty, and Raj has gleaned a few things.

Their parents went missing when Ruby was twelve, and she's been hunting them down ever since. She hasn't found many clues, but she does have one she's never been able to follow up on: the knapsack she was carrying when she and her infant brother showed up on the doorstep of the Aymaya Apostles in Artemis City was stenciled with the words *Auburn Station*.

Ruby swears under her breath. "I'm curious, only," she says finally; he knows she's more than curious, but he lets her play it cool.

"Meet me tomorrow morning at that tea shop in Selena's," he says. "I'll bring the captain along — make your decision after you meet her."

"Fine."

"I owe you, Ruby."

"You do."

"And about the headhunters? Pair of them tried for me at the link station in Nestor's."

She sighs. "So I'll take care of it when I get home."

And the connection cuts.

Raj lets his head fall back in relief. Ruby's still furious with him, but he'd also been right that Auburn Station would pique her interest enough to get her to the meeting. Now he can spend the night planning out his charm offensive to get her to say yes to the gig, and prove to her he's worth trusting again after their disastrous last job.

It'll keep him from thinking about Lasadi.

Almost.

CHAPTER 9
LASADI

THE CASUAL OBSERVER wouldn't be able to tell anyone lives aboard the *Nanshe*. Lasadi keeps her toiletries in a travel case in her locker; she washes, dries, and replaces each dish as soon as she's done with it. She splurged on a nicer blanket and pillow than the standard itchy fare the *Nanshe* had been outfitted with, but she chose the same soulless gray as the original so her new bedding wouldn't seem out of place.

Not that anyone cares. Nico and Tora know she stays here, and they don't have a problem with it. But it's not her ship, not yet.

Lasadi rocks in the pilot's chair, listening to the creak of the springs under the gravity of Ironfall's docks, feeling every familiar bulge in the seat, every place the padding's worn thin. First thing she'll do when she's comfortable calling this ship hers is to trade out this chair.

As much as she tries not to leave a mark, the *Nanshe* is the one place she actually does feel relaxed. She can take full, deep breaths here. Let her muscles unclench, her shoulders unwind — even the scars that normally pull at her thigh and over her ribs seem less taut here. She rubs her thigh absently, working at scar tissue. Jay's back — the *Nanshe* alerted her, and she can hear the occasional thump in the engine room — but he's not here to notice the gesture and make that face, like he's worried about her.

An unfamiliar lump digs into her thigh; she's tired enough it takes a moment to place it. The adventure at Sumilang's museum feels like days ago, though the dinner party was this morning, Ironfall time. No wonder she's so exhausted. She got up at the crack of Artemis City's dawn to work a catering gig.

Lasadi reaches into her pocket and slips the little mixla out, turning it over in her hand.

Creamy white Coruscan marble, shot through with a slash of turquoise. It's a striking stone, and the artisan who carved it had taken their time with every detail, working the little house god's features in among the natural characteristics of the marble to create an exquisite piece.

She hadn't really examined it back at the museum, just snatched it in a moment of impulse and ran. Didn't seem right, leaving the little guy under glass. But now, examining the craftsmanship, she can tell this is no tourist trinket or rough-hewn family heirloom. In the hands of the right buyer, this mixla is probably worth hundreds of thousands of credits. Enough to finally buy this boat and get out from under Nico's thumb without having to work any more jobs after this one.

She knows fences, she could sell it easy. Send it right back to some rich asshole's collection.

Lasadi frowns at the mixla, knowing the disapproval she feels is internalized childhood guilt, not a sign of the imminent retribution of an angry pocket god.

Still, "I'm not going to sell you," she says aloud. *Yet.*

She pulls a roll of double-sided adhesive from the toolkit under the console and secures the mixla in an out-of-the-way alcove. She can barely see it out of the corner of her eye from this chair, and no one else will notice it unless they're — *shit* — sitting in Jay's chair.

She reaches for the mixla, determined to find a less visible place for it to live.

"Brought you a snack."

Lasadi snatches her hand back and whirls, blood rushing to her cheeks. Jay climbs out of the hatch in the floor and drops into the co-pilot's chair, tossing a torn-open takeaway package on the console in front of her.

"You eat yet? The new guy, that Arquellian asshole you insisted on saving? He bought me dumplings. I figured — oh." Jay leans forward, peering at the mixla. "Well, hello there."

"I was just seeing what it looked like," Lasadi says. "Set it down while I was working on something else." She's desperately hoping Jay won't notice the adhesive.

"Sure." A faint smile plays over Jay's lips. "You steal that from Sumilang?"

"Couldn't just leave it there."

"Course not." Jay leans back in his chair. "I've always been saying we should decorate this place."

"It's not — "

"Our ship," Jay finishes. He pops open the toolkit under the console and rummages for a discarded cap, then pulls a flask out of his pocket and pours a few drops into the cap. He sets it in front of the mixla. "Little guy's probably thirsty after getting sprung from prison."

He offers the flask to Lasadi. She hesitates, feeling ridiculous, then raises it brief to the mixla, drinks, and passes it back. Jay toasts the mixla without a shred of self-consciousness.

"May the old ones keep this rust bucket flying."

"That's your job," Lasadi says; whiskey burns in the back of her throat. "Anyway, you believe in all that?"

"How old were you the first time you walked past your nana's shrine without praying?"

"Eleven."

"Bet it was the last time, yeah?"

"I was scared shitless." Lasadi ignores the hollow, ripped-empty ache that comes with talking about her family. They'd held banishing, which means even if they knew she was alive, she wouldn't be welcomed back. "I was so afraid I was going to die in my sleep I laid awake all night. I cooked it a special meal the next day."

"I was nine," Jay says. "Next day I broke my leg. Never walked past without praying again."

"That's ridiculous."

"Better safe than moxed." Jay grins. "Can't believe I caught you being superstitious."

"Sentimental," Lasadi corrects, then points to the little marble house god. "And if you tell a soul, you're dead. I'll sic the mixla on you."

"We'll see who feeds the little guy better," Jay says with a wink. "Speaking of, you want to go out for dinner? I'm meeting Chiara, sure she'd love to see you."

Lasadi laughs. "I doubt that. I took you away to Artemis City all the past week, and I'm barely giving you a night in Ironfall before dragging you away again. Tell me she's not furious."

"Maybe a little. She'll come around, though. Especially when I tell her this is the last Nico job." He slides her a look. "For real this time, Las."

Lasadi winces. Their last gig was supposed to be his last Nico job. They'd been in Artemis City to retrieve something a petty crime boss had stolen from Nico — a simple enough job, but very little had gone according to plan. After dodging assassins, getting shot at by gangsters, and stealing a mototaxi, they'd finally achieved their objective — and Jay had sworn off working for Nico again.

Then Lasadi called Tora to report success, and Tora sent them after Sumilang's data chip and offered them the gig on Auburn Station. Lasadi had agreed out of habit, not realizing until later that she hadn't run it by Jay first. And by his expression, that's not the only thing he's disappointed about.

"You knew we were going to Auburn Station," Jay says with a sigh. It's not a question. "You could have warned me."

"I didn't have all the details." At his lifted eyebrow, she takes a deep breath. "Okay. I was afraid you'd say no."

"I still could," he points out, but he's not going to. They both know that.

"This will be the last Nico job, Jay. I promise."

"For both of us?"

Olds be damned, she wants to say yes. To seal off this stage of her life and leave it behind her in the black. To smooth those worry furrows between Jay's dark brows. She can't say she'll never take another job for Nico, though. Not truthfully. Not when she's so close.

"You do what you have to," Jay says when she doesn't answer. "But I'm done."

"I'm buying the *Nanshe*." The words rush out in a tumble — she hadn't known she was going to say it — and Jay's eyes widen in surprise. "Nico agreed to sell it to me once I've saved up enough. I'm almost there, Jay. A few more jobs."

She doesn't know why she hadn't told him before this. A different form of superstition, maybe — she used to make plans with abandon, playing along with Jay's games of *What if* and *After the war we should,* spinning up fantasies of the future. Of course Anton shut that kind of talk down when he heard it. With him, it was always about the present. Their fearless leader was too focused, too disciplined for sentimental folly.

Maybe Anton had been right. Las, at least, has learned better than to indulge in fantasies about the future until they're a sure thing.

"You're going to buy the *Nanshe*?" A smile tugs at Jay's lips. "You know how much money you have to sink into repairs to keep something like this running? We'll have to pull some pretty good jobs."

"I've heard you complain about it once or twice." Relief floods through her: *We.*

"Can't believe you've saved up enough for it — I've got about ten credits in my account right now."

"You've worked as many jobs as me."

"Hormones are expensive."

Las laughs. "Bullshit. Testosterone doesn't cost a tenth of what you spend taking Chiara out."

"Then women are expensive."

"*That* woman is."

"Sorry, I meant *classy* women are expensive." Jay winks when she smacks him on the arm, his laugh dimpling his cheek. "Admit it, Las. Chiara helped you pick out the few nice clothes you own."

"And they cost as much as the *Nanshe*'s berth rent," Lasadi complains. "My sister Evvi got all the classy genes. I don't need anything fancy."

"Okay," Jay says. That puzzling — and increasingly familiar — worry flickers over his expression, almost too fast for her to notice this time. "Hey. So what did Tora have to say that she didn't want me around for?" He holds up a hand. "Don't worry, I sweep the *Nanshe* for bugs before every job. Besides. Garnets already know what I think about them."

"Still," Lasadi says. "Don't provoke them."

"Provoking people weeds out the chaff."

"It hides your big heart."

"Such lies, and in front of the mixla, too." Jay fans

himself in mock shock like a Coruscan matron, then lounges back in his chair. "Spill it."

Las still doesn't feel like she's got her head wrapped around it, but she gives the short version of the story Nico told her. Pirate queen gets cursed, builds Auburn Station into a never-ending labyrinth to thwart the curse, then does a bunch of wild experiments to help her live forever. "They think Rasheda Auburn was trying to move her consciousness into an AI," she finishes.

"And Nico wants that, too?" Lasadi nods, and Jay swears under his breath. "How is he?"

"Not good. Not good at all." She shivers at the memory of death lingering in the corners of the room. She'll be shocked if he's still alive to attempt Rasheda's solution by the time they return.

If this technology is even real.

"The Garnet organization is bad news right now, Las," Jay says. "They've been keeping Nico's illness secret, but I'm hearing things on the street. Change comes to an organization like that, people die, and I don't want to be around for it." Jay scrubs a hand over his jaw. "You trust Nico?"

Lasadi nods. "Yeah. I do."

"You trust Tora?"

"No. But she's Nico's daughter. She's not going to burn us. Not like — " She can't say his name aloud. "Not like before."

"Not like Anton did." Jay's voice is so gentle it cuts to the bone.

Three years ago, Lasadi had led Mercury Squadron into their most daring attack of the war. The operation was supposed to be a turning point in the fight against the Alliance — and maybe it would have been if tragedy hadn't struck. They'd been midflight when a neutral New Manilan medical transport was destroyed in a fiery explosion; the Alliance blamed it on Mercury and started shelling the settlement of Tannis in retaliation for its support of the rebel fighters based nearby. Mercury — already en route to their original target — had rallied to defend the settlement. But they couldn't stop the devastation on their own, and the backup Lasadi requested never came.

Instead of a decisive victory, she'd watched helpless as her fighters — her comrades — vanished one by one as streaks of blazing stars. She'd watched helpless as the civilian settlement of Tannis was reduced to ash and rubble. And then she and Jay had been hit and there'd been nothing else Lasadi could do.

The Alliance had used the medical transport's destruction to justify the slaughter of hundreds of civilians. Dozens of Lasadi's friends. At the time, Lasadi had been certain Mercury Squadron hadn't killed the transport, yet she woke up in Nico Garnet's medbay to find Anton on the news, laying the blame squarely at her squadron's feet. She'd clung to hope — maybe, assuming she was dead, he was making a strategic decision to shift blame somewhere it wouldn't matter so he could keep the cause alive.

And then she'd reached out to him, and he'd told her the horrible truth. Mercury truly was to blame. It hadn't been intentional, like the Alliance was claiming, but seven hundred and twelve souls aboard the medical transport — and thousands more civilians in Tannis — had died because of her.

Anton managed to spin the tragedy into peace talks with the Alliance, and a seat for himself on the Senate. He told her not to come back. Not to him, not to Corusca. And so Lasadi found herself in exile in the Pearls.

She finally meets Jay's gaze, and the pity there shakes her. She doesn't need pity, she needs to change the subject.

"I'm not worried about Tora," Lasadi says. "But we'll watch our backs." *And we'll leave after this*, she's about to say. *We buy the* Nanshe *from Garnet and we go wherever the hell we want, leave the ghosts in the past where they belong.* But the words die on her lips when Jay clears his throat.

"Chiara asked me to move in," he says.

He says it like he's delivering bad news, but the shy smile dimpling his cheek betrays his happiness, and breaks her heart. Lasadi likes Chiara, but the woman's made no secret she wants to tie Jay down. Adopt some rugrats. Live some sort of normal life. Secretly, Lasadi's been hoping Jay wasn't on board — but she's heard enough of Jay's "what if" fantasies to know how bad he wants a family.

Lasadi lets everything else rush out of her mind. "Yeah?" She's proud of how happy for him she manages to make the word sound.

"She brought it up again before we left for Artemis City."

Again. So they've been having this conversation for a while, and Jay hasn't mentioned it until now. He does that sometimes, when he wants to make up his own mind without letting Lasadi talk him out of it.

Well, she can respect her friend's decision — and she can *be happy* for her friend.

She finds a smile. "You're nesting," she teases.

"I had 'em cut out my ovaries," Jay says. "Means I'm incapable of nesting."

"That's sexist bullshit."

Jay waves away the charge with a laugh. "Says the cis girl who won't even leave her toothbrush out on her own ship. And getting serious with someone isn't 'nesting,' Las, it's living. You should try it sometime." Jay's smile becomes sly. "Take the new guy for a spin."

Heat creeps under Lasadi's collar. "I thought you hated him."

"He's not so bad," Jay says. He lifts his chin at the take-away package. "He bought me dumplings."

"He *bought you* with dumplings, you mean."

Jay holds up his hands in protest. "We talked."

"About what?"

"The job. Garnet." Jay starts to smile. "You. He was subtle, but he was fishing for if you're available."

Lasadi's heart betrays her with a little flip. She shuts that down with a vicious internal curse. This isn't the first time Jay's tried to set her up with someone, but it's the first time that someone has lit her up like a fuse.

"Hope you told him I'm not."

"You're not?" She knows that note in Jay's voice, and she shoots him a glare. "You start seeing someone in the last few hours?"

"I've got too much going on."

"I know what you're doing."

She knows what he's going to say: *You work too hard. You've got to get out sometimes. Remember to live once in a while.*

"You're still punishing yourself."

There's not enough oxygen in the room; something twists inside her, deep and clawing.

"What else do you call the life you've been living the last three years, Las? You buried the woman I first met so deep I'm surprised we haven't had a funeral for her." Jay's tone gentles. "You can't blame yourself for what happened at Tannis."

"The whole system does," she shoots back. "And I'm not about to fall for some Arquellian with a nice smile. Look into this Captain Demetriou — I know Tora's hiding something about him."

"She did a thorough background check."

"Which means she didn't find anything that would jeopardize the job," Lasadi points out. "Just something I might not like."

"You sure you want to know what it is?"

"Don't you?"

"Everybody's running from something here, Las. Sometimes it's better to leave the past alone and trust your gut."

"Your brain's for thinking, not your heart." Her grandmother's words.

"I'll check around." Jay pushes himself out of his chair and squeezes her shoulder. "I've gotta meet Chiara," he says. "Eat those, get some sleep. I'll catch up with you tomorrow."

"Yes, Dad."

"I'm serious, young lady." His expression softens; he's teasing her, but that worry is back. "We'll be launching again before you know it."

"Then don't let Chiara keep you up all night."

The dimple pops back into Jay's cheek. "Can't promise anything with that woman." And with one last grin, he vanishes down the stairs. After a moment, the *Nanshe* informs her he's disembarked and the security systems are armed.

Lasadi is exhausted, but after the rush of memories that conversation brought back, she's too wired to sleep. She pops a cold pierogi in her mouth and plugs in the coordinates Tora sent, chewing slow, willing the tangled lines leading her to the ghost pirate's lair to begin making sense.

CHAPTER 10
RAJ

LASADI'S THERE when Raj arrives, waiting at the bazaar entrance in Selena's Ante and surreptitiously studying a mannequin. It's wearing a silky, coppery rose dress that would make the amber in her smoky brown eyes glow, with a racerback cut that would look sexy as hell given how strong he knows her shoulders are.

He shouldn't stand here watching her, but he's captivated. Not just by the conjured image of her long legs disappearing under that flirty hemline, but by how different she seems when she's alone. The muscles in her jaw are relaxed, her gaze soft; she almost looks peaceful. She's wearing her hair in a loose braid today, a few strands drifting out to frame her face. She's even smiling.

He's dying to learn what he needs to do to make her that happy all the time.

He doesn't want to disturb her, but Ruby hates waiting, and — provided she's actually at the tea shop — he's got a short window to win her back over. She didn't answer when he called this morning, but he's scoured the bounty boards and the latest dead-or-alive prize on his head is gone. So even if she's still mad, at least she doesn't want him dead.

He's taking that as a sign she won't stay mad at him forever, which is a good thing, because he's well and truly screwed if he can't fix this relationship. It's one of the few he has left on this rock. Or anywhere, really.

"Morning," he calls to Lasadi. "Beautiful day, yeah?"

That startles a laugh out of her, drops her guard long enough her entire face lights up.

"Simply gorgeous," he says.

She tilts her head like she can't tell if he's flirting. He can't tell if he is, either. Anyone else, he wouldn't be hesitating — but they're about to head out on a job together, and the last thing he needs is to make things awkward from the get-go. Plus, even after his chat with Jay yesterday, he doesn't have a clear read on their relationship. He gets the sense that if he guesses wrong when it comes to that question, he'll lose his head. And he's not sure which of them will take it off: Jay or Lasadi.

Not to mention, she was captain of the Mercury Squadron. The most feared arm of the CLA guerrillas before the smear campaign that blamed them for the deaths on the medical transport. Lasadi doesn't seem the kind of woman who does things by half measures — even the searching look she gives him now threatens to pierce him to the core, and if he's right about her, she won't like what she sees there.

So.

Keep it business.

"An old woman who lives in a pod in my cluster, 'It's a beautiful day' is how she says hello." It's an explanation that tells them both he wasn't flirting. "She's been here most of her life, but I swear she remembers every drop of rain she saw as a kid in New Manila. She'll talk your ear off about the weather."

"Rain sounds . . ." Lasadi's eyebrows draw together as she considers the word. "Terrifying."

Raj laughs. Of course, she grew up on Corusca. "It's lovely," he says. He jerks his chin at the bazaar entrance. "Have you been to this tea house before? No? Then you're in for a treat. Best views in Ironfall."

"Views of the bazaar?" Lasadi doesn't sound convinced.

Raj winks. "You'll see."

A small percentage of Selena's Ante is living space, but most of the hub is a giant bazaar. Retail shops and services make up the first few levels, wholesalers above them, printers and manufacturers at the top. That dress Lasadi had been eyeing before he arrived was sewn from fabric purchased a few levels up, the cloth manufactured even above that.

You can get anything you want ready-made or bespoke in Selena's, so long as you know where to ask. The problem is getting lost in the maze of pods and ramps that slope so gently it's almost impossible to remember which level you're on. Makes it hard to keep your wits about you, but Selena's isn't dangerous. You won't get knifed in an alley, but pickpockets, scammers, and con artists thrive in the crowds.

They make their way past tiny storefronts smashed together, squeeze past hawkers with cases crammed illegally onto balconies and selling everything from handmade jewelry to counterfeit gentech implants. Someone's preaching about the end times in the middle of one platform, and Raj skirts past to climb a ladder shortcut to the next catwalk up, where a row of home goods printers have colorful sample wares on display.

"I didn't know you could get here from there," Lasadi says. "I'll keep it in mind."

"Selena's is full of shortcuts." Raj presses them both back against a shuttered storefront while a pair of porters with an enormous cart rattle down the walkway. Lasadi's shoulder is warm against his, and she doesn't shift away.

There's not room to, he tells himself. Don't read anything into it.

Still, he risks a touch to her arm to point out their destination; the fabric of her sleeve is rough under his fingertips.

Talia's Tea Shop is on a platform jutting out on the fifth — or maybe the sixth — level, a single door with The Best Views in Ironfall emblazoned over the top. The floor-to-ceiling screens on every wall are why: pothos vines climb the walls to frame the screens in lush greenery, and realistic video changes each day to show a different place.

Today it's like you're standing on a balcony on Sapis, overlooking the shimmering blue swirls of Bixia Yuanjin — the farthest place in the Durga System humans have dared to establish a permanent home.

Ruby's waiting for them at a far booth, absorbed in the screen of her tablet. Today she's wearing her dark, wavy hair worn loose so it frames her face and brushes her shoulders. She's got a pair of rings in her left brow and a lip ring on the right side, all three slowly shifting from neon pink to green and back. Her favorite red leather jacket is open to display the abstract tattoos sweeping across her collarbones like a necklace: the five Pearls in a graceful chain amid a scatter of smaller bodies in delicate gold ink that glints on her brown skin.

"Oh, good," he says to Lasadi. "She's here. Means she'll most likely take the job."

"You worried about that?"

"Let's just say she's a little mad at me for how our last gig together turned out. But she'll come around." He grins when Ruby glances up, waving as she lifts one perfect eyebrow in an arch of scorn. "Hey, Ruby."

He slides into the booth across from her. The molded

seats have a bit of give, the tables are reclaimed dashboards from scrapped ships, covered in plastiglass.

"Lasadi, meet Ruby Quiñones," Raj says. "The best hacker you'll find in the Pearls. Ruby, Lasadi Cazinho is captain of the *Nanshe*, and leading this little expedition."

Ruby meets Lasadi's outstretched hand. "Nice to meet you, Captain," she says politely. "Gotta say I'm intrigued by your gig. But I've got two bullet points in regards to this particular gentleman, first." Ruby leans towards Raj, swirling her tea. "First, Raj, fuck you. I got burned on our last job together, and I am done getting burned by you."

"I told you I'm sorry, Ruby." Raj runs a hand through his hair. "I can't do this without you. I need you. I'm lost without you."

"Save that shit for your exes," Ruby says. "As for the second bullet point, maybe you're following me, Raj?"

"I can go to hell."

"You can go to hell." Ruby lifts an eyebrow, daring him to turn this into a joke.

Raj leans forward. "Look. I really am sorry about how the last job went down. And to prove it, I brought you a shiny new gig for a client who always pays the bills." And access to Auburn Station, but he doesn't say that last bit aloud. Ruby already knows, and Lasadi doesn't need to wonder why Ruby'd have a special interest.

Ruby's lips quirk to the side, but she finally sits back and turns to Lasadi. "What's the job?"

Lasadi's been watching the exchange with mild amusement. Now she raises a finger. "Two bullet points," she says. Ruby laughs; Raj relaxes. "We're hitting Auburn Station. Got a client who wants something from the heart of the station and is willing to pay very well for us to procure it. We can handle the physical job, but we need someone who can hack into the station's network."

"Raj mentioned the location," Ruby says. "Not a problem. I've been studying up on everything I can find on Auburn Station's security."

And not just since Raj told her about it last night, Raj knows.

"Bullet point number two: The client is Nico Garnet."

Ruby's nostrils flare, but she doesn't look away from Lasadi. Raj can't tell if she's surprised at the client, or to hear Lasadi say the name aloud in a public place. Knowing Ruby, she's not surprised. She'd clearly been on a date when Raj called her last night, but he'd bet good money that as soon as she heard the words *Auburn Station* she ditched the girl and spent the night hacking every network in Ironfall to figure out exactly who would be interested in a visit to Auburn Station.

"That's fine," Ruby says.

"We ship out tonight."

Ruby hesitates at that. "What's the rush? Station's been abandoned a decade."

"Auburn Station got bought by a corporation and it's going to get dismantled at the end of the month," says Lasadi.

"This is going to be any of our last chance to see what's inside," Raj points out.

"I said I'm in." Ruby drums her fingers against the table. "One condition on account of the timing, only."

Lasadi lifts her chin. "Go ahead."

"You hire my brother, Alex, for your crew, too."

Raj shakes his head. "Ruby, c'mon."

Lasadi glances at him, then back to Ruby. "What's with your brother?"

"If you're trying to break into a place, he's your guy. Kid can pick any lock, get into any room and back out without even God knowing. Sensors, traps, he can see through it all, and he's got a memory for layout like a steel trap. I can hack any system you want me to — Alex can hack any physical location. We'll need him for a job like this."

"And he steals anything that isn't nailed down," Raj points out.

"He's not a klepto," protests Ruby. "But the brain on him, sometimes he's too smart for his own good. I don't have a choice, though — so neither do you if you want me to come. He's staying with me for a minute."

"You said kid?" asks Lasadi. "How old is he?"

"Seventeen."

"He's not old enough to stay on his own?"

"Sure he is," Ruby says. "But he's not staying on his own in my apartment, and I'm not throwing my little brother out to sleep in the plaza." She shrugs. "Plus, sounds like the perfect job to bring a break-in artist on. He's a fucking genius, and he'll be my problem. I'll split my fee, it won't even cost you more."

"That's fine," Lasadi says finally. "I have budget for one more crew, and if he's as good as you say, it sounds like he'll be perfect. But if he's going to be trouble . . ."

"I'll kill him myself," Ruby says. She sighs. "I'll go track him down and tell him to get ready to ship out." She leans forward, one red-lacquered nail to Raj's chest. "You and I still have some talking to do, my friend."

The knot of anxiety twisting his guts for days slowly unwinds, relief washing through like spring rain. Raj is willing to withstand any tongue-lashing he deserves, so long as Ruby answers his calls again.

"I'm counting on it," he says.

CHAPTER 11
LASADI

THE CACOPHONOUS RACKET of strangers fills the *Nanshe*: boots stomping, cargo thudding into place, unfamiliar voices shrill even from the solitude of the bridge, where Lasadi's been meticulously going through the preflight checklist. The *Nanshe*'s new — temporary — crew has arrived.

She waits, listening. Used to be her excitement swelled at the familiar sounds of her crew gathering for a training run, or a supply mission, or a raid on the Alliance. She's been trying to remember that feeling, tap into the magic and let it carry her through these next necessary days — but every memory she tries fractures under the weight of everything that came after.

She can't think of Tania teasing Anna Mara about her preflight superstitions without thinking of Anton. Can't think of Henri's practical jokes without remembering her comrades' voices cutting out one by one. Can't think of the twins' laughter without visualizing the fire raining down from the Alliance ships above Tannis.

Lasadi squeezes her eyes shut, trying to quell the rising panic, barely noting the sharp spike of pain from her nails digging into her palms, when a familiar laugh drifts up from the cargo bay to curl warm and silken and dangerously soothing below her ribcage.

Raj.

Lasadi drags in a deep breath and cuts her gaze to the little mixla, who's watching her from the stasis field Jay set up to capture any gifts they might leave it. She takes another, calmer breath, telling herself that the sound of Raj Demetriou's laugh isn't the only thing pulling her back from the brink.

He's talking with Jay, by the sound of it. There's Ruby's voice, and an unfamiliar laugh that must be her brother, and Lasadi reminds herself that if they have to run with a crew, at least it's not made up of Nico Garnet's soulless mercs. They might be strangers, but they also might be able to help keep her mind off the ghosts this job is dredging up.

And maybe —

Lasadi cuts herself off before she starts imagining what might come after Auburn Station.

"This is all going to be fine," she says to the mixla — it's *not* a prayer. Then she swivels out of her seat and grips the ladder that leads from the bridge, sliding down two levels to the cargo bay.

As she'd guessed, Raj is here with Ruby and Alex Quiñones — but Jay's nowhere to be seen. The trio are gathered near the entrance of the cargo bay at the stern of the ship. Lasadi emerged in the bow of the ship, from the cluster of cargo-level cabins.

She pauses in the entrance to the cargo bay itself, considering her temporary crew. Ruby Quiñones is wearing the same red leather jacket as this morning, with tight black pants, a low-cut black tank top, and low-heeled boots. Her hair is pulled back into a ponytail, the loose, bouncy curls spilling over one shoulder.

The lanky young man beside her is obviously her

brother. Alex has the same golden undertone to his brown skin, the same spray of freckles over his cheeks and forehead; his thick black hair is tamed into a pompadour. He shoves his hands in his pockets, shoulders slouched as he studies her ship.

Raj is laughing at something Alex said. His dark hair is clubbed back, though a few unruly locks brush over his cheekbones. He lifts a hand to absently tuck a strand back, then looks up like he knows someone's watching him, turns to meet Lasadi's gaze. Is she imagining the banked embers in his eyes?

Danger.

Raj breaks into a grin, and it's all she can do to keep from smiling back. She's the captain, she tells herself. These may not be Nico's mercs, but Anton's voice is sharp in her mind: "You're not their friend anymore, you're their captain." And she's not here to make friends — she's here to do this job for Nico and bring everyone on this ship back home in one piece. Romance isn't on the menu, despite her runaway emotions seeming to think it is. Time to get that under control, once and for all.

Ruby follows Raj's attention, lifts her chin in greeting. "Hey, Cap," she calls. She elbows her brother, who straightens as Lasadi crosses to them. "This is my brother, Alex. Alex, Captain Cazinho."

Lasadi meets Alex's handshake and wide grin with a measured smile of her own. "Nice to meet you. Call me Lasadi."

"Cool ship," Alex says; he's got a teenager's casual indifference, but his eyes are bright and alive, filing away details. Alex can hack any physical location, Ruby said this morning. Lasadi wonders what that means for how he sees the *Nanshe*.

"Thanks," she says. "It's not mine, though."

Alex shrugs one liquid shoulder, hands still in his pockets. "Still. Always thought it'd be cool to learn to fly."

"It's pretty cool," Lasadi agrees. What the hell do you talk to a seventeen-year-old about? "Where's Jay?"

"He had to run out for a minute," Raj says. "Told us to strap in our gear and pick a room."

Lasadi tries to keep the surprise off her face. They're under an hour to countdown, which is no time for Jay to have one last fling with Chiara, she doesn't care how much they've been away from Ironfall on jobs lately. "All right, then. Cabins are on the crew level — I'll give you the tour."

She pulls up a new message to Jay while the others climb up to the next level, duffel bags over shoulders.

Closing doors in 15.

His response is immediate: I'll be there.

Efficient with his trysts, at least.

"Cabins are at the bow," Lasadi calls; the ladder from the stern of the cargo level opens onto a landing with a pair of doors: storage and medbay. A short hallway leads from there to the galley, where Ruby, Raj, and Alex automatically congregate. Lasadi waves for them to continue forward into the next hallway, where the doors to four cabins and two heads circle the ladder to the bridge.

"The open doors are all up for grabs," Lasadi says. "Ruby, why don't you take the far one on the starboard side. It has a bit more space."

It's also the only one that shares a wall with her own, which means whichever cabin Raj chooses, she'll at least have a few extra meters between them at night.

"Thanks, Cap," Ruby calls, tossing her duffel in the room Lasadi indicated. "Neither of us want to share a bathroom with my brother, do we. Is the ladies' room port or starboard?"

"Port has the better shower," Lasadi says.

Ruby flashes her a grin. "Port, so."

Raj and Alex toss their bags in the two smaller cabins,

then they all reconvene in the galley.

Alex opens a cabinet, browsing the contents. "That mechanic guy, Jace?" he asks.

"Jay," Ruby corrects.

That jerk of Alex's chin could be *Yeah, him* or *I don't care*. "Where's his cabin? Or is he with you, Cap?"

"Alex!" snaps Ruby.

"Cargo level," Lasadi says. She can't tell if Alex is simply curious or still filing away details, because he merely moves on to another cabinet. Raj, on the other hand, seems relieved at the answer.

"Everybody happy with their bunk?" Lasadi asks. "Good. We're scheduled to fly in an hour. You need anything else, have it delivered quick because I'm sealing the doors as soon as Jay gets back. Any questions?"

Alex shuts a cabinet. "Do we have coffee?"

"What does a live wire like you need coffee for?" Raj asks.

Alex shrugs. "It's good."

"Plenty of coffee," Lasadi says. "Plenty of decent food, drinks, et cetera." She spent most of the day checking over the hold and refilling supplies; they're stocked for a comfortable eight days, with emergency supplies that'll float them for another month in case something goes wrong. Not that she wants to live on ration bars that long, but they'll work in a pinch.

"And plenty of hot sauce," Alex says, noticing the rack of bulbs by the table. He slides her a grin.

"Some of the best in the Belt, and a few imports that are hard to get your hands on," says Lasadi. Alex looks impressed, and she feels a strange twinge of pride. On the few jobs Lasadi had run with Nico's mercs, they tended to keep to themselves and make their own meals. The *Nanshe* had mostly been transport.

"Bridge and engineering are off-limits," she says.

"Medbay and the pantry are both locked but fully stocked, talk to me or Jay if you need anything. Help yourself to anything in the galley, feel free to use any of the exercise equipment in the cargo bay. All clear? Good. Get settled in." Lasadi turns her back on the little group, then pulls up a message to Jay: ETA?

2 min.

She heads down to the cargo bay to wait for him, and to get away from the pressure of people in her galley. She'd expected to feel claustrophobic at the thought of elbowing past Alex in the hallway, sharing a bathroom with Ruby, trying at all costs to avoid brushing up against Raj. But now that her initial moment of panic is over, she's almost looking forward to the next few days. With Alex's easy-going curiosity, Ruby's casual friendliness, and Raj's well, everything — she might just be able to relax.

"Permission to come aboard, Captain?"

Lasadi straightens at the familiar silk-and-steel voice. Tora Garnet. Lasadi hadn't been expecting a send-off, but then again, Tora isn't dressed in her usual elegant suit. Her nails still gleam gold, but her makeup is minimal, her black bob is pulled into a half ponytail, and she's wearing in a simple jumpsuit and practical boots. Lasadi's always assumed the other woman to be in her fifties, but maybe that was a trick of how she carried herself. In the simple clothes, she's dropped a decade.

"Welcome aboard," Lasadi says, then frowns when she spots the duffel Tora's carrying. "You stopping by to drop off some more gear?"

"I'm shipping with you."

Lasadi's shaking her head before Tora's finished. "No. I mean, no offense, but this isn't exactly a cruise. And the *Nanshe*'s a bit rough in terms of accommodations." And Lasadi does *not* want to spend the next six days with Tora Garnet.

"It can comfortably crew six," Tora says. "I know the specs of my father's ship."

Lasadi smiles tight against the barb. "It's your father's ship," she says, careful. "And it's your right to come with us if you want. But, respectfully, you hired me to captain it for this job. Which means orders come from me, and I make the decisions about what's best for this crew."

For a gleaming, dangerous moment Lasadi thinks Tora will fight her — and it would be a fight. Tora may be in charge when they're in Nico's lair, and Lasadi may not have asked to be responsible for these lives. But she is.

"My father claims you were a brilliant commander," Tora says.

Lasadi's smile sharpens. "Excellent." She holds out an arm to the bow of the cargo level. "If I'd known, I'd have saved you the bigger cabin. But the one here on the cargo level is still unclaimed." She half considers offering Tora her own cabin and taking the spare one near Jay's for herself, but she should stay close to the bridge — no matter how crowded the crew level is going to be. And how pissed Jay is going to be at his new neighbor.

"I don't need any special treatment," Tora says.

"Of course," Lasadi says.

"Are all the others on?"

"We're waiting for — ah. There you are."

Jay saunters up the cargo ramp as though he's been just around the corner, rather than disappearing for a tryst with Chiara in the final hour before launch. Lasadi tamps down a flare of frustration — but it's not his fault he doesn't know how rattled she is about the crew coming on.

Jay gives Tora's back a puzzled look.

"Tora's shipping out with us," Lasadi says, all pleasant and accommodating. Tora returns the smile; they both know how to play nice now they've shown their teeth.

"Show her to the cabin by yours, then get us prepped and meet me on the bridge."

She doesn't wait for his response, just turns her back on his surprised expression and manages to make her way to the bridge without having to talk to anyone else.

Once there, she settles into the pilot's chair, her heart racing with far more effort than it took to climb the ladder. She glances at the little marble and turquoise mixla.

"This is all going to be fine," she says again, then hits the general channel. "Strap in and let's get this show on the road."

A moment later the *Nanshe*'s system announces that the ship is sealed. "Request permission for liftoff," she tells the computer, then sets to double-checking everything herself.

A soft chime indicates an outside channel request.

"Control to *Nanshe*," says a human voice. "You're in the queue. Stand by for release in twelve minutes."

"Copy twelve, thank you," she says, then clicks on the general channel again. "Twelve minutes, people."

She hears noise on the ladder behind her and glances over her shoulder to find Jay. He sinks into his chair and buckles himself in. She expects Jay to have a smudge of lipstick on his collar and a mischievous twinkle in his eye, but he's deadly serious as he seals the hatch.

"What's the matter?"

"Got some news," Jay says, voice low. "About the new guy."

"Figured you were out with Chiara."

Jay shakes his head. "Got a call from a friend I asked to do some digging on his military record — what I found wasn't complete. He wanted to meet in person."

"And?" She's studying Jay's face, trying to understand what she needs to prep herself for. It can't be that bad, she tells herself, or Jay would have stopped the launch sequence before it started and dealt with the situation.

"He deserted, yeah," Jay says. "He told me he resigned in protest and was arrested. Turns out he was going to be court-martialled."

"Court-martialled for what?"

"Don't know. It's sealed. Probably because his dad's an admiral."

"Seven minutes, *Nanshe*."

"Copy seven minutes," Las says, automatic. The son of an admiral? The name rings a bell — she'd been more focused on day-to-day operations and mission planning in the CLA, but Anton had always kept tabs on the Alliance leadership. Always considered himself on a level playing field with those who held the highest power.

Admiral Demetriou; she tries the name out. It sounds familiar.

"Admiral Demetriou was in charge of the blockade against Tannis," Jay says, and it clicks into place — she remembers the admiral confirming Anton's accusations about Mercury Squadron's role in destroying the medical transport, the footage playing over and over while she lay in medbay with nothing to do but drink in the awful news of the aftermath rather than shutting it out and focusing on putting herself back together.

"What does the son of an admiral do to get court-martialled?" she asks.

"I'm trying to find out. But even without that, you think the son of an admiral just defects? Simply walks off his ship and sets up a new life on Dima — right before they started shelling Tannis?"

Lasadi's fingers spread over her left side automatically, brushing over the ridge of scar tissue beneath her shirt.

"Copy two minutes," Jay says, and Lasadi realizes with a jolt that she missed the control tower's prompt.

She takes a deep breath and turns back to the controls. "Does Tora know about the court-martial?" she asks.

"This was hard to find."

"The Garnets have a way of finding out difficult information." She types in the code for launch sequence, watching the *Nanshe*'s clock tick slow towards the one-minute mark.

"Las. He still hasn't lied to us."

"He hasn't told us the whole truth."

"Would you have?" Jay asks. "It's the Pearls. Everybody's here for a fresh start."

A voice crackles through the comms: "Sixty seconds, *Nanshe*."

"Copy sixty." Las presses Enter, feeling an eerie calm despite the new knife lodged in her ribcage. She frowns at Jay, trying to read his expression in the dim light of the console. "Do you trust him?" She needs to know; somewhere along the way she's lost the ability to make that call for herself.

"My gut says he's all right."

"Thirty seconds, *Nanshe*."

"Copy thirty." Below her, settled in his cabin and plotting olds know what, is Raj Demetriou. Grifter. Charmer. War criminal? Or a refugee from the same tragedy that left its marks blazing across her body — and psyche?

She brushes a kiss over her thumb and presses it against the mixla's forehead before she even realizes old muscle memory has taken over. Beside her, Jay murmurs a prayer she hasn't heard him say since the war.

Lasadi grips the controls.

They say Auburn Station is full of ghosts, but Lasadi's mind has been swirling with them since the minute she agreed to take this job.

She has six days to find a way to leave a few of them behind her in the black — or leave an Arquellian grifter there instead.

CHAPTER 12
LASADI

"Pass the hot sauce?" Alex asks.

They're all gathered around the dining table in the galley — all but Tora — and Lasadi isn't ready to say it out loud, but it's . . . comfortable. She enjoys the companionable silence she has with Jay, but the *Nanshe* feels more alive with a full crew. Tora's been keeping to her cabin, but the Quiñones siblings and Raj have made themselves at home. And, turns out, Lasadi doesn't hate it.

In the two days since they shipped out, Lasadi has talked with Ruby the most. The hacker has a disarming way of treating you like you've been friends for years, filling every room she's in with such a swirl of small talk and observations and funny stories it took Lasadi a while to realize what the other woman was doing.

Ruby's patter is just as much a barricade as Lasadi's tendency towards silence. Lasadi has exchanged more words with Ruby in the last two days than she has with everyone else combined in the past year — but she hasn't learned anything about who Ruby truly is. It's impressive. And weirdly comforting; Lasadi has found herself relaxing around Ruby, appreciating the safety of the faux intimacy.

Alex, on the other hand, is an open book. Anything Lasadi knows about the Quiñones siblings' past, she learned from him: They were orphaned young, left at the doorstep of the Aymaya Apostles in Artemis City, raised by the ayas. There's a decent age gap between them — Lasadi would guess a decade or more — and Ruby moved out when she was eighteen, but Alex was living there until he was kicked out "most recently."

Lasadi hasn't asked why he got kicked out, but knows he'd tell her if she did. Alex Quiñones has a teenager's self-absorption, a desire to be seen, to tell his story. He's not annoying about it, though — probably because he's equally keen to absorb the stories of the people and world around him. And now his curiosity has turned to her collection of pepper sauces.

"Which one?" Raj is sitting closest to the rainbow array of hot sauce bulbs on the galley counter — and farthest away from Lasadi. She can't tell if he's avoiding her or if he's giving her space. In the market at Selena's, she could have sworn he was flirting, but he hasn't made another attempt, and he doesn't give her any special attention now in his smile — he shares the same one with Alex. Maybe he's respecting their professional relationship, maybe he's one of those guys who moves on fast if they don't get an easy win.

She hopes it's the latter, because his presence lights her up like a beacon every time he's in the room, and she can't seem to shut that reaction down. It would be much easier if he were just another asshole looking for an easy lay.

"The orange one," says Lasadi. "With the black scorpion on the label. I picked it up on a run to New Sarjun a few months back — you've got to try it."

Raj plucks the neon orange bulb from the rack and lobs it gentle down the table towards Alex. Lasadi catches it first, squeezes a healthy dollop onto her spoonful of stew, then sends it spinning with a touch to Alex.

Jay laughs. "Don't hurt yourself, kid."

"I can handle spice," Alex says archly, matching the amount Lasadi had used. "Anyone else?" He twirls the neon orange bulb in dexterous brown fingers.

"I'm gonna see if fire comes out your ears first," says Ruby; Raj waves him off. Alex shrugs and sets the orange bulb spinning like a top above the table.

"Don't play games with Coruscans," Raj says to Alex. "Especially when the game involves New Sarjunian heat."

Lasadi pops the spoonful of stew in her mouth and chews slow, never breaking eye contact with Alex, never losing a hint of a smile. Alex winks and does the same.

At his age, Lasadi had believed she knew how the world worked, and she made sure everyone around her knew it. She'd memorized the facts and practiced the arguments, and she had the passion to back up her stances — but she'd lacked the natural curiosity to sit back and listen, or the self-confidence to potentially make a fool of herself in front of strangers.

Alex, on the other hand?

His eyes go instantly watery, fat droplets clinging to his lashes as he screws his eyelids shut, thumping a hand against the table. Lasadi laughs and pushes herself out of her chair, floating across to the cooler to draw Alex a bulb of soy milk.

"Here," she says, sending it soaring back to the table; Alex clutches at it, desperate. "That should help."

"Did I miss something?" Tora's voice comes from the hallway to the cabins, and the warmth drains from the room. It's silent but for Alex, who's still coughing frantic into his sleeve, covered in a faint sheen of sweat.

"A hot sauce arms race," Lasadi says.

"I lost," chokes out Alex. He takes another long pull of the soy milk bulb.

Tora, apparently, has no comment on the hijinks; she's made it clear already she's not here to fraternize with the hired guns.

"We dock in eight hours," she says, taking her spot at the table. They've left her one at every group meal, though this is the first time she's taken advantage of it. Tora tears open her stew packet and plucks the still-spinning hot sauce bulb from above the table, heavily anointing her meal before flicking the bulb back down the table to Raj. He catches it and tucks it back in the condiment rack's webbing with a nod of greeting Tora doesn't return.

Tora takes a bite and continues, apparently immune to New Sarjunian peppers. "However, the captain and I got word that SymTex is ahead of schedule," she says. "Their survey crew was due to arrive at Auburn Station six days from now, but it will be closer to two. This shouldn't affect us — we'll be long gone by then. But I want to impress on you that there's no time to waste."

Right down to business, that one — Lasadi had been going to wait to do this briefing until after the dinner's wrappers were cleared. The crew's glancing from Tora to her.

Lasadi floats back to the table, locking her magboots in at her spot. "Like Tora said, we'll need to be fast — but there are no other ships in the area. So with any luck we'll have undetected access to the station. And if we are detected?" She lifts an eyebrow at Jay.

"Ruby and I have an emergency plan and cover story prepped," he says.

"Thank you." Lasadi inclines her head to Tora. "Shall we?"

Tora places a holoprojector in the middle of the table, and at the tap of her finger it projects the map of Auburn

Station above their meals. A trio of habitable outer rings encircle the knot at the heart, which appears to be less like a planned project and more like a junkyard's worth of living modules, corridors, and leftover parts from a shipbuilder haphazardly gathered around a gravity well.

The station looks small, but as Tora spreads her fingers to zoom in on the station's heart, the schematic peels back in layers to reveal how extensive and complicated Rasheda's inner sanctum is. Corridors spiraling in on themselves, airlocks leading to other airlocks, observation rooms covered over by shielding plates, defense turrets aimed at other parts of the station.

Rasheda Auburn's own private fortress, a labyrinthine knot designed to keep her safe, but which cut her off so thoroughly from her own crew, living in the outer rings, that they mutinied and killed her.

Tora touches a spherical module near the exact center of the station's heart. At her touch, the sphere glows a pale blue. "What we want is in this room."

"Do we get to know what that is?" Raj asks.

"Your job isn't to know." Tora's tone says it's a fact, not a rebuff. "Your job is to get me in." She zooms back out a bit and touches a button on her cuff. A glowing orange path lights the way through the maze. "This is the fastest route through the labyrinth, which can only be accessed from the outer rings; we'll dock at this airlock in C Ring, and enter the labyrinth at this location."

"Why not dock in the station's heart?" Alex asks. He leans into the schematic, studying it. "Looks like there are airlocks."

"Because Rasheda Auburn designed those airlocks to blow trespassers into jelly, didn't she," Ruby says. "Buzz is the labyrinth's airlocks can be safely opened from the inside, only." She leans in, studying Tora's route. "This map is amazing."

The corner of Tora's mouth tugs into something that could be pride; the woman's not entirely an automaton after all. Lasadi doesn't think Tora's shipped out with a crew before; she suddenly wonders if the other woman has been keeping to herself because she's the boss, or because she's simply out of her element.

"I've seen loads of half-assed scribbles from the nets, but this is flash," Ruby says. "If anyone else has a set of schematics this detailed, they're not letting on. Upload those to our suits, and navigation shouldn't be a problem."

"That won't be necessary," Tora says. "We won't be splitting up. I'll be in charge of navigation."

Lasadi blinks at her; this was not part of the plan. Ruby's lips part in surprise, but before she can say anything, Lasadi cuts in.

"Too much of a risk," Lasadi says. "We each need a copy of the schematic."

"These are too valuable to risk getting out." The chill in Tora's eyes says this is not up for discussion. "We stay together."

Lasadi opens her mouth to argue and Jay shifts beside her, a subtle nudge of his ankle against hers before Lasadi can say something she'll regret. Tora's waiting for it, though. Waiting to see if Lasadi is willing to go toe-to-toe with her in front of the rest of the crew.

And you know what? She is.

"My top priority is getting us in and out safe," Lasadi says. "We can wipe the suits — wipe the *Nanshe*'s entire system once we're done with this job — but we need to be able to navigate."

"Then I suggest you all stay with me," Tora says. "This is not up for discussion."

A spark flicks between them, ready to catch, and of the half-dozen potential outcomes Lasadi can imagine to this fight, none of them are good. Tora's family owns this ship, which means she owns Lasadi's future until Lasadi can take it into her own hands — and despite the impression Tora gives of a gilded bureaucrat in a suit, there's a knife's edge below her surface. If Lasadi was smart, she'd keep her mouth shut and let Tora Garnet have her way.

If it was something that didn't put her crew in danger, she would.

She takes a sharp breath, but before she can speak, Raj clears his throat.

"We'll stick close," he says. He shines his good-natured smile on both women. "Not a problem."

"No need to separate," Jay agrees.

Ruby shakes her head like she'd argue but it's pointless; Alex is ignoring them, studying the schematic with head cocked to one side, pale blue lines reflected in his dark eyes.

"Fine," Lasadi says. Tora's mouth flattens; she won, but she's not happy about it. Lasadi gives her a tight smile, then turns back to the schematic. "Tell us what we're up against," Lasadi says to Ruby.

"This place is filthy with traps," Ruby says. "But the nice bit is Rasheda also left behind the rumor that there's enough gold to make a saint blush if you make it through the maze. People have been trying to crack this puzzle for the last fifty years, so there's lots of good information on the nets if you know where to look. And how to weed out the bullshit."

"I'm impressed with how much you found so quick," Lasadi says.

Ruby flashes her a smile. "You hire a pro, you get pro work."

Beside her, Alex reaches to zoom back in on the labyrinth, pointing to a star symbol. "Are these the defense turrets?"

Ruby bats his hand away. "They are," she says. "They're our next biggest worry after the labyrinth itself. They're run by the station AI from a centralized location, and not linked to each other."

"Which means disabling the turrets one by one until we get to that location," Lasadi guesses.

"Yep," Ruby says. "That's why we brought Alex along."

Jay laughs like she's joking, but Alex nods, solemn. "It's a blooming arrow trigger grid pattern," he says. "Could get through one of those in my sleep."

"And if Alex does trigger one — "

"I won't."

Ruby glares at him. "If Alex *does* trigger one, it'll likely alert the defense bots as well. So come prepared to shoot."

"On it," says Raj

"Of course," Lasadi says, nearly at the same time. He winks at her, and she ghosts him a reflexive smile. His gaze doesn't linger on hers any longer than would be professional, and Lasadi tells herself the heat below her collar is from the New Sarjunian peppers.

"Most likely Rasheda left boobytraps that aren't recorded on these schematics," Lasadi says. "We take our time, keep an eye out. Even accounting for delays, we should have plenty of oxygen to make it to the heart of the labyrinth and back to the *Nanshe*."

She glances around the table; everyone nods assent.

"Worst-case scenario is we have to make a second run," she continues. "Which we'll have time for, even with the SymTex survey crew being ahead of schedule. Anything else, Ruby?"

Ruby nods. "Last major buzz is about the door to the central chamber," she says. "There are supposed to be five locks — three mechanical, two digital. How much are we authorized to damage?"

"Anything you need to in order to get me into that chamber," Tora says.

"Fab. Then just one of the mechanical locks'll be a real challenge. Jay's got a plan for that one, though."

"And backup plans on backup plans," Jay says. "Between us we should crack this station wide open."

"Do you have plans for the ghosts?" Alex asks.

Ruby elbows him. "*Alex.*"

"I've been reading the boards, too," Alex shoots back. "Everyone says Auburn Station is haunted. Or full of aliens."

"Aliens?" Ruby rolls her eyes. "Saints save me."

"And there are no ghosts," Tora says, sharp; the warmth vanishes from the room. "Rasheda Auburn left boobytraps and rumors, that's all."

Alex shrugs one shoulder, a universal teenage gesture that says he's not arguing because it's so obvious he's right and he doesn't want to waste the energy. Ruby's glare says, *Do not fuck this up for us.*

Lasadi clears her throat. "That said, ghost stories don't come from nowhere. Drifters, pirates, scavengers — we can't assume we'll be alone, so we go in armed and keep our eyes open for trouble. Any other questions?"

When no one speaks, Tora turns off the holoprojector and pockets it, pushing back from the table. "Remember we dock in eight," she says on her way out of the galley; an uneasy quiet falls in her wake.

Alex finally breaks the silence. "Looks like a fun time to me," he says. "Pirate treasure, haunted space station, killer defense bots? Practically a vacation."

Jay laughs. "See if you can beat me to the treasure, kid. You can't even hold down some hot sauce."

"I didn't even see you try," Alex shoots back. He turns to Lasadi and makes a mock bow of respect. "I straight up thought I was going to die. You win, queen of fire."

Lasadi finds herself smiling without realizing it, and realizes the strange tension Tora left behind has all but vanished. Where Ruby uses friendly banter to make a person feel comfortable, her little brother reflexively defuses tension with his self-deprecating jokes and antics. It's not the unshakable camaraderie of Mercury Squadron, but it's nice.

"Can't wait to watch you break that mechanical lock," Alex says to Jay. "Gonna have to teach me how."

Jay winks at Alex. "It's secret sauce as much as know-how," he says. "But you can watch. And maybe eventually you'll learn."

"That's the last thing we need," complains Ruby. "Teach Alex another thing that will piss the ayas off when he goes back."

Jay laughs and catches Lasadi's eye: *This is good, right?*

And he's right, this is good. But the easy banter is conjuring up memories of other jokes, other people's laughs she'll never hear again, and suddenly the room is heavy with ghosts. A complicated band of fear and grief tightens slow around Lasadi's chest, and she pushes herself back from the table so quickly Ruby breaks off ribbing her brother midsentence.

"Ruby and Alex, cleanup duty," Lasadi says, ignoring Jay's concerned look. "Jay and I take this watch, and I want everyone else getting their beauty rest. I'll wake you all when we're an hour out."

"I'll do a supply double check," Raj offers, and Lasadi nods her thanks, forcing herself to smile like everything is perfectly normal.

"I'll be on the bridge if any of you need me," she says; her tone says they shouldn't need her. "We'll be on Auburn Station before you know it."

CHAPTER 13
RAJ

THE SUPPLY CHECK GOES FAST, even though Raj runs over his lists twice, and even though his mind is half on the woman sitting two levels above him in the bridge.

He can't figure out Lasadi.

She's been keeping him at arm's length. It's subtle, but she's pushing back on him in a way she's not doing with Ruby or Alex. Does it mean he came on too strong with the "beautiful morning" comment at Selena's bazaar, and now she's wary of him? Or is she trying to keep things professional on this job?

Either way, he'll follow her lead. She's the captain, he's a hired hand, and the last thing this fraught job needs is for him to make a misguided pass at the boss. Especially now Ruby's involved — he talked her into a second chance working with him, and he's not going to blow it.

No harm in thinking about Lasadi, though. And maybe seeing how she feels about him once this whole thing is through.

Whether or not he'd have a chance isn't the only thing he's having trouble getting a bead on, though. Tonight Lasadi had been relaxed and carefree, ribbing Alex as his cheeks turned beet red, trading jokes with Ruby like they were old friends. Raj keeps catching glimpses of the confident, playful woman he'd met in Sumilang's museum — until she catches herself, and snuffs that light as quickly as pulling a shutter down against the glare of the sun. But even when she's closed off she has her tells. The restless fingers, the tapping heel. The twitch in her cheek and spark in her eye like some fire inside is struggling to shatter through the ice.

It's as though she's taken on a forced gravitas and deliberation that chafes. It doesn't fit with his image of someone who would have commanded a squadron as celebrated and feared as Mercury Squadron.

Space travel is long hours of boredom, so Raj has spent time going through news reports and footage of the CLA guerrillas during the war for Coruscan independence. They all kept low profiles by design, their faces and identities obscured, so he hasn't caught a glimpse of her or Jay, nor heard their names mentioned.

The single name or face to officially represent the CLA, of course, was Anton Kato. A charismatic man who claimed to be only the spokesperson, though Raj had sat through plenty of intelligence briefings showing that he was in fact the leader.

After the slaughter at Tannis — the slaughter Raj had failed to prevent — Kato managed to convince the public that the CLA had been divided. That he had represented a more moderate faction that was willing to negotiate a peace with the Alliance. Kato had blamed the death of the New Manilan medical transport on his own people — on Mercury Squadron, to be exact.

It was a lie, though few people know it. Raj doesn't know if the Alliance — if his *father* — fed Kato that lie, or if he came up with it on his own. But either way, Mercury Squadron had been the perfect scapegoat. A feared unit, all either captured or killed in the fighting that followed the death of the transport. No one spared to refute the slander — or so at least Raj had assumed.

Anton Kato had gone on to spin that lie and the negotiated cease-fire with the Alliance into a seat in the Coruscan Senate, while most of his colleagues in the CLA had either been arrested by the Alliance or vanished back into the population that had supported them. Maybe it's true that the rest of the guerrillas had obscured their identities to focus the story on the cause rather than themselves. Or maybe, Raj wonders, Kato insisted they obscure their identities to keep all the attention on himself.

"You done here, then?"

Raj looks up so fast he bangs his head on the lid of the crate he was checking. Ruby's floating gracefully behind him. Raj has learned to navigate easily in zero G, but Ruby has the sort of natural skill that comes from growing up with weightlessness. They've discussed it before; like the knapsack stenciled with the words Auburn Station, it's another clue to a past she doesn't remember.

"Double-checking," he says. Her lips are pursed, like she has something she wants to say but doesn't like the taste. "What's up?"

"I've been thinking I owe you an apology," Ruby says. "So if we're going to be murdered by ghosts in a few hours, I should say it."

"You don't owe me anything."

"No? I was maybe too harsh when I said I didn't want to work with you anymore."

"I screwed up that last job pretty bad."

"Yeah, you did. But I could've been kinder. I don't actually think you have a death wish — you've been a bit lost, only." Her expression softens. "I was worried about you. Seemed you'd stopped caring if you came out of a job alive."

"Maybe I had."

"Yeah? What changed?"

"Somebody cared enough about me to tell me to fuck off."

Ruby laughs; he'd missed that sound. "Good on them, then."

"And I also may have gotten myself tangled up with a domestic dispute in one of the big Artemis City families."

"You did not!" Ruby's eyes are wide. "Who'd you sleep with?"

"No one!" Raj waves it away. "Just what should have been a simple job got complicated, and when I made it out I realized you were right. Something needed to change."

"So you got right in with Nico Garnet and a pair of grumpy Coruscans, then?"

"I was going to walk away until I heard where they were going. I figured even if you didn't answer my call, I could bring you back something that would help your search. Make it up to you."

"The ego on you," and she laughs again. "You wouldn't know the first thing about where to look."

"Then it's a good thing you came."

"It is, isn't it."

"Does Alex know why you wanted to come?" he asks, and Ruby shakes her head.

"I don't think he cares." She exhales softly. "This is the third time in as many years the ayas have asked me to come deal with him. I can't keep dropping everything to get him."

Raj hasn't asked Ruby exactly what Alex did to get himself kicked out of the Aymaya Apostles boarding school this time, but he assumes it has to do with being insufferably seventeen. And probably getting caught traipsing somewhere he wasn't supposed to be.

"When he goes back, it won't be for much longer," Raj

says; her eye roll says she knows that. "Will he stay with you?"

She shakes her head. "You can imagine that, can you? He's too much, runs me ragged. I can see why the ayas need a break from that one, time to time. He needs a job — something to keep him focused."

"He seems extremely focused here."

"He's getting paid to dismantle things and be a general sneak-about, so he's only delighted. And he's stuck on Jay like holy on a saint, so God knows what else he's learning."

"Maybe it'll come in handy," Raj says. "Plenty of jobs for mechanics."

"You know my brother. He'll use it to break into some place he shouldn't be, only." Ruby's teeth catch her lower lip; she's got something else on her mind. "Not that it's any of my business," she finally says, "but what's the captain's story?"

"You checking her out?" Raj says it teasing; Lasadi is about as far from Ruby's type as it gets. Ruby likes her women bubbly and spontaneous and playful, party girls who won't be much of a distraction from her work. Raj can't see Lasadi out clubbing in a minidress — though that doesn't stop his imagination from taking an instant left turn to picture it. He shuts that down fast, though. He doesn't need Ruby to guess his new obsession.

"Not on purpose." Ruby lowers her voice. "Walked in on her toweling off in the bathroom before dinner — the door was unlocked and I didn't hear her in there. Walked right back out, obviously, but couldn't help seeing her."

Raj swallows, his rogue imagination gleefully running with a new scenario.

"She's got a lot of scars," Ruby says. "Like, bad. I wondered if you knew why."

That cools him right back down. Jay had told him she'd been injured in the Battle of Tannis — that she'd almost died. Raj had nearly forgotten the offhand comment, but it's yet another reason he's desperate to make sure Lasadi never learns what's in his sealed military files. It's one thing to be a deserter; if they found out what he was convicted of, he'd be in trouble. He might be able to explain it to someone else; with her, it would be far too personal.

Ruby's giving him a strange look, he needs to say something fast. "CLA," Raj says. "She and Jay both fought for the CLA, got shot down at Tannis."

"I knew the CLA bit," Ruby says; Raj doesn't ask how. She did her research, like she always does, ferreting out the truth. She's presumably done her research on him, too, a fact that's always been reassuring to Raj. If anyone could find his sealed military files, it would be Ruby — and if she'd found them, she would have called off their friendship long ago. His father may still put bounties on his head, but at least he's done Raj the one favor of making sure the records from the court-martial are thoroughly locked down.

"Since you already know everything," Raj says, "what's the deal with the Garnets? Tora's a piece of work."

"Nico Garnet's about next in line to shake hands with the maker," Ruby says. "That's the buzz, at least — they've been keeping it quiet so no one panics, but he's been sick for months and doing all these experimental treatments. Whole organization's going to fall apart if he doesn't get better or pass on power."

"You have any idea what they want from Auburn Station?"

"Not a clue, and I'm not going to ask." But he hears the faintest click: pinkie nail flicking against thumbnail. She does know, or she suspects. She's not going to tell him, though.

Before he can decide if he wants to press, voices sound from the ladder well: Jay and Alex, coming down from the galley.

"Heya," Ruby calls, waving them over. "My brother being a pest, is he?"

"He's fine," Jay says with a grin. Where Lasadi closes down in the face of newcomers, Jay's opened up with the camaraderie. "We're arguing about the best way to beat this last mechanical lock."

"I say we torch it with the plasma saw," Alex says.

"Won't work," Jay says. "We'll trip the backup explosives."

"Not if Sis can get those turned off, first."

"Show me," says Ruby, leaning in. She glances at Raj, but her smile slips away, oh so briefly. She's worried. It could be the usual nerves, but Raj would bet money it's anticipation. Whatever ghosts are waiting on Auburn Station, they might hold the key to the questions Ruby's been asking her entire life.

CHAPTER 14
LASADI

IN THE SCHEMATICS, Auburn Station looked like a disorganized junk pile. In person, the station is a hulking ruin.

The three outer rings are stark and utilitarian, but appear to have held everything a small settlement would need to survive out in the black: crew quarters, grow labs, repair docks, other station services. Two of the rings appear mostly intact, though the middle one is cracked open in multiple places, chains of refuse trailing from the breaches. Some of the devastation is a side effect of being unprotected from the debris of Durga's Belt, but most was caused by humans — both in the original mutiny that killed Rasheda Auburn, and by wanderers afterwards.

Scorch marks char the station's surface. More than a few ships have used Auburn Station for target practice, Lasadi would guess. She wonders what the station's ghosts have to say about that.

C Ring, the innermost ring, still has power — as do parts of the sprawling tangle of construction that makes up the station's heart. Rasheda's inner sanctum. Jay's been giving her regular updates as they approach, and the station's power levels have remained a perfectly constant background hum that indicates passive systems running on their own rather than any human activity. The bioscanners haven't picked up any signs of life.

Lasadi leans back in her chair, watching Auburn Station fill her view: a strange, twisted metal monument to a woman who thought she could build a fortress to protect herself and ended up getting killed by her own crew instead. Better than getting them all killed and being the only one to survive.

The *Nanshe* is ringing with the sounds of preparation, and Lasadi should be down there with the rest, teasing out the preboarding jitters with jokes and laughter. Back in the CLA, she'd loved the electric rush of anticipation before every mission launch. The other members of the squadron swapping stories of near misses, ribbing each other about the blast marks on the wings of their ships.

They'd been a bunch of idealistic kids. A few were more experienced pilots, but most of Mercury Squadron had been young hotshots driven equally by the patriotic fire in their veins and their addiction to the rush of dancing with death.

Tania, round-faced and wide-eyed, her infectious laugh bellowing from her petite frame. Henri, with his lopsided grin and bear hugs. Chayña and her sibling Yunxi, the practical jokers. Nolan with his lucky streak, Saul with his pragmatism, Anna Mara with her constant superstitions.

Lasadi can still remember the last words each of them said before their comms went offline and their ships exploded into flame.

Logically, she knows she did the best she could. The mission had been going according to plan when someone destroyed the medical transport — she still can't believe it was anyone from Mercury Squadron, but she has no other explanation. Maybe the safe thing would have been to return home to base after the Alliance started shelling

Tannis, but Lasadi wasn't going to run when civilians were dying, and neither would anyone under her command. She'd called for backup, and Mercury Squadron had flown to defend Tannis.

Backup hadn't come.

She still doesn't know why. When she finally reached Anton, from Nico's medbay, he told her she'd never sent a backup request. Had her comms failed? Had he not received it? Or is he right, and she's misremembering after the chaos of the battle and her injuries. The last reply she ever received from Anton — she'd watched it over and over from her hospital bed — is playing on a loop in her head.

"You can't blame yourself for what happened," Anton had told her. "It's my fault; I let my feelings for you cloud my judgement when I promoted you. You weren't ready yet for command."

It's taken her three years to realize how precisely he'd used words as weapons to manipulate her. Isolate her. Shatter her own sense of self and rebuild it the way he wanted it. She knows that last message was just another tool in his arsenal of head games — but it doesn't stop the words from feeling true. Doesn't stop them from circling her now like wolves.

Every person on this ship is counting on her to bring them back safely, and the pressure clenches like a fist around her ribcage. She tries to slow her breathing, and then she remembers the way her own ship shuddered around her and she digs her fingers into her temples, trying to shut the torrent of memory down. Flames blaze up her side, something ice cold pierces her gut, Jay frantically calls her name.

"Captain?"

She's torn free from memory by the clinking of magboots on the lower deck, the creaking of the ladder behind her. Lasadi twists in her chair, and Raj's face appears in the hatch. "Permission to come up?" he asks.

She turns away, forcing ragged breath into her lungs. Olds, now is not the time for company. She almost sends him away, but she's afraid her voice will betray her. So she breathes deep again, quiet calm finally seeping through her enough that she can speak.

"Of course," she says.

Raj floats up the rest of the way, then settles into Jay's chair and leans forward to study the station. The light from the screen cools the warm undertones of his tawny skin, catching the gold flecks in his dark eyes like stars. His hair is tied back in a short ponytail at the nape of his neck, but a few strands float loose to brush his cheekbones.

If he's noticed anything's wrong, he doesn't show it.

Even before Lasadi knew who Raj Demetriou was, she'd known he was dangerous. She'd like to think she's immune to the charms of charismatic men, after Anton, but Raj has cut straight through her defenses.

And, somehow, she doesn't mind it.

He's an Arquellian admiral's son, she tells herself. The disgraced captain of an Alliance ship who was court-martialled in absentia, and he hasn't told the whole truth about why he deserted. Not that she's asked — and not like she's interested in showing off her old wounds to a stranger, either.

Jay's comment echoes in her mind: "He hasn't lied to us. It's the Pearls. Everybody's looking for a fresh start."

"Are we prepped for boarding?" Lasadi asks.

Raj lifts his chin, *Yes*. "All good to go," he says. "This place looks a lot worse off up close, doesn't it?"

"It's a trash heap."

"I keep thinking about that curse," Raj says. "That Rasheda would die once she found a home. Building this station did make her a target."

"Sure. But the attack came from her own crew."

"She cut herself off from them."

Lasadi flashes him a look, but he doesn't seem to mean anything by it. He's still studying the station.

"When I was a kid, my mom took me to an aquarium on the north coast of Arquelle," Raj says. "The thing I remember most is a fish that lives so deep in the ocean that the water's pure black. The fish developed this symbiotic relationship with a bioluminescent parasite that lives in their mouths, so when they open their jaws, other fish come to investigate. And get caught."

Lasadi's never been on Indira; she's only ever seen the vast blue oceans through the observation domes of Corusca, the lush turquoise planet above her more an interesting thought experiment than somewhere she'd ever expected to visit. For a moment her mind paints a picture. A young Raj standing on an Arquellian beach, staring up at the pale disk of Corusca in his own night sky, all silver dust and glittering lights. She wonders if he ever thought of visiting.

Ahead of them, Auburn Station blazes against the black backdrop of the void. The active systems in C Ring must include some sort of security beacon, because a ghostly blue light has been sweeping the interior at regular intervals, glinting through the portholes. The airlock they'll be docking with in about an hour glows red as a warning sign.

In the vast darkness of space around it, the station's light is mesmerizing. Drawing attention away from the potential danger held in the black, and dazzling away any thoughts of the trap held in the light. And, like any light, the closer you get, the harder it is to spot the trap within.

"What's the moral of the story?" Lasadi asks. "Don't trust hope in the darkness?"

Raj turns his full attention to her, gaze lingering; she wonders what he's found so fascinating. Those eyes don't just kindle feelings that are better left cold, she thinks, they see too much. Another reason he's so dangerous.

She doesn't look away.

"I think the moral is to know when you're walking into a trap, and to have good people at your side." Something about that makes him smile. "Thanks for the view, Cap. I'll go do a triple check on our gear." Raj shifts as though he's about to head back down to the cargo hold, but his gaze slips past her to the little shrine tucked in the corner.

He laughs, and her jaw tightens with anticipation of whatever he's about to say about the mixla.

"Look at you," he says with a smile. "I didn't get a thing out of Sumilang's museum, but you nabbed the totem *and* the mixla. You're supposed to leave something when you go on a journey, right?"

"It's not a good-luck charm. It's a — " She cuts herself off from saying *superstition*. That's what Raj and Sumilang had derisively called it, back at the museum.

Or, Sumilang had been derisive, she realizes. Thinking back through the conversation, she can't remember Raj saying anything disrespectful, even in the middle of his grift. Maybe he'd even been telling some of the truth.

She clears her throat. "Did your Coruscan nanny teach you that? Or was the nanny part of your con?"

Raj slides her a secret smile. "Her name was Meri, and she was one of the most genuinely loving people I knew." He slips a bangle off his wrist and suspends it in the stasis field Jay set up to hold the necklace and the whiskey shot he'd left there. "Keep an eye on the captain," Raj says to the mixla. "She's our way home."

She wants to believe he's not just telling her a story about the Coruscan nanny — needs to *know* it, for certain. But at some level, trust is about the not knowing, isn't it? The understanding that you can never know another person as intimately as you do yourself, but you can still step into that gap with them, have faith they'll catch you.

"Your father," she says, and he goes still. She can almost see him running through a catalogue of stories to find the perfect one to tell her. He'll be guessing what she knows, deciding how to spin it. She braces herself for excuses, for a tall tale, but instead she sees the moment of decision. Raj's eyelids slide closed. He breathes deep, lets it out slow, and the gesture carries with it years of old wounds, far older than whatever transpired during the war.

"My father is Admiral Demetriou," Raj says, meeting her gaze, steady. "Who led the blockade against Corusca."

She waits for the spin; it doesn't come.

"I don't know why I thought I could keep that hidden," Raj says. "But I should have been the one to tell you. I'm sorry."

"You were about to spend a week in the black with a couple of Coruscans," Lasadi finally says. "I probably wouldn't have mentioned it, either."

The furrow between his brows smooths; his exhale is audible. "Jay knows?"

"He's the one that found out."

"Then I can apologize to him, too."

"Tell him we're an hour out," she says. "And thank you."

Raj frowns. "For?"

For breaking her out of her dark swirl of panicked thoughts, for gifting her the story about the fish in the aquarium, for being respectful of the mixla, for not lying to her about his father — she doesn't know how to say any of that.

Lasadi waves a hand vaguely at the screen in front of them, and the tangled mess of a station they're approaching. "For your help," she says.

A gentle smile touches his lips, and again she gets the

dizzying sensation he's seen too much. But, "You're welcome" is all he says. Raj unbuckles himself from his chair, turning his back on the ghostly lights of Auburn Station that beckon in the dark.

She watches him disappear down the hatch to the crew quarters. Ahead of her, Auburn Station looms like a trap — but she knows it this time, and Raj is right. She has good people at her side. A part of her died with Henri and Tania and all the rest, but a part of her has been waiting patient for the right time to come alive.

Lasadi removes one of the small Coruscan opal studs from her earlobe and sets it in the stasis field in front of the mixla. It floats in the pale yellow light beside Raj's bracelet and the necklace Jay left earlier.

Every person on this ship is counting on her to bring them back safely.

And she'll do it.

CHAPTER 15
LASADI

WHEN LASADI GETS to the cargo bay, Tora's standing apart from the others, wearing an environment suit like she learned how to put it on from an instruction vid. Lasadi isn't sure if the others haven't noticed or are too spooked of Tora Garnet to correct her, but no one seems to have offered to help her with it.

Jay and Ruby are engrossed at the airlock, heads together over a tablet and arguing about some sort of breach protocol Lasadi can't follow. Raj is at the weapons lockers, directing Alex in distributing sidearms.

"Can I have a plasma rifle?" Alex asks.

"Did the ayas teach you to shoot since I saw you last?"

"I'm a quick study."

"Then negative," Raj says. He floats Alex an electric barb, then lifts his chin in greeting to Lasadi. "Flick down the safety, then the big red button zaps people. Leave the shooting to the queen of fire."

Raj's smiles have the capacity to ignite feverish heat, but this one isn't flirtatious. It's comrade to comrade, filling her with steady, slow warmth. She returns it, something unknotting deep within her.

"How's it going, Jay?" she calls, drifting to Tora and clicking her magboots into lock beside her with a soft thud.

"Just about got it," Jay calls back. "Scans show the life support systems are still running in the inner rings."

"Doesn't mean they're working right," Lasadi says. "Either way, we keep our suits on. We'll get a good three hours of oxygen before we need to recharge — that should be enough time to get us to the heart of the station and back, but watch your levels. We have plenty of time before SymTex arrives, so we don't need to take any chances. Understood?" A chorus of assent around her. "Good. Double-check your neighbor."

She turns to Tora while the others run through their own checks, adjusts the seals on the other woman's gloves, tightens the straps of her O_2 pack. Tora's wearing minimal makeup today, her hair swept back under a cap. Her expression is set fierce as if she were about to head into a contentious meeting, but Lasadi can tell she's nervous. Tora's probably had a lifetime of walking into fraught and potentially deadly situations; nerves won't be her problem. Her problem will be following orders.

"I want to be clear on command out there," Lasadi says. "You're in charge, but orders come from a single person. Me."

Tora's mouth flattens into a line, but she doesn't argue.

"If I override you, it's because I have a good reason. My number one goal is to fly out of here with every single person safe — and that includes you. Best-case scenario, we achieve that along with your objective."

"That's fine."

"Good." Lasadi hits the systems diagnostic check at Tora's collar; lights flare green, one by one. "You're good to go. Give me a hand?"

Lasadi doesn't need a hand with her own suit, but Tora needs to learn and Lasadi isn't about to say that out loud.

She talks Tora through the steps, watching her wordlessly file information away. It occurs to her that Tora Garnet probably hasn't had much opportunity to learn on her own. Always needing to be the fiercest, strongest person in the room, always trying to be the capable leader her father was. Maybe one of the reasons she came on this trip was for a chance to prove herself outside of her father's shadow.

"All systems good," Tora says when Lasadi's systems diagnostic check is finished. She takes a sharp breath to hide her nerves, but doesn't speak.

"Then let's go," Lasadi says; she turns to the others. "Jay? How are we looking?"

"Ready when you are, Captain."

"Let's go."

Jay breaks the seal, wrenching Auburn Station's airlock door open manually when it sticks halfway. "All clear," he says, and pushes himself through. Lasadi watches Tora, curious, waiting for her to balk, but if the other woman is still nervous, she's buried it deep.

Lasadi follows Jay in.

They've entered C Ring through a service airlock that accesses the ring's central corridor, which Lasadi scans as the rest of her crew joins them. The corridor stretches away from them in both directions, curving gently out of sight. The sweeping security light Lasadi had glimpsed from the *Nanshe* runs at regular intervals along the strip of emergency lights, illuminating a ransacked mess in gentle strobes. Panels have been pulled open, wiring stripped, and valuables looted. Debris floats in the corridor like an obstacle course.

Beside her, Alex reaches out and touches an object floating in the gloom, brushing it with a single gloved finger that sends it spinning towards his sister. In the lights of Ruby's helmet, it becomes horribly clear what it is.

"What the fuck!" Ruby bats the human femur away before it can drift into her helmet. "Alex, that's not funny."

"I don't see the rest of it," Alex says, cheerful.

"It's over there," says Raj, pointing at a skeleton floating farther down the hall. "Good thing we're not going that way."

"Don't think it's going to matter which way we go," Jay says, and as Lasadi draws closer to his position, she spots what he's pointing at. A desiccated corpse, lodged in a partially open door. The face mask is cracked, spidering out from a bullet hole in the center.

Lasadi shakes off the worm of uneasiness crawling down the collar of her suit. "We don't have time for sight-seeing," Lasadi says. "Come on."

As Tora had promised, the airlock they chose offers a short journey to one of the entrances to the labyrinth, which is hidden inside a closet. The access panel beside the door has been stripped for parts like the rest of this hall-way, and anything useful in the closet has been cleaned out.

Ruby floats in, gloved fingers probing behind the top shelf. "Got it," she says, then snakes a cord out of her gauntlet and plugs it in. She hums to herself as she works, an eerie tune that Lasadi finally recognizes as an old funeral dirge. Both of the Quiñones siblings have a morbid sense of humor, apparently.

Lasadi opens her mouth to tell her to keep the channel clear, when Ruby straightens. "I'm in. The security on this door's been disabled already, someone's been this way before."

And she hums again — or no. That's not right, Lasadi realizes with a chill. The funeral dirge in a woman's voice had continued even as Ruby spoke.

"Tora, are you humming?" Lasadi asks. Tora frowns at her, and Lasadi shakes her head. "Never mind. I'm just getting some weird feedback. Everyone, let's keep this channel clear."

The humming fades as they cross through the internal airlock into the labyrinth itself, leaving behind an equally eerie silence. They've entered a cube antechamber with six identical doors — one in every wall. The walls and doors had at one point been finished with glossy white ceramic; now the finish is scuffed and stained by years of benign neglect and active defacement. Lewd graffiti is scrawled across one wall, numbers are scratched into the ceramic coating of each door.

"Nice of someone to leave us distinguishing features," Raj says.

"There's a whole subculture of people who've tried to find Rasheda Auburn's treasure," says Ruby. "We're definitely not the first people who've gotten into the outer layers of the labyrinth."

Lasadi's suit flashes a notification that the life support is working. Temperature, oxygen levels, atmospheric toxicity — everything is reading as within tolerable levels.

"Is everyone getting positive life support readings?" Lasadi asks. Alex and Tora answer verbally over the comms channel; Raj, Ruby, and Jay sign assent nonverbally.

"That's good, right?" Alex says. "In case things take longer than expected."

"We're not trusting fifty-year-old life support," Lasadi says. She catches Jay's eye; the life support shouldn't still be running at all after this long. Someone's been maintaining it, and Lasadi wants to know why. "Keep your suits on and your eyes open. We may not be alone here."

"There weren't any signs of life," points out Ruby.

"Who else would be maintaining a life support system?" Lasadi asks. "Tora? Which way are we headed."

"Door number four," Tora says, pointing to a door smeared with what Lasadi hopes is grease.

Ruby snakes a cord out of her gauntlet and into the access point, then makes a puzzled sound. "There's a security screen — these defenses were put in recently."

"Not part of Auburn's original design?"

"Nope. Somebody else thought they'd have some fun." Ruby pulls her jack out, snakes it back into her gauntlet. "I cut power to the screen, we're good to go."

"Jay?"

He swings in with his plasma rifle aimed and ready, beckons them after when he's determined it's safe.

Lasadi holds out an arm to Tora. "Lead the way," she says, and to her credit, the other woman doesn't hesitate. If she's not going to share the map, she doesn't get to share the responsibility of taking point, though Lasadi stays close at her side. Last thing she wants is to head home to Nico with news she got his daughter killed.

Now they're in a hallway that twists, like someone put one end in a vise and twisted, the walls spiraling so it's impossible to maintain a consistent orientation.

"Why the fuck?" Raj asks brightly.

"They call this the Drill Bit," Ruby says. "It was one of the last pieces Rasheda added on — it goes parallel to some of the older passages, which is where we need to get if we're going to make it to the heart."

"How do we access the older passages?" Lasadi asks.

"There are three known connection points," Ruby says. "At least one has been permanently destroyed, but Tora and I mapped out the other two. Ahead, about thirty meters — right?" She glances at Tora for confirmation.

"Correct."

"Then let's go."

Other adventurers have left their mark on the hallway, too. More graffiti, a few scorch marks indicating plasma bolts from a firefight. Trails of magboot scuffs indicate most people have chosen one wall to be the floor and stuck with it — as Tora is trying to do. Lasadi ignores up and down and launches herself gently down the hall, pulling herself along the occasional handholds.

"Stop that, Alex," Ruby says, and Lasadi turns back to them in irritation. They don't have time for shenanigans, everyone's too high-strung.

"I'm not doing anything," Alex says. "It's coming through the channel."

And that's when Lasadi hears it. A woman's faint, mocking laugh. The same voice as the humming she heard earlier.

"Everyone hears that, right?" Ruby asks.

Lasadi glances ahead of her to get confirmation from Jay and Tora. For a moment no one speaks.

"Old recordings," Tora finally says.

"Then we ignore it," says Lasadi.

But when she looks back, Raj, Ruby, and Alex are gone.

CHAPTER 16
RAJ

RUBY'S STUDYING her gauntlet when the trap springs; Raj reacts without thinking, pulling her back as a door irises shut right where she'd been standing, chopping the hallway neatly in two. He grabs onto a handhold to keep them both from floating away, tugging Ruby to a stop. Her eyes are wide.

"What the fuck was that?" she asks. She catches herself and spins gently back to face the direction they were going. A smooth, segmented panel has emerged from the wall so precisely that it's like it was always there. Lasadi, Jay, and Tora are gone.

"The first of Rasheda Auburn's traps," Raj says. "You all right?"

Ruby raises a fist and nods it: *Yes.*

"Alex?"

"Yeah, fine." The kid's staring at the wall with shock.

"Cap?" Raj asks. "Jay? Tora? You all good?"

Lasadi's voice comes first; relief floods through him. "We're fine. What's your situation."

"We triggered something," Raj says. "Wall sprang shut, but we're all okay." He runs gloved fingers around the seam, searching for a way to open it again. "You see any control panels? Any way to get leverage? There's nothing on our side." He turns, scanning the corridor. They could probably head back out into C Ring and find something to use as a pry bar, but there's no place to wedge the end into where the door disappears into the wall.

"Looking now," Jay answers, and Raj bites back a curse. Means nothing is immediately obvious, which isn't a good sign.

"Is there a way around?" Raj asks. "We haven't passed any other doors — at least none I could make out."

"Tora's on it," Lasadi says.

Right. Because the plan was for them all to stay together so Tora wouldn't lose control of her precious map. A map that's about to become obsolete as soon as SymTex scraps this station anyway. Which means either she doesn't trust Lasadi and the rest of the crew, or there's something on that map she doesn't want the rest of them to know.

Ruby rolls her eyes and switches to a channel that includes just the three of them. "Alex? What've you got for ways around?"

Alex makes a big, exaggerated shrug — but the corner of his mouth is tugging into a smile.

"Alexander Abdul Quiñones," Ruby snaps. "As I am standing here before God and Raj, if you are messing with me I will kill you."

Alex grins. "Relax, Sis." He taps a gloved finger against his helmet. "It's all right here. Gimme a sec, I'm figuring it out."

Raj thumps a fist against the door in frustration, leaves his palm flat and feels a corresponding bang from the other side. He imagines it's Lasadi, her fingers separated from his by mere centimeters of steel and ceramic.

No time for daydreaming, loverboy — anyway, it's probably Jay thumping around.

"Can we cut through it?" he asks over the general channel.

"Negative," says Jay.

"Absolutely not," says Ruby. "Half of her traps are rigged with a secondary system that triggers something worse if you try to cut through."

"This one definitely is," Jay agrees. "I see the motion sensor that triggered it, my scans are picking up charges embedded in the panels. Can't tell if they're armed, but I'm gonna assume yes."

"Auburn tied all her security systems to a central hub only she could access," says Ruby over the main channel. "Probably she had a portable way of connecting to that hub while she was alive, but it's impossible to work backwards from any one part of the defense system to disable the others. Once I get to the main hub I can turn it all off. But until then?"

Alex waves an arm for attention, then points to a vent a few meters back down the corridor. "That connects with the parallel passage," he says on their private channel.

Raj nods. "There might be a way around," Raj says over the main channel. "Alex says this vent leads into the parallel passageway. Is there a place we can rendezvous ahead?"

"I see it," says Tora. "I'll give you directions."

"We need the map," Raj says.

Tora ignores him. "Alex's memory is right," she says after a minute. "Follow the passageway the way we were going, and there will be a T after about twenty meters. Head left, look for the third door on the right. We can rendezvous in that chamber."

Alex is nodding along, gaze towards the ceiling like he's tracing the steps in his mind. He holds up a thumb when Tora finishes.

"We got it," Raj says. "Opening the vent now."

"Stay in contact," Lasadi says. "And pay attention."

"Will do."

Raj joins Ruby at the vent panel, using his utility knife to help wedge the cover out of its hole. Alex carefully pokes his head in, then pulls himself through in a single, fluid motion. A moment later his head appears back through the vent, eye level with Raj but upside down.

"All clear," Alex says. "But you've *got* to see this."

Raj draws his pistol, pulls himself through.

Where the corridor they left is sterile and white, this new corridor is awash in reds and golds. Plush fabrics are stretched over the walls, pulling free in places to reveal even older fabrics below those. Shapes float in the middle of the corridor, shadows flickering as Raj sweeps his light over the area. A cushion floats nearby, torn open so stuffing drifts like summer clouds.

This new corridor feels lived-in, but instead of being homey, it's wild and untamed, a human place that hasn't so much been abandoned as gone feral.

"Lasadi, sending visual of new corridor," he says. "We might be in Auburn's private sector."

It's a moment before Lasadi answers. "Not a fan of that limited visibility. Be careful, and don't touch anything."

"Copy that."

Ruby runs her fingers over the place they'd removed the vent panel from. "Looks like this could also be completely sealed off from the other passage," she says.

"So she could cut herself off, even this deep in the labyrinth?"

He likes the idea of modular, but Rasheda Auburn's station is built like a trap — for its own inhabitants as much as for attackers. She should have made it more agile. Each module able to break free on its own, maybe set like spokes on a wheel — no, like strands of a spider's web. Surprisingly strong when woven together, but flexible enough to give way and rebuild if need be.

Raj leads the way, rifle at the ready, the strangeness of the corridor setting his skin crawling. A few of the doorways gape open, one jammed that way by an ammo chest. The chest's lid is open, the contents gone. Raj shines his light into the rooms as they pass. Living spaces, complete with beds, cushions, furniture.

"We've got crew quarters," he says over the main channel. "Auburn's? Or did someone else stay here?"

"I thought she was the only one who lived in the labyrinth?" asks Lasadi.

"These all seem like they'd been occupied," Raj says.

"Ghosts," says Alex, and Jay laughs.

"Keep this channel clear for emergencies," Lasadi says.

Beside him, Ruby shakes her head. "Has she never heard of relieving tension by joking?" she says on their group's private channel. "Or, never heard of relieving tension, has she. We need to get that woman laid when we get back to Dima."

Raj doesn't think he's reacted, but Ruby lifts an eyebrow at whatever she sees on his face. "Oh, no," she says with a laugh. "Not you. You should stay far away from that trouble. Plenty of women in the world who aren't your boss and don't work for Nico Garnet."

"I don't know what you're talking about," Raj says.

"I know some single straight girls who'd think you were a catch."

"Ugh, Ruby," Alex says. "Captain said keep comms clear for emergencies."

She laughs, but the smile on her face slips back into serious. That's Ruby on a job — she may banter, but she's always sharp.

"Heya, Alex," she says, glancing at her scanner. She gestures ahead to where the corridor Ts off. "Something's drawing a lot of power up there, reads like a defense turret. Go turn it off without getting shot up."

Alex snorts. "Love you, too." But he pushes himself forward; he'd been lingering in one of the doorways to the crew quarters, and Raj drifts over to see what the kid found so fascinating.

Unlike the other rooms, which don't seem to have been touched in a decade, this one is tidier. Objects still strapped down, the cot made. A stash of food in the corner.

Raj motions to Ruby. "Someone live here?"

She frowns at the room, a faint line of worry sketching itself between her brows. "Our scanners didn't pick up any signs of life."

"What are the odds they're wrong?" Raj asks. "Or that there's still some sort of shielding active?"

"Those odds are good. I need to find an access panel that's connected into the main system. Everything I've tried so far is siloed."

"So no records access, either."

She shakes a fist *No*. "Local access logs, but that's it."

So she hasn't found anything pertinent to her missing family yet. He's not about to ask directly, he knows her well enough to know that'll get Ruby to seal herself off tighter than that trap door — with just as much explosive force set to blow if you try cutting through her defenses.

He's known Ruby for almost three years now, long enough to see how easy it is for a casual acquaintance to think they know her well. She presents herself like an open book, but getting to know the real Ruby is more complicated than navigating this labyrinth: a maze of half-told mostly true stories about the past, secret pains hidden under friendly facades, and at the heart of it all, a secret, locked room not even Ruby knows how to open.

There are parts of Raj's childhood he'd rather not

remember, but he can't imagine not knowing anything about his life before the age of twelve.

"Let me know if there's anything I can do to help," Raj says, and Ruby gives the lived-in room one last worried look, then turns away as Alex's excited whoop comes through the channel.

"You get it?" Ruby asks.

"Who's the king?"

"Nobody's giving you a crown for disarming one defense turret, only," Ruby says.

"I did two, didn't I."

"Mildly impressive."

At the T, the corridor is in a shambles both directions. "Damaged in the attack?" Raj asks. "Or a project abandoned midconstruction?"

Ruby raises her hands in an exaggerated shrug. Down the corridor they're supposed to take to the left are coils of cables, workers' tools. Alex is floating near a pair of defense turrets on the left. Ruby joins him, snaking the port from her gauntlet to log in once more. She shakes her head. "This one's siloed, too. Which means I still can't turn off the general system until we get to the central hub."

"Which is what we expected," Raj says. "How are your O_2 levels?"

"Good," says Ruby. Alex holds up a thumb.

"Then we keep going slow and steady." Raj opens the main channel. "We got to the T. Had to disarm a couple of turrets, but we're almost to the rendezvous."

Something groans, long and low, the station shifting around them, and Lasadi's reply takes long enough that Raj checks the channel. He opens his mouth to speak again, and Lasadi's voice cuts through the faint static.

"Copy that," she says. "We ran into a couple of defense drones, but all good. Watch for something that looks like recessed light fixtures."

"Will do." Raj studies the hallway around them — with the fabric stretched over the walls and drifting aimlessly, he's not sure how they'd ever spot them. "There's some debris in the corridor ahead, but we should be able to get through."

But Ruby's shaking her head at him. "It's not debris," she says over their private group channel. "It's a ninety-degree bend — straight into a dead end. Alex, is Tora lying to us?"

Alex raises his gaze to the ceiling as though thinking. "That's not how it is on the map," he says. "Not that the passage is blocked off, it's just completely different."

"So we took a wrong turn."

Alex gives his sister a withering glower, then closes his eyes. "The rendezvous point is thirty meters that way," he says, pointing to a wall. "Worst-case scenario we take a little space walk."

"Tear down some of this fabric," Raj says. "Let's see what we have to work with here."

"If that part of the map's wrong, can we trust the rest?" Ruby asks.

No one answers her; the answer is clear.

"Let's get to work," Raj says. "Captain, come in? We have a problem." He reaches for the fabric wall nearest him as he waits for a response, but stops when Alex's eyes widen. He's staring over Raj's shoulder, back down the corridor they came from.

"Oh, heya," Alex says. "Who're you, then?"

CHAPTER 17
LASADI

Lasadi catches a smoking drone in one hand, turns it carefully to study the design. She didn't see any shipside combat during the war, but she trained for it, and she's spent time studying the obstacles they might come across in Auburn Station. She was expecting a historic artifact, but this drone appears to be one of the newer models the Alliance uses — and there are fresh scratch marks on the cover. A gouge in the coating where someone's screwdriver slipped while doing a repair.

She floats it gently across the corridor to Jay. "Anything odd about this to you?"

He frowns at it, turning it over in his hand.

"It's new," he finally says.

"Yeah." Lasadi keeps her plasma pistol in her hand, unease crawling down her spine. They hadn't seen any signs of life in their scans, but that doesn't mean someone wasn't here recently. Could be someone's been using this as their base and stepped out to go raid some prospector's settlement. Or maybe the station's shielded somehow.

Lasadi turns slow to study the rest of the corridor. The frame and exterior walls are up, and Jay keeps reassuring her it's solid enough for the life support system to keep working. But as they've gotten deeper into the hallway Ruby called the Drill Bit, it's felt less stable. The interior walls aren't fully covered, and the work was abandoned in a hurry. A few stray tools still float untethered near pallets of plating that have been measured and marked, but not cut.

The walls are now marred with fresh scorch marks from their fight with the drones, along with older layers of graffiti and wear. Someone's scrawled a ship's name and a date — not that long ago.

"Someone's been here recently," she says to Tora. The other woman hadn't helped out in the firefight against the drones, but Lasadi hadn't expected her to. Tora is armed, like they all are, but to Lasadi, Tora's simply an asset Lasadi's been charged with getting to and from the central chamber without any damage.

"We expected that," Tora says. "In the outer part of the labyrinth at least. Any drifter could luck their way into these outer corridors, but the central chamber is still sealed."

"As far as you can tell."

Tora gives her an arch look. "As far as we can tell."

Lasadi knows Tora's not sharing everything, and she's still not certain it matters. It hasn't mattered in the past. Nico Garnet never told her everything about a job; he also never led her astray. The old man saved her life. Gave her a fresh start when no one else in the system would have touched her. Is he secretive? Yes. Did he send her on a job that will get her and hers killed?

She can't believe that.

But Tora?

"How far are we from the rendezvous point?" Lasadi asks. She doesn't like being separated, doesn't like what the newly sealed corridor behind them means for a quick exit back to the *Nanshe* if it turns out they need it.

"There's an airlock straight ahead," says Tora. "It's through there."

Lasadi had seen airlocks on the map that led to other corridors. Some looked like sections that had been built after the airlock was already there. But a few of those airlocks were part of the original design, a way for Rasheda to isolate certain parts of the station, or simply to create more chaos in the layout.

Can't ask a ghost.

"I'll take point," Lasadi says. "Jay in back — everybody stay close."

Jay slips back, his own weapon drawn, watching for more of the drones, defense turrets, or any other booby-traps Rasheda Auburn may have left behind to deter attackers decades after her death.

Lasadi doesn't like the debris, how much unsecured junk is floating through the hallways. They're not on a ship, where any one of those screwdrivers or welding torches could become a missile under sudden thrust, but they still make her uneasy.

Here one day, gone the next. An entire bustling world blinked out of existence, without time to finish the day's work.

Something moves out of the corner of her vision, and Lasadi twists, trying to catch a glimpse of it.

"What's wrong?" Jay asks.

Shadows. Paranoia. Absolutely nothing.

"I thought I saw something," Lasadi answers. "This place is fucking with me."

"I feel that," Jay replies. "Let's get out of here soon and never come back."

They manage to make it another few dozen meters before it becomes clear the promised airlock is not to be found. Instead, the dizzying Drill Bit hallway comes to a four-way intersection, with each new corridor heading off at its own bizarre, nonstandard angle. The effect is nauseating, triggering the wave of vertigo Lasadi had managed to stave off in the slowly twisting hallway.

One corridor sweeps away in a curve, truncating the sightlines. The second is sealed by the same type of iris door that slashed them off from Raj and the others. And the third is completely black; Lasadi shines a light into the darkness but can make out only a nondescript hallway lined with ladders that don't go to hatches.

"I hate this place," she says, forcing herself to ignore the warped effect. "Tora, is this where the airlock is supposed to be?"

Tora floats past her into the junction, spinning in place to study it. Whatever her overlays show, it doesn't make her happy. "Yes. This doesn't line up with the map."

"We don't have time for this," Lasadi sighs, then turns to Tora in surprise. "What did you say?"

Tora shakes her head. "Nothing."

"You said — " Lasadi pauses, listening as the whisper comes again.

You're in my house.

Tora's lips aren't moving.

"What?"

"Neither of you heard that?" Tora's frowning at her, Jay's shaking a fist *No*. "Then never mind. I'll call the oth— "

A flash of movement and Lasadi reacts without thinking, shoving Jay backwards down the corridor, sending her own mass drifting into the junction.

A knife-bladed grate slams into the opposite wall, right where they'd both been standing.

Lasadi stares at the blades. Even without touching the edges it's clear they're razor sharp; they would have gone through them both like butter. Jay's eyes are wide, Lasadi's heart is racing. Beside her, Tora swears soft.

Lasadi shoves away fear, reaching for anger that some-one — dead woman or no — tried to kill Jay. She does a quick sweep for potential secondary traps that might have been triggered, noting Jay doing the same thing on his side, then floats closer to check the gate.

"At least this one has leverage points," she says. "Jay, see if you can find something down the hall to pry back this gate."

"Here," says Tora, tearing one of the short ladders from the wall and floating it back to Lasadi. Lasadi fits the legs into the grate and locks her magboots, testing the give. The ladder is surprisingly strong, but so is the grate. It shifts slightly, but it'll take more than her strength to shove it back in the wall.

She bites back a growl of frustration, putting her anger into the ladder.

They expected this, they expected traps. But in her mind they'd be working through these together. Instead, the station itself is trying to separate them, picking them off one by one and forcing them to filter out into the labyrinth on their own. Well, Lasadi isn't going to let that happen.

She checks the levels on her environment suit; she's still got 70 percent in her tank. It should still be enough time to get to the central chamber and back before needing to recharge the systems. They're still doing fine on time. Even with two trips, they'll have time to spare before the SymTex crew gets here.

She gives another lunge, then hears Raj's voice in her ear.

"Lasadi, come in? We have a problem."

Of course they do. She sighs and motions for Jay to join her with the pry bar he managed to scavenge from farther down the hall.

"What is it?" she asks Raj, then grunts as she shoves her shoulder once more against the ladder. Working at the same time as Jay, the grate is finally starting to move. The blades ease out of the wall, their tips just visible. With any luck they'll get this cleared in a few more minutes. She shoves again, then waits.

"Raj?"

She checks her channel, glances at Jay. He shakes his head.

"Raj, come in. Raj — "

Something explodes beside her, knocking Jay away from the grate and jamming her painfully against the junction where her ladder meets the knife-edged blades of the grate. Her suit's overlay flashes red — breach — and she drags herself away from the blades.

Someone's screaming her name. She barely registers Tora before hands grab her arms, pulling her back and slamming her into the wall.

A woman's voice is laughing, sharp and brittle above the high-pitched whine in Lasadi's ears.

CHAPTER 18
RAJ

THE FIGURE FLOATING in the corridor behind them is dressed in shreds of fabric that must have been torn from the walls around them, fashioned into a rough cloak and tied at the waist. Beneath the rags is a child: pale olive skin streaked and filthy, thin brown hair a greasy rat's nest floating gently around her head. Dressed like that, staying still and silent — Raj could have walked a hands-breadth away without noticing if she hadn't wanted them to.

"A ghost," Alex says. "It's not wearing a helmet."

"Jay said the life support was working in this section," says Ruby. "My suit says it's safe."

"Doesn't mean it's real," Alex points out.

"Alex." Raj holds a hand out to shut Alex up, not taking his eyes off the girl. She's tense, but she hasn't tried to run away. Wherever the hell she came from, she decided to make herself known — he's got that in his favor. Raj crouches down to the girl's level, trying to make himself as harmless-looking as possible. Triple-checks the readout saying it's safe to remove his helmet, then reaches for the catch.

"Raj!"

He ignores Ruby. Unseals his helmet to fold back into the collar of his environment suit with a whir. He takes a lungful of stale air, breathing in a half-century's worth of decay and dust, and a faint undercurrent of rot and scorched metal not screened out by the ancient air recyclers.

"Hi," he says. "My name's Raj. We're lost."

The girl's gray eyes dart over his shoulder, but she doesn't speak.

"These are my friends, Ruby and Alex. What's your name?"

The life support system may be keeping the air breathable, but it's cold in these corridors; the tremor in the girl's hand could be fear, or she could be shivering. Her cheeks are sunken, her eyes bright. She swallows hard, uncertain.

Ruby breathes out a curse, then her helmet hisses unsealed, too. She pushes herself to float gently beside Raj. "We won't hurt you, love," she says.

The girl's eyes flash between them, knuckles whitening on a handhold as though she's about to rabbit.

"Maybe she doesn't speak standard," Ruby says.

Raj could try greetings in a half-dozen other languages, but first he'll try something universal. He unzips a pocket on his thigh and pulls out a ration bar, holds it up with a friendly smile: *Are you hungry?*

The girl doesn't answer, but when he pushes it towards her, one bony hand darts out from her makeshift cloak and seizes the bar. She tears into it, swallowing big bites without chewing. Her fingers are grimy, knuckles covered in layers of scrapes and nicks.

Raj pulls out his second bar and she holds out a hand. "Easy with these, kid," he says. "What's your name?"

The girl rubs the back of her hand across her chapped lips, then swallows. "Lisbeth," she finally says.

Raj lets himself float forward, closing enough of the gap that he can reach out and hand the bar to Lisbeth. She snatches it out of his fingers, but she doesn't tear into it like she did the other. She hides it somewhere under her cloak. Whoever she is, she's used to being hungry and rationing food.

"We're lost," Raj says again. "Can you help us?"

"You can't go that way."

"We figured that out."

"They can't see you if you stay here," she says. The singsong pitch of her voice, the way she moves — Raj is reassessing her age. With those gaunt cheeks and wrapped in rags, he thought she was maybe ten years old, but now he'd guess she's much younger than that.

"Who can't see us?" Ruby asks.

"I don't know," Lisbeth finally answers. "The bad men."

Raj glances at Ruby; her skin has an ashen undertone that has nothing to do with the dim lighting. "Did the bad men bring you here?"

Lisbeth squeezes her eyes closed and shakes her head, a pair of fat tears breaking free to float down the corridor. "My parents."

She doesn't flinch when Ruby reaches for her, doesn't resist when Ruby pulls her gently forward to enfold her in her arms. Ruby presses her cheek against the girl's filthy hair, eyes screwed shut as the girl shudders with sobs.

Raj's mind is racing. Lisbeth and her family must have landed here and run into trouble. The *Nanshe*'s scanners hadn't picked up any signs of activity, which could mean whoever attacked her is gone. But they hadn't seen any sign of Lisbeth, either, so there's a very real chance the labyrinth shielded its inhabitants.

Which means they might run into trouble, too.

After a moment, Lisbeth opens red-rimmed eyes. "Can I go with you?"

"Of course you can," Raj says. "We need to find our

friends first, though. Do you know this place? Can you help us?"

She nods, and Raj motions Alex forward. "Alex. Tell her where we're trying to go."

"Sure thing."

Her frightened gaze darts behind him again.

"Take your helmet off," Raj says.

Alex sighs, but unseals and folds it back without arguing. "Heya, I'm Alex," he says, giving her one of his signature grins. The girl smiles back almost reflexively. He pulls a piece of chalk out of a pocket, and turns to a wall, pulls the fabric back and starts drawing a simple map on the metal beneath. "We're here, right? Does this make sense? Good. Okay, and we came from this way? So we're trying to get here." He stars the chamber Tora wants to break into. "Is there a faster way?"

She's staring blankly at the map.

"The door with a sun on it," Ruby says. Raj frowns at her. Tora hadn't told them that particular detail. "It will have a big gold sun on it."

Lisbeth's eyes widen.

"You know it?" Raj asks. "Can you get us there?"

But the girl's shaking her head. "The bad men are in the way. You can't get there."

"Can we get around them?" Raj asks.

A bony shoulder lifts, falls. "Maybe? We could ask *her*, but I don't think she likes you."

Tora, he immediately thinks — because Tora has the map. But how would Lisbeth know that?

"Who?" Raj asks, but Ruby cuts him off.

"Is she in the room with the sun?"

The girl shakes her head. "She's everywhere. But she has to want to talk to you. She doesn't talk to the bad men."

"Ruby?" Raj asks. "What's going on?"

"The station AI," Ruby says. "Rasheda Auburn put her

personality in it — I've been sensing it off and on when I plug in, but the rumor boards say it gets more active the closer you get in."

"What do you mean, active?"

"Some people say the traps get more personalized, but I think that's bullshit. And I've dealt with AIs before. Once I can get into the main system I'll take care of it." She clears her throat. "If that's still the plan."

Whatever the plan *was*, right now Lisbeth comes first. Raj hits his comm. "Captain? Come in. We've got a complication."

Nothing. With the surprise of Lisbeth's appearance, he hadn't realized until now that Lasadi hasn't answered his last hail.

Ruby gently releases Lisbeth to tap at her gauntlet. Lisbeth floats with her back to the wall, sticking close to Ruby.

"Our suit diagnostics are fine," Ruby says. "Comms shouldn't be having a problem, unless they turned theirs off."

"Try to connect again. Something's wrong."

"Everything's wrong, isn't it," says Alex. "Do we head back to the ship?"

Raj shakes his head. "Not if the others are walking into a potential trap. Can you see where they are?"

Ruby nods. "I've got their location beacons — would be more helpful if we had the schematics, but they're about where we expected them to be. All three still together."

And then the whole station lurches, rocking Raj against the connection of his magboots, throwing Lisbeth free from her perch. Raj catches her in his arms before she can slam into the other wall; when the shuddering of the station stops and he releases her, she stays pressed into his side.

"Captain," he yells into the comms; he gets no answer. "Lasadi, answer me."

Static crackles from the severed connection in his earpiece. From far away comes a sound like screeching metal against metal and a high, tremulous whine.

"Jay?"

Silence.

"Tora."

"Their comms must not be working," Ruby says, but she doesn't sound like she believes it.

"We're going to find them," Raj says. He needs that to be true — but right now these three are his responsibility. Around them, the station groans. Raj points at Alex and Ruby. "Helmets on," he orders. Lisbeth's eyes go wide in terror as she understands what's happening. "It's going to be okay," Raj tells her, though nothing about this situation seems that way. The bare skin on his face prickles; he'd love to put his own helmet back on, too, but he's not going to make this kid think she's about to be abandoned again.

"First things first," he says to his tiny crew. "We need to find Lisbeth a suit."

CHAPTER 19
LASADI

Rough hands tear Lasadi away from the bars; she hits the wall at an awkward angle, the breath forced from her lungs in a rush. She twists, trying to spot her assailant, reaching for her sidearm while her lungs scream for air. But while she's focused on the person who first grabbed her, someone else seizes her arm from behind, wrenching it painfully into the small of her back.

She kicks back. Her boot makes contact, but the grip on her arm doesn't loosen — and the kick earns her a punch to the kidney from whoever's behind her.

The person in front of her — they're wearing a mismatched scavenger's suit with a white star scrawled over the faceplate — draws back an arm to punch her in the gut.

And their faceplate shatters, red globules spraying free along with white shards from the fractured star.

Jay, still trapped behind the grate, but able to fire at their attackers.

Lasadi kicks the dead scavenger's body down the hallway, using the momentum it gains her to slam into the person behind her. Just in time, too; the blast that was meant for Jay flares wide, scorching the wall.

She finally wrenches herself around to face the person behind her — another scavenger with a blood-red helmet — slashing him across the chest with her utility knife.

Where the hell's Tora?

There. She's grappling with a third attacker, a bit farther down the hallway that had, until a moment ago, been sealed with a door. Must be where the pirates came from; Lasadi curses herself. She should have checked it, secured it, before going back to try to free Jay. Lasadi slashes again — she's only hitting armor — trying to get out of Jay's shot and reach Tora, whose attacker slams her faceplate-first into the wall.

Lasadi screams Tora's name through the comms. Gets no response.

The man in the red helmet swings wide. But when she ducks, he doesn't follow up. Instead, he fires at Jay.

Red misses, but sparks catch in the corridor behind Jay. A nauseating lurch shudders through the station: shrieking metal, a blast of pressure there and gone. And as the smoke clears, Lasadi sees only jagged metal and empty, star-filled space where Jay was standing.

Lasadi's throat is raw before she realizes she's been screaming Jay's name, doesn't stop until someone yanks her down the hall. Their remaining two attackers are yelling at each other, shoving Tora's limp form and Lasadi's shocked body down the corridor. A few meters on, one of them slams a fist on a control panel, and the door irises shut once more, sealing them from the breach.

Sealing them from Jay.

Lasadi kicks off the wall, driving her shoulder into Red's sternum. He growls out a curse and swipes a blow at her — she twists so it glances past, then pulls him off balance and uses her new momentum to land a heel blow on the back of his neck.

The other pirate slams her into a wall, again, and before she can pull herself back around her wrists are pinned behind her back. She kicks out, but now both of the pirates are on her, crushing her face-first into the wall until she finally goes still.

"You done fighting?" growls a man's voice. She's flipped around to be face-to-face with her attacker. Red's helmet is scored with deep gouges, darkened the way pirates often do, so she can barely make out his eyes in the gloom. She catches the faintest glint of Red's teeth as he smiles.

"Who the fuck are you?" Lasadi snarls.

"I don't think you're asking the questions," Red says. "Seeing as you're on our turf now."

"This is no one's turf," she shoots back. "The station's been abandoned for a decade."

"Says who?" The other figure has the number 13 sprayed over his chest, a drifter's face mask obscuring everything but his eyes under his helmet. He grabs Tora by the arm and hauls her to him; she blinks like she's stunned, blood rimming one nostril and spattering the inside of her helmet.

"Your friend's dead," Thirteen says. "Play nice or we'll kill this one, too." Then he laughs, malice in the crinkling of his eyes. "Slower, I mean. Come on."

Lasadi barely notices Red shoving her forward, doesn't pay attention to his painful grip above her elbow. Communication's cut off with Raj and his team. Jay's on his own — he was wearing his suit, she tells herself. He practically grew up in an environment suit, helping his dad keep the domes of Corusca running. He can handle himself, unless his suit was compromised in whatever caused the explosion. Unless he was shot. Unless —

She shuts down the runaway train of thought with a soft *click*, letting her mind go still and calm.

She can't get herself and Tora out of this if she's overwhelmed with worry about what's happened to Raj and Ruby and Alex and Jay. And she can't help any of them if she doesn't get herself and Tora free from their captors.

She can't overwhelm two of them — they're both armed, and Tora isn't going to be any help in her state. When Lasadi catches Tora's eye, the other woman's lips are pinched in pain. What happens to Lasadi if she comes back home to Nico Garnet without his only child? There won't be a safe place for her in the entire Durga System then.

Don't you dare die on me.

She doesn't know how she can tell, but her gut says they're being dragged closer to the heart of the labyrinth. Emergency breach lights strobe along the floors and ceiling, and Red and Thirteen seal airlock doors after them as they go, as though worried that whatever breached the wall and sucked Jay out might have destroyed the integrity of the rest of the station. They don't seem worried about booby-traps, though, which means they've probably disarmed them.

And set up some of their own — she remembers the fresh scratch marks around the screws in the drones she and Jay took out.

They're scavengers, that's obvious enough. The ragtag suits that have been repaired again and again, the deadly weapons fired without much care for the damage they might do to their current home. Auburn Station is haunted, all right. But as she suspected, the ghosts are nothing but pirates using the reputation of the station to their own benefit.

After nearly fifteen minutes, Lasadi and Tora are pushed through a doorway into a suite of rooms in the heart of the labyrinth, where the pirates have made a home. Central sleeping area, kitchen, a door that must lead to the head. Is it just the two of them? The bedding has been stowed, so it's impossible to tell if there's more gear than the original three pirates that captured them would need.

She'd guess yes. But how many more? Lasadi's not going to wait around to find out.

Red reaches for his helmet, and Lasadi tenses for the opening. If he does it, she'll twist, try to bash *his* head against the wall. She tenses to move, but Thirteen rounds on him.

"Environment's compromised," Thirteen yells. "Idiot."

Red pauses. The warning lights are still blinking in the corridor, flashing subtle in this chamber. "My suit reads levels are safe in here."

"Sure, try it. It's your own funeral."

Red's hand stills near the seals to his helmet, thinking, then drops back to his side.

Olds curse it all.

Lasadi shoves back against Red, then pivots, kicking him in the chest and launching herself in the other direction in one smooth movement. She didn't get a grip on his weapon before he went flying, but at least she kicked it free of his hand. She hits Thirteen square in the chest and they ricochet against the wall. She's grabbed his gun when she realizes Tora is screaming.

Screaming at her to stop.

She can't see anything of Thirteen's face but his eyes, but she can tell he's grinning.

Lasadi's surrounded by the drawn weapons of four more members of this ragtag pirate band. Without the element of surprise, without a weapon, and severely outnumbered.

A feral, primal scream in the back of her mind shouts for her to launch herself at them, to make them take her down in a hail of bullets or not at all. To fight to the death before she gives in.

But Tora's injured. Jay might still be alive out there. Raj, Ruby, Alex — they need her to make it through this.

Lasadi slowly raises her hands; Thirteen wrenches them behind her and into cuffs.

CHAPTER 20
RAJ

WARNING lights pulse red up and down the corridor, flickering between scraps of tattered fabric to create an unsettling scene. "Environment compromised," a woman's voice tells them pleasantly, crackling and distorted in the speakers.

The girl, Lisbeth, wraps her arms around herself.

"It's just a warning for another part of the station," Raj tells her; Ruby shoots him a skeptical look, then goes back to prying open the cover of an access panel. She snakes a cord out of her gauntlet and frowns down at the display. Raj checks his own suit's stats for the hundredth time — despite the warning from the station, his suit's still telling him the environment is stable.

"Do you have a suit?" he asks the girl.

She shakes her head, knotted hair floating around her filthy, pale cheeks. "They have it," she says.

"The bad men?"

"I think I know where they are," says Alex. His eyes narrow in concentration; Raj can almost see the scenarios running in his head as he studies the station's plans in his mind, puzzling through escape routes, rendezvous points.

"There are only a couple of spots in the station you could set up a camp. Ruby, where's the breach?"

"Main corridor," she answers. "Near where the others were headed."

"Did they trigger something?"

"Maybe. The station sealed it off on both sides, can't tell if that was manual or automatic. We need to get back to the ship." Ruby blinks at whatever's on her lens. "Put your helmet on, Raj."

Terror flashes across Lisbeth's face.

"You're going to be okay," Raj tells her. "Any sign of the others?" Without his helmet he's cut off from the visual overlay.

"Yeah, they — shit." Ruby looks at him. "They split up. Captain and Tora are still together, moving steady towards the heart of the labyrinth — or at least where I assume it is, goddammit Tora. She couldn't make us sign a nondisclosure like a normal boss?"

"Jay?"

"I don't know. I don't see him."

"Can you tell what happened? External impact?"

External impact wouldn't be out of the question — and from what he saw on the approach, small asteroids and other space debris have punched more than one hole in the station throughout the years. A living station would have defenses: AI systems to monitor the void around them, automated weapons and human guidance to protect their home. But even if the station's AI is still active like Ruby says, it wouldn't have been able to protect the station from everything on its own.

"Station diagnostics say a power relay was overloaded and detonated," says Ruby. "That's what caused the breach."

"They tripped a boobytrap."

"Or they were attacked."

Raj takes a deep breath, calculating. Their sensors clearly missed signs of life on this station — one of them is standing right here in front of him. Maybe the girl's bait in a trap, but unless she's some sort of grifter savant, her terror's too real to be feigned. Lasadi and the others could have tripped a boobytrap, but they wouldn't have left Jay behind. Even if he'd been hurt or killed, Ruby should have his suit's location beacon.

Only one good explanation for why they couldn't find lifesigns from the *Nanshe*, and why they might not see Jay's suit now. "Could Jay have gone outside the station?"

Ruby purses her lips. "Maybe."

"Something went wrong, so we go after them," Raj says. "We have to assume whoever attacked Lisbeth's ship also attacked the others." He turns to the girl. "How many of them are there?"

Lisbeth stares at him.

"We're going to get you out of here, but we need to get our friends first. One of them is our pilot. And we need to get your suit, right? How many of them are there?"

"A lot," she says finally.

"Helpful," says Alex, and Raj shoots him a glare.

"You steal food from them?" Raj guesses; Lisbeth nods. "Good, really impressive. Show us how you do it, okay? And then we'll all get out of here."

Ruby takes a sharp breath; Raj recognizes that set of her mouth, the downward twist of her lips that means she's run into something unexpected.

"What's going on?"

"The system," Ruby says. "Something's . . . I don't know how to say it. Hold on." She catches her lower lip between her teeth in concentration as she taps a sequence into her gauntlet. Then she flinches back, sparks flying from the access panel, the surprise of the blast throwing Ruby back against the far wall

The sparks have caught in the fabric on the walls, and Raj snatches a cushion floating nearby, beating at the fledgling flames until they're smothered. The acrid stench of scorched fabric and melted wiring stings his nose, black smoke coiling out from the access panel.

"What happened?" he asks.

"Another boobytrap," Ruby says. "I just get a sense. . . I don't know. It sounds crazy."

"Everything on this station sounds crazy," Alex points out. "It's haunted."

Five minutes ago, Ruby probably would have rolled her eyes at her little brother. It's a testament to how rattled she is that she doesn't now.

"Before, we were triggering automatic defenses, but this time someone was actively stalking me. They tried to hack me back."

"The pirates," Raj says.

"Probably. Whoever it was, they were fast."

"Doesn't change our plans," Raj says. "Lisbeth takes us to where we can get to the pirates, we reconnect with the others, and then we get our asses out of here. Only now we assume the pirates know about us and have control of the station's system."

The wall Raj is standing beside shudders with a hollow thud. A glancing blow from some of the station's debris, maybe — but it comes again. And again. Rhythmic, like someone's kicking at the wall, or pounding a fist against it. He tears away the fabric; a faint layer of dust poufs out of the folds to mingle with the rest of the particles in the musty, smoky air.

It's an airlock.

"That's not on the schematic," says Alex.

"I officially no longer trust the schematic." Raj powers on the screen beside the door, then bites out a curse of relief. He knows the figure on the screen. "It's Jay." Raj jabs a finger towards the button to open the outer airlock doors.

"No!" Ruby shouts, and Raj pulls up short of the button. "Let me — there are too many traps here. You hit the wrong thing it could kill him. You three get back."

Ruby hesitates, then snakes the cord out of her gauntlet and plugs it into the panel, fingers a blur on the screen as she types in a code. Raj can hear her panting through the comms. He calls her name.

"Hold on," she says. "He's in, the chamber's pressurizing. And, *fuck*."

She yanks the plug and pushes herself away from the airlock with a strangled cry. Alex catches her.

"You all right?" Raj asks, and she holds up a hand for *Yes*. She doesn't look it, though — her lips are bloodless, nostrils flared, chest heaving. If he didn't know Ruby so well he'd guess that was fear on her face. "The other hacker again?"

"Help Jay," she says. "I'm fine."

The inner airlock doors hiss open, then grind to a halt after a few seconds; the opening too narrow even for Jay's lean frame.

"Pretty thrilled to see you all," Jay says. He tries to smile, but there's pain in it. His suit is scorched, a tear in the side filled with emergency foam tinged pink with blood, blast marks blackening the material and discoloring his faceplate.

"Good to see you, too, man," Raj says. "Hold on." Jay isn't in much shape to help, but Raj and Alex grab either side of the doors and wrench them open with a shudder of bent metal and rust. Raj grabs Jay under the arms and pulls him through the gap, steadies him until his magboots click into place.

"What happened?" Raj asks.

"We were attacked," Jay says. "We triggered another

boobytrap, like the wall that got us earlier. We were trying to pry it back open when some guys came around the corner with guns blazing. I shot one, but they hit something that tore open the wall and I got sucked out." He glances back at the airlock. "I thought I was a goner. Guessed where you might be located best I could and started banging on anything that might be an airlock."

"Lasadi and Tora are still together," Ruby says. "They've stopped moving."

"Then we go after them," says Jay. "I don't care if we have a map, we tear through every wall of this gods-damned place until we get through."

"We have a guide," Raj says, and Jay blinks at him, then refocuses over his shoulder. Lisbeth's hiding behind Alex, one eye peeking out from behind the teenager's elbow.

"Oh, hello." Jay's smile dimples his cheek; Lisbeth returns it, shy. "Where'd you come from?"

"She was here. We think the same pirates who attacked you all attacked her family's ship. She escaped, and she's been hiding ever since." He beckons Lisbeth closer, and she finally pushes herself into view. "Lisbeth, this is Jay. We need you to tell us everything you know about the bad men, okay? I think I have a plan."

CHAPTER 21
LASADI

TORA'S BARELY BREATHING.

Lasadi nudges her with her bound feet, and the other woman's eyelids flutter open, focusing on Lasadi a heartbeat before closing once more. There's blood on her lips, blood spattered on the inside of her faceplate. The automed system in her suit should be doing what it can to stabilize her, but she looks terrible.

After her last attempt to break free of their captors, Lasadi had been bound hand and foot and shoved into a corner. The asshole with the red helmet didn't bother to restrain Tora, since it's clear she's not going to be doing much fighting. For the moment, they're being ignored — but only because a more pressing matter has their captors' attention. The breach warning lights have kicked into overdrive, a woman's voice pleasantly informing them that the systems in this sector have been overloaded and are destabilized.

Lasadi watches them work, testing her restraints, calculating her exit strategy.

They're in a chamber that might have been a galley or a gathering space back when Rasheda Auburn was queen of the station; now it's been turned into a base of operations. It's set up like Rasheda originally had some sort of artificial gravity to create a distinction between floor and ceiling, but is now a directionless cube. Bales of goods are webbed along one wall, a row of cots along another, then a kitchen unit that looks like it's been scavenged from another part of the station. The pirates aren't disciplined about strapping things down — there's a toolkit floating free, a pry bar, plenty of things Lasadi could use as a weapon, if she could get close enough to do so.

Her whole body aches from the first beating she took in the fight, then the second one she got from Red after they cuffed her. Her temple throbs dull and a sharp pain jolts her elbow when she tests her bonds. Her side and thigh ache where Red's boot struck. She'd humiliated him, but taking it out on her when she couldn't fight back apparently wasn't enough to assuage his pride: While the others are ignoring them for the moment, Red's watching her and Tora like he's looking forward to another go.

Let him try. She's not going down like this, and neither is Tora. Las may not like the woman, but even if she wasn't Nico Garnet's daughter, it wouldn't matter. She's on Lasadi's crew, and that means she'll be fought for, tooth and nail.

Lasadi has counted five more pirates besides Red and Thirteen. The one in the scarred silver suit is giving orders like he's the leader; he'd sent two in newer black suits out to check on something Lasadi didn't catch, then retreated to the room next door with Thirteen. A smaller person with a welding helmet is working on the other side of the common room, tearing into a control panel as though trying to fix the system from here. The one with stylized metal spikes around the collar of his helmet is arguing with Red about how Welding Helmet should be working. Spikes's voice comes out muffled by the old-fashioned internal breathing mask under his helmet, the type of system still sometimes used in deep asteroid mining.

The mishmash of suit styles and contentious leadership says this group was cobbled together over years. So, not a military unit who deserted together, not a branch of one of the organized pirate bands that succeeded legends like Rasheda Auburn. Most likely a group of opportunists and indenture dodgers who holed up here to go after easy pickings. They work together, but they're not a team — and there's plenty of tension in the way they're sniping at each other and shooting their leader glares behind his back. Maybe Lasadi can't fight her way out, but she might be able to use that.

Finally Welding Helmet laughs in triumph, and the breach warning lights go off. Spikes claps Welding Helmet on the shoulder. "I told you," he says to Red. "Works like a charm every time."

Tora's eyes are closed; Lasadi nudges her again with her feet. "Stay with me," she growls. "Tora. *Tora!*"

Red's attention's never been far from them, and now he pushes himself away from Spikes and Welding Helmet to float nearer. A predatory gleam lights up his eyes.

"She needs medical help," Lasadi says. "You have to let me help her."

The corner of Red's mouth twitches into a leer, and he reaches for the seal of Tora's helmet. "Does she, now? She definitely will once I'm done with — "

A distant explosion sends tremors through the room, and the environmental warning light kicks into overdrive once more.

"Figure out what the fuck that is," Red yells back at Spikes and Welding Helmet, who rush out the door. He swears again, though Lasadi guesses it has less to do with the explosion itself and more with the environmental breach warning ruining his fun.

Lasadi can commiserate. It's ruining her plan, too.

Red is distracted by the chaos again, but he hasn't moved away. She could catch him in the side of the knee if she kicked hard, but the cuffs around her wrists are clipped to the wall. No. She needs to get him to release her.

The robotic voice warning about station breach shuts off again, midsentence, and the pulsing warning lights turn solid yellow for caution.

"Circuits got overloaded," calls Spikes as he comes back in, his voice still garbled by the internal breathing mask. Welding Helmet follows him and gets back to work on the control panel. "Got this level sealed off, but we need to reroute power before another one blows. Helmets stay on until we get it sorted."

Spikes drifts over to join Red, and if he's feeling as opportunistic as Red, Lasadi can't tell. His eyes are shadowed, face obscured by the breathing mask. He points at Tora. "What's the matter with that one?"

"I was about to peel her out of her suit and find out," Red says.

"You better hope it's nothing." Spikes wrenches Tora to her feet and she coughs, droplets of blood floating from her lips. "You know who she is?"

Red shakes his head. Adrenaline courses through Lasadi — she's been debating using this card, but she'd hoped to get more information before invoking Tora's father out here. In the right place, it could mean special attention in the hopes of getting a hefty sum for her safe return. But say that name in front of the wrong people and they'll be dead in the black without a backup plan.

"Nico Garnet?" Spikes says. "The Butcher? The asshole who runs half of Dima? This is his daughter. We'll get a good payday so long as you can keep your hands off her. At least until we can send him proof of life."

"No shit." Red grabs Tora's arm from Spikes, tugs her closer. "That true?"

"It's true," Tora wheezes.

"She's a goldmine," says Spikes.

"And that one?" Red digs a toe into Lasadi's already sore side and she doubles over against the pain.

"Nobody." Spikes unclips her from the floor and hauls her to her feet. "But hands off. Boss wants to take a look at her first."

Red grins. "Dibs on the princess."

"Just bring her," Spikes growls, dragging Lasadi along with him towards the room their leader disappeared into.

There's something odd about the way Spikes is holding her arm, Lasadi realizes. The way his grip is tightening: pulses, sets of threes. A weird tic? Some game he's playing? She struggles in his grip, trying to get a better view of him, but he shoves her forward again.

She waits until Red is a few paces ahead of them, then locks her magboots and spins, jamming her shoulder into Spikes's solar plexus and shoving him back. He's too quick, and she's too winded from her earlier fight — he catches her, fingers digging into her upper arms, then slams her into the wall.

Lasadi braces herself for the impact.

It doesn't hurt.

Spikes pulled back at the last second, she realizes, absorbing the full impact with his own arms. He pins her to the wall, helmet pressed against hers. "I already let you hit me once before," he says, and there's a hint of amusement under the muffled growl. "So let's play nice this time around."

She frowns at the wording, at the way he'd tried to avoid hurting her. Only Red and Thirteen had been in the original fight, and she hasn't landed a good strike on anyone since then. In fact, the last person she hit was Raj

Demetriou. She searches for his eyes in the gloom of his helmet, catches a faint spark of gold in his irises.

Her breath catches in her throat.

Spikes and Welding Helmet had left together when the last explosion rocked the room. If Raj took this man's suit, what happened to the other? She risks a glance at the figure still rooting through the electrical panel. Welding Helmet's only half paying attention to the job at hand. The rest of their attention is on Raj and Lasadi. Their hand, hidden from Red, is wrapped around a plasma pistol.

She allows herself a flicker of hope, nods slightly to acknowledge she got the message.

"Fuck you," she snarls, and Spikes — Raj? — laughs. It's gravelly and broken and almost familiar through the muffled breathing mask.

He pushes her — gently — after Red and Tora.

Tora's not resisting; she's barely still conscious, her feet dragging against the floor as Red propels her forward. Lasadi is so distracted with worry for her that it takes a moment to realize Spikes is pressing her bound hands against something at his side. The handle of his knife, she thinks, and her fingers close around it by instinct.

He moves her hands away, two squeezes around her wrist.

Not yet.

Lasadi bites back a curse. Raj may have a plan, but Tora doesn't have long to wait.

CHAPTER 22
RAJ

"WHAT THE FUCK is wrong with the electricals."

The pirate leader in the silver suit barely notices Tora and Lasadi; he rounds on Raj the minute Raj walks through the door wearing the dead pirate's suit — the one with the ridiculous decorative spikes around the collar.

They've entered what must be the leader's personal suite. It's luxurious, filled with features that suggest Rasheda Auburn might once have called this room home. It might have been incredible back then, with its gilded panels and silken fabrics; now it's been set up in a caricature of a throne room. And the king? A stringy man in a silver environment suit who's barely managed to keep one leg up on the assholes he's surrounded himself with.

The leader jabs a finger at Raj. "I said what the *fuck* is wrong with the electricals?"

"Overloaded," Raj says. "Relay got hit, and that janked the nearby circuits. The one out in the corridor failed, but Zerrel's getting it under control."

That was the pirate in the welding helmet's name, right? Raj only heard it once before Jay took the guy out; Raj's throat tightens as the leader gives him a skeptical look, but it's the pirate in the red helmet who speaks up.

"When did you learn so much about electricity?" he scoffs.

"Since I keep getting stuck on patrols with that asshole," Raj says. "Learning something's good for you. Oughta try it."

Gods, but he doesn't have long on this ruse before one of them asks him something he can't answer, or helmets start coming off.

"Shut it, both of you." The leader pushes himself from the bed, alighting gracefully like someone born to Durga's Belt, his magboots connecting with the floor and bringing him to a sedate stop. "Now. What did you bring me."

"Nico Garnet's daughter," Red cuts in, obviously eager for the glory.

"She's injured," Lasadi speaks up. "She's not worth anything if she's dead."

Raj jerks her arm as though to shut her up, and to get her in a better position. She seems to understand, stumbling forward and to the right a touch so she's between him and the pirate leader, where the others can't see her hands. She lets her momentum drift her backwards until her shoulder blades are resting against his chest; Raj slides his hand down her arm. Her fingers find the hilt of his knife again immediately. He squeezes her wrist once, then readies his thumb on the release to her restraints.

The pirate leader leans closer to Tora. "Life support says stable," he says. "Get her out of this suit and see where she's injured."

Tora moans as he reaches for her, doubling over with a coughing fit that racks her entire body.

Lasadi slips Raj's knife from its sheath, and he senses more than sees the way she draws up her knees, the soles of her magboots coming to rest against his shins. Feels the deep, readying breath that flows through her body against his.

He locks his own magboots, braces himself, and clicks off the restraints.

Lasadi launches herself at the pirate leader, Raj's knife in her hand.

With their attention on Tora, the pirate leader and Red don't see Lasadi rushing them until the last moment. The leader notices first; he twists so her knife glances off his helmet rather than sinking into the neck seal where she was aiming. Lasadi pivots midleap, catching his throat in the crook of her arm to stop her momentum, and dragging him with her away from Red and Tora.

Raj takes aim at Red, but someone's shooting from the doorway to another chamber. Not at him — at Lasadi. The pirate with the number 13 emblazoned across his chest isn't expecting Raj to be on her side, so his face screws up in confusion, then shock, when Raj turns and fires into his chest. More shots sound from the other room, probably Jay cleaning up the two others who've returned to check on what's going on.

By the time Raj turns back, his clear shots are gone. Lasadi is grappling with the pirate leader and Tora has surprised Red, catching the knife he slashes at her and twisting it back on him, then launching them both against the wall with all her might. He screams as they hit, and she shoves herself back, his pistol in her hand and the blade buried in his side. Tora locks her magboots gracefully, her aim at Red's head not wavering in the slightest.

Lasadi catches herself against the ceiling and shoves back down until her own magboots connect, then bends to undo the restraints around her ankles. The pirate leader's body floats above the bed, his neck at an impossible angle.

Lasadi has somehow acquired a plasma pistol of her own; she aims it square at Raj's chest.

"Raj?" she asks. "Tell me that's you."

Raj shoves the pistol back into its holster, fumbling with the antique clasp of the old-fashioned helmet until it clicks open. He tosses it away, taking a grateful breath that doesn't include the stench of another man's suit.

Relief washes over Lasadi's face. "Thank the olds you're all right," she says. She holsters the pistol and takes a step towards him. He's been dreaming about touching her again since their first tussle in Sumilang's museum, and his chest burns with the remembered pressure of her shoulders leaning into him a moment ago. He can still feel the way her back moved as she breathed, the way her body moved against his readying for action, the certainty he'd felt as they prepared to fight together.

"Are you all right?" he asks. Her lips are pinched with pain, and now that she's not fighting he can tell she's favoring her ribs.

"Bruised is all." Her brows draw together in worry, fingers stilling on the collar of her own helmet. "The life support?"

"Is stable," Raj says. "It was a ruse."

Lasadi hesitates, then folds her own helmet away. Strands of hair have come free from her braid, floating to frame her face. She's an arm's length away. He could close the distance between them again in a heartbeat, tuck one of those stray strands back behind her ear. For a wild moment, he almost does; something in her eyes says she would let him.

And then her gaze slips past him, to the doorway they entered moments ago, and whatever tentative affection Raj imagines in her face transforms into a burning sun of joy.

"Jay!" Lasadi launches herself past Raj, across the room;

the other man catches her in his arms. They tangle together in a hug.

Raj clears his throat, pushing aside irrational pangs of jealousy he has no right to feel. Lasadi was worried, he tells himself. She must have thought Jay was dead, or injured, so of course she'd be overjoyed he's alive. And either way, Ruby's right — Raj is a hired gun, and there are far more appropriate women for him to get wrapped in a knot about.

Once they get back to Ironfall, he'll find one of them and get Lasadi Cazinho out of his system.

A groan from across the room shakes him out of his thoughts, and he turns to find Tora's still guarding her prisoner. Red has his hands wrapped around the knife in his side, blood soaking crimson into the fabric of his suit. Raj crosses to them.

"You all right?" Raj asks Tora. "You're injured."

"I'm fine." Tora touches a button and folds her own helmet back into her collar, wipes blood off her lips onto the back of her sleeve. "Biting your tongue can produce an impressive amount of blood."

"You were very convincing. You had me worried." He's still worried. Blood soaks the collar of Tora's suit; biting her tongue isn't the only thing making her eyes glassy with pain.

"I could say the same to you. I almost shot you."

"Glad you didn't."

"Me, too." Tora eases back the safety on the pistol and turns to Red. "Get his helmet off," she orders Raj, and he complies, watching for any sudden movements. When Red's helmet folds back, his face is revealed: sickly pale; thinning, greasy hair; a scar down his jaw that ends where his left ear had been.

"Hey, asshole," Tora says to the pirate. "I'm looking for a door with a sun on it. How do we get there?"

"Fuck you."

She kicks out, toe catching the blade in the man's side. He howls with pain. "That's the hill you're dying on?" she asks. "Refusing to give a lady directions?"

Red's voice comes in sharp pants. "You're going to kill me anyway, princess."

"If you're not going to be useful, then yes." Tora steadies the pistol.

"Wait, wait," Red says, holding up a hand. "Sun door's easy to find, down the corridor we came in through. Where we took a right? Go straight instead. But there's nothing there worth stealing. I can show you where the real treasure is."

Tora lifts an eyebrow.

"Rasheda left a fortune. We've been selling it off a bit at a time when we needed money, but there's millions still there."

"Where."

Hope creases the corners of the pirate's eyes. "In our secret stash, better hidden than the damn sun door." He licks his lower lip, gaze dropping to Tora's body. "I'll show you, princess. Then maybe you and I — "

Raj flinches at the blast — a sharp sear of energy from Tora's plasma pistol. Red jerks back, then drifts slowly to his side, a smoking hole in his forehead.

Tora lowers her arm. "I'm Tora fucking Garnet," she says to the body. "Not your princess." She slips the pistol into her belt and turns to Raj. He barely stops himself from taking a step back — this is not the woman he thought she was, he realizes. He'd gotten comfortable being around Tora and stopped thinking of her as heir to the Garnet organization.

"You know where the door is?" Tora asks.

"We can find it. Here."

Tora accepts the wad of gauze Raj holds out to her, pressing it against the side of her neck with a wince.

"Where else are you hurt?" he asks.

"That's it," she says. "Piece of shrapnel, I think. It can wait until we're back on the ship."

She lets Raj tape the gauze in place, then takes a deep, shaky breath. "Let's go."

CHAPTER 23
LASADI

THE AIR in the pirate's den reeks of fresh blood and electrical fire, layered sharp over an archaeological bouquet of food decay and stale alcohol. The life support may be working but the air scrubbers are no match for the bastards who'd nested here.

Let this place burn, Lasadi thinks. Let SymTex tear it to pieces, let it shatter into dust.

She fills her lungs with the scorch of plasma and unwashed bodies, releasing the breath and letting the adrenaline from the fight drain away. Time to assess their mission.

Jay's hurt, but he's alive. Raj and his team are reunited with them. Tora — she's injured, but apparently not as bad as she was putting on. And she just killed a man in cold blood, so she's still Nico Garnet's daughter. Lasadi has to admit, for all her fancy manicures and suits, Tora held her own back there. Even if Raj hadn't arrived, Tora's act might have bought them the element of surprise they needed.

They may have lost their stars for a minute, but they can still get back on track.

"Jay," she says. He lifts his chin. "How stable is this life support?"

"Stable for now," Jay says. "Wouldn't count on it forever. I know that's not helpful, but things shift quick around here."

"Fair. Tora, Raj — let's circle up. Where are Ruby and Alex?"

"In here," Ruby calls from the other room.

Lasadi slips past Jay, through the doorway, and is startled to find three figures instead of the two Quiñones siblings she was expecting. The third figure — a child — comes up to Ruby's elbow. The kid is staring at the bodies still floating in the outer chamber.

"Who the hell is this?" Lasadi asks.

"Lisbeth." Ruby wraps an arm around the child's shoulders. "We found her in the other passage. She told us about the pirates, and led us to where they were keeping you. This is Lasadi," Ruby says to Lisbeth. "She's our captain, love."

There's naked fear on Lisbeth's face, so Lasadi locks her magboots and crouches to her level. Tries to remember what to do with children. The kid's wearing a well-patched environment suit that's a touch too small for her, and her pale face is gaunt and filthy. Olds bless her, how long has the poor thing been eking out a living here among the ghosts?

Lisbeth spears her with a feral stare, so Lasadi smiles as gentle as she can. "Thank you for your help," she says. "We're friends, and we're going to get you out of here."

The kid nods slow in response.

"She also knows where the entrance to the central chamber is," adds Alex. "It's not far from here, we've figured out the best way."

"Is she alone?" Lasadi asks, wincing as she straightens.

The beating she took is going to hurt once she's under gravity again.

"She said she is," Ruby answers. "And she said there were eight pirates." Her gaze flickers past Lasadi to the open doorway — if they were waiting out here the whole time, they surely heard Red's agonized scream and the single shot that finished him. Hopefully the kid hasn't seen or heard worse, but somehow Lasadi doubts that. Those eyes are too haunted.

"Eight? Then we're good. Jay took one out in the initial fight." Lasadi turns slow, taking in their little group. Her ribs and thigh still ache. Tora's face is splashed with blood, and Jay's favoring his left arm. The gash in his suit is filled with foam tinged pink with blood. The other three seem fine, though their newest charge is probably going to be a liability if they run across anyone else in this labyrinth — although that's unlikely. Could a second band of pirates be living this close and undetected to the ones they've already dispatched?

Every face in the group — even Tora — is watching her for instruction, and for a moment the heady interplay of power and responsibility makes it feel like the old days. Those days when she didn't second-guess herself, when pressure created clarity and sliced away the noise to help her plot a clear path with confidence.

She's missed this. She's really fucking missed this.

"Tora," she says; damage assessment first. "What's your status?"

"I'm fine," Tora says. She's got a bandage on the side of her neck, but she seems much more alert — and angry — than she had a few minutes ago. "That was an act. Mostly."

"Have your suit send me a report," Lasadi says. She doesn't trust Tora not to downplay something critical. "Jay?"

"I took some shrapnel, but it didn't hit anything important and the suit gave me the good stuff. All systems are go, sending the report now."

"Good. Any other injuries I should know about?" At the shaking heads, she moves on. "We can't trust the life support, and this delay cost us time. I've got a quarter left on my suit — so maybe an hour. The rest of you?"

"Lisbeth's got a full tank, so three or four hours?" says Ruby. "I'm about twenty-five percent, too." Alex nods beside her.

"Same," says Raj.

"Fifteen," says Tora.

Jay's lips thin. "I'm at five percent," he says. "Suit estimates it'll last about twenty minutes."

It will take them at least twenty minutes to get back to the ship from here, let alone getting farther into the station; she can't risk Jay running out early. "Then you take the girl and get back to the *Nanshe*," she says.

"You need me to open that door."

Lasadi swears under her breath. "Alex? Can you do it alone?"

Alex shakes his head, mouth pressed into a tight line. "It'll take us both."

The smart thing to do would be to go back to the *Nanshe* and make a second run once they've assessed everyone for injury and recharged their suits. It's a maddening choice, given how close they are to their destination and what it cost them to get this far. But her number one priority is everyone's safety, and this is a risk they don't need to take.

"Jay, check in with the *Nanshe*. We don't know what we'll find in that chamber, and I'd rather go in fresh if we still have the time. Alex? You and Tora get together and find us a clear path back home."

Tora looks as though she's about to argue with the order to return to the *Nanshe*, but Lasadi cocks an eyebrow, daring her to go back on their agreement that Lasadi gives the orders out here. Tora's lips press into a thin line, but she nods.

"Raj, Ruby, do a quick check of these rooms — grab anything that might be useful and easy to transport. Hopefully we won't be coming through here on our way . . ." Lasadi trails off; she knows that stitch between Jay's brows. "Back," she finishes. "What is it, Jay?"

"Proximity alarm," he answers.

"More pirates?"

"I don't think so. It's a new ship — the drive signature is coded with the Alliance flag." He glances up. "I think it's SymTex."

"Already?" Lasadi curses. "How far out are they?"

"An hour or two, maybe. I'd love to get my hands on whatever's powering their engine."

"Then we trust the life support for as long as we can — but no chances." Lasadi turns to Lisbeth. "Have you seen anyone besides these men?" The girl shakes her head. "Okay. Then we're probably good — and the pirates disabled the boobytraps in the area we came through. Anything else we need to know before we head out?" Lasadi is greeted with a chorus of *No*s, but a shadow flickers across Ruby's face. "What is it?"

Ruby's mouth quirks to the side; for a fraction of a second, it looks like she's going to pretend nothing's wrong. But, "We know about the mechanical lock at the final door," she finally says. "I'm concerned about additional security we might find once we get inside, only. No one's ever documented that."

"Anything you can't handle?"

"No, Cap."

Raj clears his throat. "Back when we were letting Jay in the airlock, you said there was another hacker in the system."

"It was the pirates," Ruby says. "And we've taken care of them."

Something sparks in the air between them all, some thread she can't quite put a finger on. It's in the look of concern Raj turns on Ruby, the way Tora's nostrils flare. The way Lisbeth melts closer to Ruby's thigh and Ruby's thumb rubs absently against the girl's shoulder.

Nerves? Or something more.

"Stay sharp," Lasadi tells Ruby. "And let us know if you sense them again." She crouches in front of Lisbeth again. "Will you show us where to go?"

The kid nods once and turns as though she's fleeing — and maybe she is. Lasadi has been so focused on salvaging the plan, she's tuned out the bodies floating around the edge of this room.

Lasadi motions for Jay to go ahead with Ruby. "Keep watch for traps — the pirates may have cleared out this section, but we can't trust they got everything."

"Copy that."

Lasadi lets Tora and Alex go ahead, too — they're still discussing the route back in hushed tones — and hangs back to bring up the rear with Raj. She'd been paying more attention to their captors than their surroundings when she'd come through here last, but she had noticed it was different from the other wing of the labyrinth. It's older, more well-worn and repaired, compared to the half-constructed corridors they'd initially accessed. Part of Rasheda Auburn's oldest build, maybe.

She waits until the others are out of earshot. "What's going on with Ruby?" she asks.

Raj takes a breath, thinking through his answer, and she wonders if she'll get the truth. Ruby and Alex and Raj all have a history together that doesn't include her, and there's not much incentive for him to give up whatever secret his friend wants protected. But something tells her this is about the job, and Raj wants to get out of here alive as bad as the rest of them do.

"She's spooked," he finally says. "She said she's sensed someone else's presence in the system when she's been hacking in. The last time she tried it, they actively resisted her. Shoved her back out."

"You don't think it was the pirates?"

"Maybe. Ruby's pretty fast, but whoever this was is faster." He rubs a hand over the back of his neck, then frowns down the hallway behind them.

"What is it?"

"That girl, Lisbeth. She said she heard a woman talking to her through the station. I know it's not a hired gun's place to ask, but you heard that laughing, too. Tora isn't telling us everything about what happened to Rasheda Auburn."

Tora hasn't, of course, but there's no reason now for Raj not to know. "Rasheda was experimenting with AI," Lasadi says. "She wanted to live forever."

"So she copied her brain into a computer so it could remix her memories into a plausible facsimile of eternal life."

"I assumed it would be something localized — but my guess is she imprinted on the station AI."

"Creepy." Raj scans the corridor ahead, looking for trouble. "But is that really immortality?"

"My grandma always said death was a doorway." Lasadi doesn't know why she's saying this; something about this man makes her think he'll understand. "That the ancestors lived on in your memories, the old ones watching you from a place you couldn't yet see yourself. You're only truly gone once no one remembers you."

And if you're still alive, but everyone who loved you believes you're dead and held banishing to forget your memory? Lasadi's cheeks flare with sudden shame.

Rasheda died fifty years ago but hasn't let anyone forget her; Lasadi might as well never have existed.

She clears her throat, acutely aware Raj is watching her. "You did good work back there. You just about had me convinced."

"Glad you figured it out." Raj grins, and she looks away before she lets herself enjoy too much of the warmth of that smile. She keeps her attention up, scanning the hall ahead. She'd almost rather face danger, because this calm is making it too easy to slip into uncomfortable thoughts.

Maybe she's still riding high from the fight, but she can feel the gentle pressure of Raj's hands on her upper arms, the sensation of her shoulder blades against his chest. The illusion of being held. Adrenaline, she tells herself, and the fact that in the past three years, only doctors have seen her wreck of a body — let alone touched it. Maybe when they get back to Ironfall she needs to hire someone who won't mind her scars to scratch the itch and get it out of her system.

Or maybe Jay's right, and they could try building a crew once more. Raj, Ruby, Alex — they've all fit in well. Raj is pretty good company for an Arquellian. They could talk, at least, even if she can't expect more.

"You're a good leader," Raj says, startling her from her thoughts.

She cuts her gaze to him, but there's no guile in his face, no sense he's making a joke at her expense.

"It's been a while," she says after a moment.

"Jay told me about Mercury Squadron," he says, almost apologetic. "I heard a lot about them back in the day."

"Then you heard they're all dead or captured, right?" she says; it's a sharp lash meant to stop the conversation and cut deep both ways — and it does. A phantom ache stabs through her gut, below the scar in the hollow of her abdomen, right where the physical debris of the battle had lanced through her. "Sorry to shake your confidence."

"You were dealt a bad hand at Tannis, Lasadi." Raj's voice is pitched with such quiet conviction that she misses her step. She pauses, searching his face; light glints in the gold flecks of his irises.

"A bad hand?" Lasadi can't help but laugh, suddenly exhausted. "Mercury started that whole battle by killing a medical transport, you might have heard."

"Sure," he says with a shrug. "Everybody's heard that lie."

"Then you know — " His choice of words flashes through her train of thought, leaving the high ring of breaking crystal. "What do you mean."

"About the medical transport, that Mercury wasn't responsible for it? You were set up." He frowns at her, confused. "You knew that, right?"

Her lips part, but she can't speak — she can't even think of what to say. He sounds so certain, he'd said it so casual, like he assumed she knew, not like he was intending to drop a bomb into the center of her psyche.

Raj is telling her the truth. She knows this with all her soul.

Dizzy vertigo lurches through her, as if the station were moving underfoot. Three years of guilt and confusion and grief skip subtly to the side, leaving her clutching at an empty place where knowledge used to be.

Anton had said — fucking *Anton* — and maybe he was trying to do the right thing for Corusca by using her and her squadron as scapegoats. Maybe he thought she was dead when he made his deal with the Alliance. But when she reached out to him? Did he know the truth by then, and still let her believe the lie? She's had three years to detangle herself from his mind games and she's never once shone a light on that dark place.

"Lasadi?"

She forces herself to focus on Raj. "What do you know about that?" she asks, and when something dark and weary moves across Raj's face, a chill curls up Lasadi's spine. The stale air between them turns brittle, a cracked pane of glass that could shatter at any moment, slicing them both with the broken pieces. Lasadi almost retracts the question. She won't like this answer; olds save them both, she won't like this answer.

"Heya! We found it!"

Ruby's voice echoes down the hall, tumbling through Lasadi's racing thoughts and pulling her back into the moment. The others have reached the door. It's a perfect circle, heavy ceramic-coated steel, marked by a stylized sun in burnished gold.

"Lasadi," Raj says.

"Don't. Whatever you were going to say, don't." She tears her attention away from Raj, dragging breath into her lungs and leaving him — and everything else that should stay unsaid — suspended in the hallway behind her.

CHAPTER 24
RAJ

SOMETHING HAS SHIFTED, sharp and dangerous, and Raj isn't entirely sure what happened.

How could she have believed her team was responsible for the medical transport's destruction? She'd been there. She knew her people. The Alliance, they lied to everyone about what happened, and Anton Kato went with the lie to cement his own power — but why would Lasadi have believed it?

Raj is going to have to tell her what he knows, a conversation that's been increasingly inevitable the closer he's become to Lasadi and Jay. If he does it right, he might still be able to salvage the budding friendship — or at least manage an amicable-enough parting that they don't march him off to the nearest Alliance outpost to collect the bounty on his head.

As soon as they get back to the ship. He'll tell her everything as soon as they get back to the ship.

He locks his magboots at her side; she spares him a glance and turns her attention back to the door. A muscle jumps in her jaw.

"Scan it for traps," she orders, and Jay pulls a hand

terminal off his belt and turns to paint the door with pale blue light.

"Looks like all the mechanical traps have already been sprung or dismantled," Jay says after a minute. "But there's no sign of atmosphere on the other side of that door. My guess is the room's lost pressure."

"Helmets on, then. And Jay, as soon as that door's open, you're heading back to the *Nanshe* with Lisbeth. Alex, you'll go with them to make sure they don't take any wrong turns."

"Understood." Jay beckons Alex forward. "Ruby, you're up."

Ruby plugs into the access panel as Jay unzips his toolkit and gets to work on the mechanical lock, working in sync with Alex like they've been practicing over the last few days on the *Nanshe*. Raj watches Ruby, wary. Could be it was a human hacker working against her earlier, but Lasadi's comment that Rasheda Auburn had been trying to imprint herself in the station AI bothers him. Ruby can handle a normal station AI — but what if this one has somehow mutated beyond the norm with Rasheda's intervention?

Jay grins as something clicks into place, a faint ping deep within the door. "We're through the first lock," he says, then holds out a hand to Alex. "Plasma saw."

"Last thing my brother needs to know," Ruby complains absently, though her attention's obviously on her own work. "The ayas are going to love his new skill set."

Alex shrugs and hands Jay the plasma saw. "Ayas aren't taking me back."

Ruby blinks, but if she loses her concentration it doesn't show. "What?"

"The ayas aren't taking me back," Alex says again. "They say I'm too old to stay." He gives his sister an apologetic look. "Sorry I didn't tell you earlier, but you can't kill me if we're in the middle of a job."

Ruby stares at him, then goes back to her work. "Permission to kill him later, Captain."

"Granted," says Lasadi. "Not on my ship, though."

"You hear that, you little punk?" Ruby says. "The minute we set foot in Ironfall docks you're dead."

"Jay, man. Can I stay with you?"

Jay laughs and slots the plasma saw carefully where the locking mechanism should be in the center of the sun. "Yeah, no. My girl wants to adopt kids but I think you're a little old. Ruby?"

"Yeah yeah, hold on. If I rush this, the door will melt shut permanently, won't it." And then she whoops. "I'm through the biolock. Shutting down the internal tripwires. You're golden, Jay."

Lasadi draws her pistol and Raj follows her lead. "Keep her back," Las orders Tora, gesturing to Lisbeth; the other woman obeys.

Jay's helmet automatically goes dark as the plasma saw flares, and after a moment something rings inside the door, hollow as a bell. The door whirs open. Raj's jaw drops.

"Holy shit," Lasadi breathes.

There are trees.

Everywhere the eye can see.

The door with the golden sun opens into an enormous spherical chamber. From outside the station, and in the schematics, the chamber's size was obscured by the mishmash of corridors and modules welded into the chaotic labyrinth around this central heart. Raj was wholly unprepared for how small he feels when standing in the doorway.

The spherical walls shimmer with holographic waves of light, and at the distant center of the room, a knot of blue light flickers faintly, trapped by a tangle of what seem to be tree roots. The trunks of the trees stretch out in all directions, their branches arching and intertwining to form more pathways throughout the room.

Alex is the first to speak.

"That can't be real," he says. He floats closer to the doorway, his shoulders forced into false relaxation.

"They're not," Raj agrees. It occurs to him he might be the only one here who's been in a forest. "They're symmetrical, and you see the leaves? That one's a vine oak, the branch beside it is some kind of willow." Ruby gives him *So what* eyebrows. "They wouldn't grow on the same trunk."

The light captured by the roots of the trees is beginning to spread — or maybe it's been moving this whole time and Raj is just now noticing. Dozens, hundreds, *thousands* of fireflies flicker out from the center of the room and flow through the chamber. But they're not alive, they're tiny points of blue-green light programmed to look like they're spreading through the structures, reaching all the way out to the tips of the leaves, glittering along the edges of every lobe like droplets of water. It's stunning, surreal.

But it's far from welcoming. Alongside the beauty of this room is menace. An intent, like something old and dark and malicious watching them. The rest of the group seems to sense it, too. Alex shifts uneasily, his grin at opening the room fading. Light plays in Lasadi's eyes alongside worry. Even Tora hesitates, here on the edge of victory.

Welcome, travelers.

Raj stiffens.

"Did anyone else hear that?"

But before the words are out of his mouth, the room fills with faint, mocking laughter — loud enough for them all to hear. Alex slinks back from the doorway, all false casual like he meant to leave all along.

"It's her," whispers Lisbeth. The girl's plastered against the far wall of the corridor like she's about to run.

"Who?" Raj asks.

"The woman who lives here."

"You said no one else was here," says Alex.

"Because there isn't," Tora says sharply. "Not anymore."

"It's just a station AI wearing Rasheda Auburn's voice," Lasadi says; Raj doesn't miss the sharp look that gets from Tora. "We still have a plan. Jay, Alex. Take Lisbeth back to the *Nanshe* and get the ship fired up. I'm ready to get gone."

Jay stands and grabs his toolkit; Alex floats his plasma saw to Ruby, then holds out a hand for Lisbeth. Neither argues, though worry is clear in Jay's face. Lasadi clasps his arm as he leaves, then turns back the rest of them.

"I don't like any of this," she says. "So let's make it fast and get out of here. Ruby, we're looking for a power source, or anything else unusual in this room. What do you see?"

Ruby, still plugged into the access panel, doesn't answer for a long moment. Worry grips Raj's gut. He's about to call her name when she jerks.

"A dais, only," she says, waving a hand to the right. "If we head that way out of this door, we should find it about ten meters in."

"Then let's get going." Lasadi meets Raj's gaze; something complicated flickers across her expression before she shuts it down behind a mask of command. "Shall we?" she asks.

He nods, and together they unlock their magboots, reorienting in the hallway so the door to the chamber is up, and gently floating into the forest chamber with weapons drawn.

Nothing happens.

The tips of the branches stop about a meter above their heads, leaving a uniform amount of space between the wall and the forest throughout the chamber. From this vantage point, Raj can see that the walls aren't entirely holographic. A swath through the lights creates a path that starts and ends at the door, presumably encircling the room.

"I can see the dais," Raj calls. Ruby's right, it appears to be about ten meters out along the path, a dark protrusion against the wash of light.

"All clear," Lasadi says. "Come on up, you two."

Raj scans the room again as Tora and Ruby join them, but there's no shift in the light to signify that anyone — or anything — cares they're here. The branches are solid, the leaves immobile, a strange caricature of a living, breathing forest.

"Let's all check out the dais," Lasadi says. "Then take a quick sweep around the rest of the room to see what we might be missing."

Holographic waves of light undulate around them as they make their way along the path to the dais, which holds a simple terminal. The screen flickers to life when Ruby passes a gloved hand over it, and her fingers fly over the screen.

"No extra encryption here," she says. "Rasheda never expected anyone to get this far."

"She didn't know we were bringing you," Raj says.

"Careful, you," Ruby says. "The ego on me already, I'll float away. There — I put the station's remaining defenses into standby, so we should have an easier time getting back."

"Are you in Rasheda's database?" Tora asks. "We need those files."

"It's all here," Ruby answers. She slots a data cube into the dock to siphon up files; the progress bar ticks up a minuscule amount. She sighs and snakes the cord out of her gauntlet. "Give us a look, then? See if we can speed things up?"

"Download everything you can," Lasadi says. "Raj, stay

here with her — Tora, you and I can check out the rest of the room."

"You got it, Cap," Ruby says. She plugs her cord into the port on the side of the dais.

And stiffens.

"Ruby?" Raj asks.

She's laughing, a faint, girlish giggle like nothing Raj has ever heard come out of Ruby's mouth. The giggle broadens, deepens into a full-throated chuckle.

"Ruby, what the fuck?"

The laugh cuts out with a strangled choking sound; Ruby screams.

Raj lunges for the plug to pull her free, but a bolt of electricity flares along his arm and shoves him back, knocking Ruby's magboots loose and sending her drifting towards the center of the chamber. Her physical connection to the station tears free, the cord snapping in a batch of sparks and severed wires, but blue light arcs over her suit from the tips of the leaves, suspending her in a web of power.

Raj catches himself on the wall and spins back to face her, faintly aware of Lasadi's voice coming through the comms, calling Ruby's name. Ruby's stopped screaming and is now arched back, eyes wide in terror, as though whatever energy has her trapped has stopped her from being able to move or speak.

Lasadi's voice cuts out.

"Welcome, travelers."

The way Lasadi freezes, she must hear it, too. The woman's voice isn't inside his head, it's coming through the comms.

"I'm glad you finally made it," says the voice. "I was beginning to despair."

"Who are you?" Raj asks.

"I think you know." A low rumble of laughter, Raj feels it in his bones, as though the whole station is shaking.

"Rasheda," whispers Tora.

Her personality embedded in a station AI, at least.

The voice rumbles again. "I've been here so long, and no one has gotten this close. No one has been tenacious enough to break in. This one kept giving me tastes — tastes of herself, tastes of all of you." The rumble of laughter comes again. "Maybe I was wrong to make my heart so secure. This one's internal knowledge base is vast, but it's a single drop. Once I'm free, I'll drink as much as I want."

"Let her go," Raj says, and something in the room *shifts*. The focus, the *attention* — which shouldn't be possible to say of a room — is on him now, the points of light changing from a subtle twinkle to a steady pulse that seems to surround him, watch him.

"Ah," says the AI; the sigh slithers through the comms and down his collar. "Captain Demetriou, the murderer. This one has a fascinating file on you. I bet you thought this secret would stay hidden."

The words shiver through him like a stone through deep water, churning up currents of dread.

There's no way this AI can know what's in his sealed files, is there? Because if the information was in a file Ruby had, that would mean Ruby knew. And Ruby's been irritated with him. Been angry with him. But she's never treated him with the disdain she would if she *knew*.

But he can see it in her face now, lit up by the web of light holding her in place. *I'm sorry*, she mouths; tears glisten on her lashes.

"What do you want?" Raj is hoping to shift the conversation, but the voice keeps going as though he never spoke.

"Seven hundred and twelve innocent souls, shot out of Coruscan orbit," says Rasheda Auburn's AI. Raj sees that all-too-familiar number hit Lasadi like a punch. "An unarmed medical transport, which you ordered destroyed to spark a battle you expected to win glory in . . . along with the approval of your father? But you ran away like a coward instead, and meanwhile Tannis burned."

He recognizes the words; he's read the trial transcripts, the passionate, eloquent speeches given to condemn him and cement his reputation from a rising star in the Arquellian navy to a glory-seeking coward. But those records were thoroughly sealed. They shouldn't be parroted back to him in a dead woman's voice.

Lasadi is staring at him, eyes blazing with fury. "What is she talking about?" she asks, and he knows she's not asking about the reference. *Seven hundred and twelve innocent souls* had been a rallying cry for the Alliance. It had been splashed through the media in defense of the massacre of Tannis, crowed in victory over the bodies of civilians dressed posthumously as CLA soldiers.

"It's a lie," he says. "I was framed."

"You just said *I* had been framed."

"You were. Lasadi — "

"He didn't simply grow a conscience and desert," says the AI. "He was arrested for ordering the New Manilan medical transport shot down. A disgrace to his rank and name." Every word lands like a blow; that last sentence is a direct quote from Raj's own father.

"That would have been all over the news," Lasadi says, but even as she says it, he can tell the pieces are starting to click into place. "Except that it looks terrible for the Alliance to admit it wasn't the rebels after all. That they were wrong to shell Tannis." Her eyes grow cold. "And your father being an admiral, after all, of course it could be covered up."

"That's not what happened," Raj says. "The trial was all lies."

"Was it?" Lasadi turns on him. "This whole time everyone blamed Mercury Squadron. This whole time —

and that's what you meant, isn't it? It wasn't our fault. It was yours."

"You have to trust me." Desperation fractures Raj's voice.

"I did." She laughs, a manic edge of frustration in the sound. "Which should have been my first clue."

"You and I are on the same side," Raj says.

"You don't know a fucking thing about me," Lasadi says coldly. Then her attention shifts over his shoulder, and whatever else she was about to say dies on her lips.

Lasadi curses and shoves past him, launching herself off the wall and into the branch-filled void.

CHAPTER 25
LASADI

Lasadi leaps without thinking.

She can figure out what to do with Raj Demetriou later: murderer, war criminal, the cause of her friends' deaths, the cause of her scars, the reason she had to be rebuilt in Nico Garnet's medical bays — fuck, the reason she works for Nico Garnet now.

But all that can wait, because they've been played.

Played. By an AI wearing the voice of a long-dead pirate, and Lasadi lets the fury wash over her in pure waves, sharpening her focus as she navigates the branches of this fake forest at the heart of Auburn Station.

As she and Raj had turned on each other, the energy field that held Ruby had slowly been drawing her away, towards the center of the room and the flickering blue knot of light held in the roots of the trees. Why? Lasadi has no clue. But she sure as hell isn't going to find out by letting it happen.

The web had jerked Ruby back as soon as Lasadi leapt after her, and the branches, which had seemed solid and fixed, are now shifting around her. A thin narrow one — that fucking Arquellian had called it a willow — lashes at her, catching around her ankle, and Lasadi snatches the utility knife from her belt and slashes through it. It comes free in a satisfying shower of sparks.

When she risks a glance back, she can see that Raj leapt seconds after her. He's having as much trouble with the branches as she is — a heavy one catches him across the chest, flicking him easy to the side, and Lasadi's heart lurches in worry before she shuts that down with a vicious curse. He can save his own hide — he's plenty good at that. Lasadi returns her focus to Ruby.

The force pulling Ruby back isn't taking much care with the human body it's seized. She's ricocheting off inconvenient branches as she's pulled backwards, arms flailing as though trying to maintain control of her trajectory.

Ruby is still conscious, her eyes wide with fear. Her lips are moving, though whatever she's screaming isn't being transmitted through the comms. Instead, all Lasadi can hear is the AI's laughter and continued, constant babble. It's still pontificating about Raj's record, though Lasadi has stopped listening. Her system's recording everything so she can listen later if she cares to hear it, but right now the voice's logic has taken on a sort of circular thinking, an AI in a closed loop, a hall of mirrors feeding and elaborating on what it has available, creating patterns from the source material that sound like logic, but fracture slightly more with every mirror that reflects them.

The source material — Raj's sealed record — exists, though. That's enough proof for her.

A massive branch shifts in front of Lasadi, blocking her view of Ruby, but she glances off it nimbly, kicking off another solid section and slashing another whipping branch that tries to wrap around her throat. There are fewer branches once she gets closer to the roots, which means both fewer things trying to attack her, and more difficult maneuverability in the open void. As she gets closer, she can make out the source of the light.

It's a reactor, encircled by a platform. It can't be the main source of power for the station — this chamber is completely cut off from the rest of the station's systems — but it must run the systems in this chamber, the whipping branches and flowing light a proxy body for the AI.

The "roots" of the trees form a cage around the ball of light, and Lasadi slashes free of one last vine and launches herself in a spray of sparks through the blessedly empty space to the platform that surrounds the reactor. She can't find Raj anywhere behind her, and she's lost sight of Ruby, too, but she was being pulled towards the reactor last Lasadi saw. It has to be her destination.

Her magboots hit the platform and lock. "Ruby?" she calls over the open channel. "Tell me where you are."

A strangled scream pierces through the comm, cutting off in a burst of static.

"She's alive," says Rasheda Auburn's AI. "Don't worry, I just need her body for a moment."

"What do you want her for?"

No response. Lasadi slowly walks the circular platform; to her left, the reactor flares with captive energy, a half-dozen concentric metal halos revolving around it and casting flickering silver-blue shadows over the scene. Under her palm, the platform's railing thrums with power; the grating below her feet shivers with energy.

Their scans had noted that this room was cut off from the power grid that supplied the rest of the station. What the hell is a reactor this big powering?

"Rasheda?" Strange to name an AI, but this one is different from others Lasadi has encountered. It may be communicating with remixed words in logic spirals, but there's something of true cunning in the way it played her and Raj against each other to distract them. A station AI couldn't do that on its own.

"Mmmm?" The AI's voice hums through the comms with an odd vibration. Lasadi shudders, shakes her head to clear it.

"This reactor, it's all for you?" she asks. "It must take a lot of energy to power an AI."

"It took a lot of energy to power me when I was human, too," the AI answers. "All that growing food, recycling water. Hot and cold, bathing, sickness, healing wounds. And look at you, Lasadi Cazinho, worrying about the air counting down in your little suit."

"Ruby has a file on me, too?" Lasadi asks; something lurches against the platform. Ruby, on the other side of the reactor? Is she still struggling?

"You and I are more alike than the others," the AI says. "Given we're both technically dead."

"Can an AI really be considered dead if it never lived?"

The circular walkway seems interminable — is it actually this big? Or is she being led on like a dog, chasing her tail with nothing to be found. There are no markings, no way to indicate if she's circled back to where she started. The tree roots above her head are perfectly symmetrical. Lasadi draws her pistol, picking up her speed.

"Are you going to shoot me?" The AI wearing Rasheda Auburn's voice booms through the comms, so loud and concussive in her ear that Lasadi loses her footing. She stumbles against the railing, tightening her grip on the pistol reflexively to keep from losing it.

Something else is shaking the platform, she realizes — the whole thing moved, that wasn't just the deafening pulse of Rasheda's voice causing her to trip.

Someone's singing, the same lullaby Lasadi noticed when they first entered the labyrinth. Only now she recognizes it: an old Coruscan tune, one of her grandmother's favorites. The familiar tune flows around her, bringing with it the sensation of her grandmother's arms, her little sister's legs tangled with hers, her little brother's breathing softening to a snore.

Her grandmother kissing her on the top of the head. "Think with your brain, Lala, not your heart. That's what it's there for."

Lasadi flips a switch in her mind and the memory vanishes, the old Coruscan tune becoming the tinny rendering of a machine that thinks it knows her because it read her file.

"How have you found being dead?" the AI asks. "Is it freeing? No more obligations, no more responsibility for anyone but yourself. Although, you do have responsibilities, don't you? Your friends, racing back through my veins to your ship, I could destroy them in a heartbeat." There's that laugh again. "Not that my heart beats anymore."

"They're not a threat to you," Lasadi says. Steady, calm. "So don't waste your energy."

"I'm nothing but energy," the AI laughs.

Of course it is — Rasheda Auburn's AI may be able to control what happens throughout the station, but this chamber is its mind. Lasadi has been picturing a computer powering the AI, but she's standing *inside* it. At the heart of it. She peers up at the cage of roots surrounding her, drawing in the energy from the reactor, light running the length of the trunks and flashing from branch to branch. Not like a forest, but like neurons firing flashes in the dark.

"What do you need Ruby for?"

"At times, being dead is mildly inconvenient."

The platform lurches again, this time throwing Lasadi so violently against the railing that it slams against ribs already bruised from the pirates. She cries out in pain, her pistol thrown from her hand and spinning out into the tangled roots of Rasheda Auburn's mind. Lasadi blinks away involuntary tears, breathing deep against the ache until it diminishes.

When her vision clears, she realizes she's finally made her way around to the far side of the platform.

And found Rasheda Auburn — what's left of her, anyway.

The great pirate queen herself is a husk of pale, papery skin and brittle black hair, her clothing perfectly preserved. She's seated in a surgery chair, the type sold throughout Durga's Belt and programmed to take care of relatively standard issues: stitches, broken bones, appendicitis, amputations. The life support system in this room must have been turned off after her death, because Rasheda is wearing a simple floral jumpsuit, slippers, and a crown.

The crown is a skull wreath, similar to the ones that come with holosense projectors to tap into the wearer's senses and immerse them more fully in the holoplay. But this one is heavily modified, tight clamps keeping it in place. Lasadi is so caught up by the skull wreath she doesn't at first notice what it's obscuring.

Holes drilled through Rasheda's skull, the surgery chair modified in its programming from fixing the complaints of asteroid settlers to . . . whatever procedure copied Rasheda Auburn's thought patterns into a machine and discarded her body like an afterthought.

Ruby is floating near Rasheda's body, her limbs frozen though she's awake, eyes searching frantic. When she spots Lasadi her mouth opens, shouting something the AI isn't allowing to be transmitted through the comms.

Not the AI, Lasadi realizes with a shiver of wonder. This was never a simple AI.

"What did you do to yourself?" Lasadi asks. She takes a step forward, then another. The AI — fucking *Rasheda* herself — isn't trying to stop her from approaching Ruby, so

Lasadi closes the distance between them. Ruby's gaze darts down, and again; she's trying to communicate something.

"I made myself immortal," Rasheda says.

"But you must have made a mistake," Lasadi says. "Or you wouldn't need us to help you out."

"Not a mistake, girl. A miscalculation. I couldn't imagine true freedom until I discarded my human body. But when your mind is truly infinite, what once seemed limitless suddenly becomes a cage."

"And you want out," Lasadi guesses. Rasheda Auburn built a station to seal off and protect her human body, but once she managed to unleash her mind into it, she found it far too constricting.

"Strap the other one into the surgical chair," Rasheda orders.

Ruby's eyes are still moving — but not darting around in fear like Lasadi had originally thought. She's trying to indicate something below their feet.

"Do it yourself," Lasadi says.

"I may lack a body, but I can kill the others with a thought. You may pretend not to care, but you do. After all, you came after this one without hesitation. As I knew you would."

"Yeah?"

"I read your file, Captain."

The platform shudders again, and this time Lasadi sees what's causing it. And what Ruby's been trying to show her. One of the spinning halos capturing the reactor's energy is slightly off, running slower than the others and binding up occasionally with a grinding lurch. A dent in the metal reveals the probable reason for the deformation, and the loss of life support in this room. Some piece of space junk must have punctured the heart of the station, a random missile of iron and ice nearly missing the reactor itself.

If the reactor fails, so does Rasheda's ability to control the station. She's not just bored — if she doesn't find a way off the station before it's destroyed, she'll die for real this time.

"So you read my file," Lasadi says. "And I'm sure you've modeled all possible outcomes for what might happen once I get into this situation."

"In most of them you try to fight me," Rasheda says. "I would advise against it."

"Noted." Lasadi reaches for Ruby, stopping her gentle spin and pulling her down beside the surgical chair. "You wanted her strapped into the chair?" Ruby shakes her head, frantic. "And if I do it, you'll let the rest of us — her brother — leave?"

Ruby stills, lips parting; if she speaks, Lasadi can't hear it.

"Of course," Rasheda says. "I've read her file, too."

"Okay." Lasadi reaches past Ruby as though for the straps holding Rasheda Auburn's corpse to the surgical chair. Ruby's not struggling anymore; she nods once and her eyes squeeze shut: *Do it.*

And Lasadi grabs the plasma saw from Ruby's side. "Go!" she yells to Ruby.

She launches herself for the dented metal halo.

CHAPTER 26
LASADI

SOMEONE IS SCREAMING — she doesn't know if it's her, Ruby, or Rasheda Auburn. Whoever it is, the volume is so loud her eardrums throb, her eyes narrowing involuntarily against the assault of sound.

She forces herself to tune it out. Pulls the trigger on the plasma saw; it flares to life even before she lands on the damaged outer halo. Her helmet darkens automatically at the blaze, and she aims the saw at the weakened place where the halo had previously been hit.

Whatever alloy the halos are made of, they're not built to be load-bearing, and the plasma saw slices free with a pulse of molten metal. The halo jerks, the two cut ends grinding together with a screech that rivals the screaming coming through her comms.

Lasadi secures the plasma saw to her belt and finds a grip on the halo as near to the pivot point as she can, bracing her feet against the longer arm that has now been severed. She shoves with all her might, bruised and exhausted muscles howling in pain. Shoves again, and the halo finally gives — enough to catch the edge of the undamaged halos below, which are still rotating at full speed. It collides with a shower of sparks and a shriek of metal on metal, the impact bucking her loose.

She flies backwards, crashes into something solid — must be the platform around the reactor. Stars burst across her vision, blurring together with the sparks spraying from the grinding of the seized-up halos. The impact forces the air from her lungs, and for a brief, terrifying moment she can't tell if she's simply too stunned to move or if something has been severed in her spinal column.

Either way, the message to *reach out, grab something, flail, do ANYTHING* isn't getting through. Lasadi is drifting, course reversed so she's approaching the rapidly disintegrating halos once more. She's moving slow enough she can appreciate that her plan worked, at least. The outer halos are splintering and buckling, lodging one by one in inner halos and shattering them in layer after layer of spectacular catastrophe. It's a dazzling display of sparks and folding, jagged, windmilling metal.

She can't hear Rasheda's voice.

Lasadi's foot kicks, sudden — she's not paralyzed, she realizes in relief, though the motion sends pain flaring through her lower back. She kicks the other foot. She can move, but she has nothing to grip, nothing to push off of until she reaches the toothy, splintered maw emerging from the reactor's shining halos. The initial slow destruction is speeding up now, bits of halos breaking free and churning like rotors, whipping through the air like chaotic blades.

She hadn't been thinking when she grabbed Ruby's saw and leapt. She didn't have an escape plan; she'd simply been trying to stop Rasheda, shut the reactor down so Ruby could go free. So Jay and Alex and Raj and Tora and the little girl — all of them — could get out of Auburn Station alive.

Lasadi's already dead anyway, after all — Rasheda was right about that. She'd been presumed dead in the Battle of

Tannis; her family held banishing on hearing of her death. Anton had told her that during their final call. Her grandmother, her sister, her brother, her cousins — they'd declared her name unspoken and memory wiped because of what they thought she was responsible for. "Imagine the pain you'll cause them if you come back home," he'd said, and she'd believed him.

But Anton had been wrong about the medical transport. Maybe he was wrong about her family, too. He may have tossed her aside when she was no longer of use to the cause, but she earned captain of Mercury Squadron on her own. Even if she isn't always sure who else she is, she can be certain of that.

Lasadi has the plasma saw. She has the ability to move — if not to change her course. She can only hope Ruby took her order and fled to safety. Lasadi braces herself for impact, searching calm for a safe space to push off of and finding nothing. She's close enough that the wild, windmilling arms of broken halos are whirling by her with centimeters to spare. She screws her eyes shut, and flares the saw to life in front of her as her final stand.

Something jerks her back, igniting screaming pain from earlier injuries — but it's not the sharp tearing, chewing she's expecting. Hands catch under her arms, pull her out of the dancing reach of the shattered halos, away from the churn of the rapidly unspiraling reactor. Hands haul her backwards over the railing and onto the platform she'd leapt from moments earlier.

"Captain." The voice belongs to Raj. "Lasadi."

His suit is lashed to Ruby's, who's still gripping the railing; she must have acted as the anchor for Raj to leap from the platform to grab Lasadi. The heady realization that she's safe spirals through her, but the relief doesn't last long. The entire platform lurches, the chaotic torque of the disintegrating halos finally breaking it free from its moorings.

She shakes her head to clear it, takes a ragged breath. "We have to go." But pain screams through her when she tries to push off.

The others don't hesitate. Ruby grabs one of her arms and Raj grabs the other, and between them, they propel her back to the door. The branches of the trees rustle around them but are no longer trying to capture them. It's more like the twitching impulse of muscle in the moments after the soul is gone, insensate spasms of an artificial thicket.

"Tora, come in," Raj says. "We've got the captain."

"The power levels are flaring." Tora's voice holds an edge of panic. "I'm at the door."

Lasadi can barely make her out, a silhouette with one hand braced on the doorway, the other reaching to help the others. She catches Lasadi when Raj and Ruby push her through, then turns to help them wrestle the door shut.

Ruby snakes a cord from her gauntlet.

"Wait — "

Lasadi and Raj say it at the same time, but Ruby waves them off. "All Rasheda's energy is going towards keeping shit from disintegrating," Ruby says. "I just need a second." Her fingers fly on the access panel, typing in a row of numbers and hitting Lock. The door seals shut with a hiss. "Get back," yells Ruby, and Lasadi pushes herself clumsily away, biting off a cry of pain as she overcorrects. Tora gently catches her arm.

Ruby launches backwards herself as sparks pop and flare in a flaming circle around the door, leaving the edges glowing angry red with molten metal.

"What was that?" Raj asks.

"One of Rasheda's boobytraps that I disabled earlier. It should seal the door shut permanently."

"And can that door withstand the reactor blowing?" Lasadi asks.

"Rasheda built the heart of her station for an attack that strong," Ruby says. "And this chamber is cut off from the rest of the power grid. So, hopefully? But if it can't, we're already screwed."

At that, the station shudders around them, a violent lurch that sends Lasadi flying; Tora still has her arm, though, and a handhold to steady them both.

Lasadi's eyes screw shut of their own accord, but, no sudden death blazing through the door in a fury of fire and shrapnel. She waits, frozen. Lets out a breath as the tremors die down; still nobody moves. Finally, Ruby pushes herself forward, tentatively plugging herself back into the access panel.

"Did we live?" asks Raj.

"I think so?" Ruby types something into her gauntlet. "Looks like a section of wall on the far side of the chamber failed, but this part of the station's golden. Rasheda was a clever one with her partitions, wasn't she."

"Is she . . ." Lasadi doesn't know the proper term, so she goes with classic. "Dead?"

"As far as I can tell."

"Fantastic." Lasadi straightens, breath catching with pain.

Tora frowns at her. "How bad is it?"

"Just got the wind knocked out of me," Lasadi says; her suit doesn't seem to think she's in danger of dying, but it does keep offering her a pain cocktail. She hits Yes — fuck yes — and a needle pricks her neck, a slow trickle of cool release spreads through her muscles. She opens a channel. "Jay? Come in."

"I'm here," Jay says, and relief floods through her, riding the wave of meds. "You all good?" he asks.

"We're good." Lasadi takes a deep breath. "We may

have caused a small reactor failure, but it seems to be contained. Heading back to you."

"Figures." The edge of humor in Jay's voice overlays tension. "But we've got bigger problems. Get your asses back here fast."

CHAPTER 27
RAJ

"WHAT DO you mean SymTex is here already?" Lasadi tears her helmet off the instant the airlock has finished cycling, though Raj isn't sure whether it's her need for action or the growing desperation for oxygen. Raj's suit's gauge has been on zero for the last five minutes, and even though he knows there's always a margin of error built in, he's been practicing the art of trying not to breathe heavy while also hurrying through the station. "How far out are they?"

Jay catches the helmet Lasadi tosses at him. "About ten minutes. They just hailed us again."

"What did you say?"

"Nothing, it was an automated message. 'You're trespassing, prepare for boarding, if you try to run we are authorized to shoot.'"

"And can they back that up?"

"They came with a small fleet," Jay says. "We might be able to outrun them, but we're definitely outgunned."

Jay, Alex, and Lisbeth have all come to meet them in the cargo bay — the entire raggedy band looks like they've been through hell. Jay is calm as ever, but Tora's lips are thin and ashen — she's holding on, but barely. Ruby's dark skin is salt-streaked, her eyes bloodshot and worried. Alex is chewing on his lower lip, Lisbeth at his side. And Lasadi . . .

Lasadi is a fierce and exhausted goddess of war: battle-worn, furious, and untouchable. She'd hardly been able to help herself when he and Ruby hauled her out of the inner chamber, but by now her suit has probably pumped her full of painkillers. Still, she's moving like she broke something. They can deal with that in a minute.

"The contingency plan," Raj says. "We have time."

Anger smolders in Lasadi's smoky brown eyes. Her gaze flickers past him and she lifts her chin to Jay. "Ship's prepped?"

"Yep. Caches are ready, repair log's been doctored to make it look like we just wrapped up a fix on the drive."

"Good. Then I need the rest of you in the caches." She points at Raj's chest. "Including you. Jay and I will do the talking."

Jay shakes his head, startled. "Las, Raj is the one — "

"Captain," Raj says. "I think — "

"You think what?" Lasadi cuts in. "How good a pardon you could get if you turn in a couple of wanted CLA terrorists?"

Her words are meant to wound, and they do; accusation slices through him like a knife. A stitch appears between Jay's brows, Alex is frowning at her in surprise. Neither of them were there for Rasheda's big announcement.

"I hadn't planned on it," Raj says through clenched teeth. "Are you wondering how big a payday you could get from turning in a deserter?"

"That's rich, coming from a war criminal and a two-faced grifter."

"Las," says Jay quietly. "Raj. What the fuck."

"He was responsible for that medical transport at

Tannis," Lasadi says before Raj can answer. She turns on Tora. "Did you know about this?"

"I knew." Tora arches an eyebrow. "And my father knew. But we don't have time for this."

What little color is left in Lasadi's cheeks drains away at that. "Nico never would have trusted Raj."

"Which is why he gave me explicit instructions not to let him return with us."

And Ruby's stepped in front of him, fists curled. "You'll be going through me."

"Relax." Tora doesn't even flinch at Ruby's threat. "Is my father here? I don't give a shit about whatever war you were all fighting, I only know my father poured a lot of resources into a lost cause." The smile she turns on Lasadi is cold. "And that Raj saved your life back there."

"Because you let Ruby get possessed by Rasheda's consciousness," Raj points out. He's not interested in being used as a weapon in whatever fight the two women have going on, and if Tora's not planning on leaving him to die, he's got another bone to pick with her. "You knew, didn't you? And you didn't tell us what we were up against."

"*I* knew," Ruby cuts in. "I read between the rumors and figured out what I was getting into, so don't get all self-righteous on my account, Raj. You don't exactly have the moral high ground."

"You got possessed?" Alex asks. "What are you all talking about?"

"They can tell us about it later," Jay says sharply, voice raised above whatever anyone else might say. A stunned silence follows. "Because if you all are done fighting, SymTex is at the door."

For a brief moment, no one moves. Then Lasadi takes a sharp breath. "All of you, get in hiding. *All* of you. I'll take care of it."

Raj laughs. "You just got finished calling me a two-faced

grifter," he points out. "Which is exactly who we need right now. I'm not staking my hide on your ability to bullshit SymTex. Or Jay's for that matter. No offense."

"None taken," Jay says. "Folks, let's move."

"The ident cards I made are keyed to biosign from you and Raj," Ruby says. "If they do even a basic scan . . ."

Lasadi's nostrils flare, but Raj can tell she's done arguing. "Fine," she says. The word cuts like a knife, and Jay catches Raj's eye with a little frown. He'll get the rest of the story later, but for now he turns to usher the others into the shielded concealed cargo compartments.

Two people on a ship like this could have an innocuous cover story. A group of five who are obviously not related makes it much harder for the "we were stopping for a resupply" story to work without the corporate security guards assuming they're smuggling something and giving the ship a thorough shakedown — along with a more thorough search on their ident cards. Better to look like a down-and-out family.

Jay's voice shakes Raj out of his thoughts. "It's okay," he's saying to Lisbeth. She's staring in fear at the dark compartment, magboots locked, arms wrapped around herself. "It's only for a few moments, then we'll get you settled in a room."

"I can't," she whispers, a terrified creature about to bolt.

"Hey," Raj says, crouching and beckoning to Lisbeth. The girl swings her stare between him and Jay, wild fear on her face. "Do you think you can help us? We're not supposed to be here, and we need to pretend we broke down. Have you done that before, with your parents?"

Half the drifters out in Durga's Belt are smugglers of some sort or another, and odds are Lisbeth's parents ran these sorts of drills with her. Lisbeth nods slowly.

"These guys might believe me more if you're with us," Raj says. "You don't have to say anything. Just stand with me, and we'll get through this. Then we'll get you back to your auntie and uncle in Ironfall."

Lisbeth straightens, then pushes past Jay, soaring to Raj as graceful in zero G as any child born out here. Raj catches the girl in his arms and turns to Lasadi with a smile.

"Trust me," he whispers, and her jaw tightens — maybe that wasn't the right thing to say. But when he holds out his hand she takes it, sealing the illusion of family between them as the airlock unseals and armed men step out, pulse carbines raised, fingers alongside triggers.

"Hands up," one of the SymTex soldiers barks, and Lasadi drops Raj's hand like it burns. Raj raises his right, the other holding Lisbeth close. One of the men sweeps his carbine over Raj and Lisbeth and she shivers closer into him with a cry of fear. It's not feigned — he can't imagine what happened to bring her to this station in the first place, what horrors she's already witnessed at the hands of armed men who looked a lot like these.

"It's going to be okay," Raj murmurs into her stringy hair. Maybe he's screwed up the rest of this beyond repair, but he can make sure Lisbeth is safe.

"This station is property of SymTex," the man says. "You're trespassing in violation of International Code AC.381."

Raj lets his hand drop, relief pouring over his expression. "Thank the olds," he says, accent as Coruscan as it comes. He grins at Lasadi. "See? It's going to be okay."

"Hands where we can see them," barks the leader, and Raj jerks his hand back up like he forgot about it.

"Sorry," he says. "But it's good to see you."

The soldier scowls, puzzled.

"You're with SymTex," Raj says like it's an explanation. He gestures to the soldier, like the reason for his relief is self-evident. "We heard rumors about pirates, but our drive broke down. We knew stopping here was a risk, but if we didn't we were — "

He cuts himself off, glancing at Lisbeth as though not wanting her to hear what he was about to say.

"We were in trouble," he finishes. He smiles at Lasadi, who's managed to shift her defiant glare into something that might resemble relieved nervousness. They'll have to work on her acting ability for next time, he catches himself thinking, before a pang of chagrin eats through his core like acid. After what she's learned about him, there's not going to be a next time.

"It's okay, love," he says to her. "They're with SymTex."

"Identification?"

Raj sets Lisbeth down beside Lasadi and steps towards the soldier. He can feel Lasadi's anger burning a hole into his back, a feral animal who scents a trap closing around her.

Because she's right. He could say who she is. Use his father's name and claim he's infiltrated this group to catch Tora Garnet and two CLA soldiers — some of the system's most wanted. That would be enough to start repairing bridges and bring him back home. He could say Ruby and Alex were in on his ruse, of course — but even without them to consider, it's not even a question.

He meets Lasadi's gaze, sees her hand lowering slightly to her sidearm, and there's that same flash of fury that was in her eyes when the guard at Sumilang's mansion had her in his grasp, when the pirates had her bound hand and foot, when she was drifting back towards the splintering reactor: *I am not going down without a fight.*

I'm not letting you go down without one, either, he thinks. He owes her that much, at least.

He holds out his wrist for the soldier to scan the credentials Ruby mocked up for them. "Oscar Dusai," he says.

"And my wife, Izabella. Our drive broke and we had to stop if we were going to make it to Artemis."

The soldier glares at the readout, then steps forward to scan Lasadi's arm. He studies their faces. Names, biosigns, history — it's all in the new ident chips, and Ruby does impeccable work.

Lisbeth lets out an involuntary whimper of fear, and the soldier's expression finally softens. He swipes away Raj and Lasadi's false identities and touches the release on his helmet to fold it back. With a quick glance of permission at Lasadi, the soldier crouches in front of Lisbeth. His encouraging smile says he knows kids, maybe has a few of his own.

"It's okay, kiddo," he says. "We just needed to talk with your parents a minute. What's your name?"

Raj tenses. He hadn't thought about this. She's probably not in any system, but there's a nonzero chance the soldiers have seen a bulletin about a missing little girl named Lisbeth.

"Andie," Lisbeth says without hesitation.

"Good kid," the soldier says with a grin. "You keep taking care of your parents, okay?" He stands, and Raj squeezes Lisbeth's shoulder. She's shivering.

"Thank you for checking in on us," Raj says, scooping Lisbeth back into his arms.

"Don't get too dependent on this particular pit stop," the soldier says. "We're about to start scrapping it."

"Good to know."

"You need anything else to get on your way?"

Raj glances at Lasadi as though checking with her, then shakes his head. "We're just looking forward to getting home," he tells the soldier, who lifts a hand to send the rest of his team back through the airlock. "Safe travels," Raj calls after them.

And the airlock closes behind them.

Beside him, Lasadi lets out a long, slow breath. When she finally looks at him, he can't read her expression.

"I didn't blow up the medical transport," Raj says. He needs her to know that. He needs her to know everything. "But I do know what happened. I know it's not enough, but I was planning on telling you — my only excuse for not saying something earlier was fear."

She doesn't seem angry anymore. She looks exhausted, glassy-eyed with pain, her pale skin ashen. "I'm sure it's a great story," she finally says. She lifts her chin to Lisbeth. "Get her settled in and prep for a burn."

"Do you need me in — "

"No." She's already turned away. "I don't."

CHAPTER 28
LASADI

"I'M FINE, JAY," Lasadi calls through the medbay door; it's only been a handful of minutes since she sent him away with a promise she was getting some painkillers and heading to bed, and he's already knocking again. She hadn't thought setting up a scan would take this long, but it's her lower back that's bothering her, and she's having trouble reaching.

She'd waited until the others had settled into their bunks or left the crew deck before opening the hatch to the bridge. She'd told herself that the *Nanshe* needed her, that the diagnostics she was running were critical, that she wanted to wait until she had plenty of black between her and the ghosts of Auburn Station — but the truth is she doesn't feel like talking. Not to Jay, not to anyone.

Her muscles are sore and screaming, stiff from sitting for so many hours in the pilot's chair after the adrenaline of the escape wore off. Something grates painful in her lower back; she might truly have injured herself when she got thrown against the railing.

It's nothing, she tells herself. And the others are fine, too — she'd used her captain's login credentials to check on their visits. Ruby, Tora, and Jay each took their turn in the chair and were cleared, though the autodoc has Tora on a concussion watch and the shrapnel wound in her neck required four stitches.

The knock comes at the door again; the autodoc blinks at her. Error. Scan incomplete.

She's about to start the scan again when her cuff chimes. It's Jay: Open the damn door.

Lasadi sets the scanner back in its dock, then unties her jumpsuit's sleeves from around her waist and pulls it on far enough to cover her arms — even that movement is painful, she wrenched something in her shoulder. She unlocks the door; it retracts with a hiss.

"Jay, I don't — oh."

Raj Demetriou is leaning against the far wall, hands in his pockets. He's showered, damp strands of his loose black hair smoothed out of his face, and changed into a pair of loose joggers and a tight green tee with sleeves pushed up to the elbows to show tawny, well-toned forearms.

She tugs the left side of her collar to make sure her jumpsuit's fully covering her shoulder; Raj clocks the gesture, but doesn't comment.

"You need a hand?" Raj asks. "Jay said you might."

"I told Jay I didn't need any help," Lasadi says.

"You apparently weren't convincing."

"So he sent *you*?"

That flash of a rueful smile is so fucking disarming. Raj runs a hand through his hair. The damp strands are already starting to form curls around his ears.

"I didn't think it was a good idea, either," Raj says. "But he figured you needed to hear this story sooner rather than later."

Slow curiosity unspools in Lasadi's gut, unwinding the knot of anger that has been coiled there since she heard about Raj's record.

Auburn Station had messed with her head, between the whiplash of learning Mercury Squadron wasn't responsible for the transport's destruction and the minefield of shifting alliances and withheld information. Tora had known about Raj and hadn't warned her. Ruby and Tora both had known the true nature of Rasheda's experimentation and hadn't shared it.

Despite all that, though, nothing's changed. She didn't trust Tora before. She didn't trust Ruby or Alex or Raj. She didn't trust her own gut.

But she trusts Jay — who's already heard Raj out. And Jay believes him.

"Fine." She steps out of the doorway and he closes it behind him. He grabs a bulb she hadn't noticed floating beside him and hands it to her. A warm, bitter-earth scent rises from it.

"I brought you coffee," he says. "And a couple of ration bars. Figured you could use it since you haven't been down to the galley in hours. You take your coffee black, right?"

"You've been watching me?"

"It's a small ship." He takes the scanner she'd been trying to use, then glides to the far side of the medical chair and hits the button that morphs it flat. "It's your back bothering you, yeah? You hit that railing pretty hard."

When she doesn't move, he sighs. "I'll go ask one of the others to help you. But please listen to me for a minute. Even if we never see each other again, I need you to know the truth." Relief floods through Raj's face when Lasadi finally nods.

She shifts herself onto the bench so her back's to Raj, but she doesn't shrug back out of her jumpsuit — the scanner will just have to do its work through a double layer of fabric. She sips the coffee, trying to ignore both the pain in her muscles and the feeling of Raj's strong fingers smoothing over her lower back. Breathes in the bitter scent to obliterate the hint of citrus and sea salt from Raj's cologne, now that he's so close.

She doesn't think she winces, but he backs off the pressure. The scanner beeps soft, compiling data on the screen in front of her.

"You already know who my father is. If you'd ever met him, you'd know there wasn't room for alternate career paths. I was meant to march right along in his footsteps, and be excellent at it. Maybe if I'd had siblings, things would have turned out different. But there was never room for another choice."

"It was just you?"

He laughs; there's a brittle note in it. "Only child."

"I had a sister and brother." Lasadi means to say it offhand, as a peace offering, but something lurches in her chest. She *has* a sister and brother. If Anton had been wrong — or lied — about the medical transport, why wouldn't he have done the same with the story about her family holding banishing? She wouldn't even put it past him to have embellished her grandmother's anger — he'd needed to keep her away from Corusca and out of touch, and this would have been the perfect way.

Even if they *had* held banishing, it could have been because of political pressure on her grandmother the senator, rather than because of their crushing disappointment. She tries to remember how he phrased it, tries to sift the things she actually knows from what she heard him say. But he'd spent years training her to rely on him for the truth; now he's woven such a web of smoke and mirrors in her own mind that she barely trusts her memories, let alone her intuition.

And here she is, letting Raj weave even more complications into the tangled mess of what she knows to be true.

She trusts Jay, she reminds herself. And Jay believes Raj.

She forces her shoulders to relax, forces herself to listen.

The scanner beeps again in its search for bruised tissue and splintered bone; Raj shifts it gentle along her spine, his fingers sure.

"So I joined the navy," he continues. "Worked my way up — I know, I know. Didn't have to try hard when my dad was an admiral."

"I didn't say anything."

"You'd be the first not to." He laughs: a touch self-deprecating, mostly weary. "When the fighting on Corusca started, I was captain of the *Lisaro Chaves Symes*. Our original mission was supposed to be peacekeeping. Obviously that turned out to be a farce. But back then, we were told insurgents were obstructing the will of the Coruscan people to join the Alliance, and we were there to help."

He takes a deep breath, shifts the scanner. There's an electric current in the air; wherever this story goes next, this is what Raj came here to say. She suppresses a shiver, the fine hairs at the base of her neck rising.

"Because of my father, I sat in on meetings someone of my rank normally wouldn't have," he says. "I was on my father's ship with the rest of the navy's command when the medical transport exploded. I was there when command was shown the ship's logs, and we all realized the explosion was an accident."

The scanner trills to let them know it's finished compiling data; the screen in front of her flashes green: Show results? Lasadi can barely read the words.

"An accident." Nausea washes through her, and she tries to set the bulb of coffee in a nearby stasis field; it bounces back off the wall and begins to drift away. Raj catches the bulb and settles it back in the field.

"Command made the decision to hide the records and treat it like a rebel attack."

Which gave them the excuse they needed to shell Tannis, while this whole time, Lasadi had believed they were reacting to something that had happened on her watch. But it hadn't been her fault. It hadn't been Raj's fault. No one was to blame — for that, at least.

"Do you know how many people died at Tannis?" she finally whispers.

"I do. I know exactly how many people died, and at the time I could guess how many were going to die. I spoke up then, which was a mistake I'll never forgive myself for. I thought I could make a difference — I thought I could sway command. But if I'd kept my mouth shut for ten more goddamn minutes I could have gotten the word out and maybe done something to stop it. Instead, they threw me in the brig."

She glances over her shoulder; there's raw grief on his face. "How did you get out?" she asks.

"I was supposed to have an accident," he says finally. "Before I could tell the truth to the wrong person. But a few friends found out and helped me get off the ship before that could happen." His smile has no mirth in it. "And I ended up in Ironfall."

"Your father would have let that happen to you?" She's shaking her head involuntarily, she can't imagine it.

"You don't know my father. The Alliance — and image — means everything to him. He'd rather mourn the memory of a dead son than have a living one who could destroy everything he'd built."

She lets that sit in silence for a long time.

"Why not say something when you got to safety?" she finally asks.

"I tried to contact my father when I got to Ironfall. I told him I'd tell everyone the truth — and he told me about the court-martial. He said all he has to do is unseal those documents and who would believe me? It would be a blow for him, but it would be my death sentence out here. And it wouldn't make a difference."

"Every headhunter from Indira to Bixia Yuanjin would be after you."

"I'm dead the minute we dock in Ironfall, if Nico Garnet knows." He doesn't sound upset, merely resigned.

"Tora will talk to him. *I'll* talk to him."

"So you believe me?"

Lasadi takes a sharp breath; she doesn't know how to answer. "How do I know what to believe?"

"What does your instinct say?"

"My instincts are trash."

"You *do* work for Nico Garnet," Raj points out, and when she's about to protest that point, his lips quirk to the side. He's teasing her. After all of this, he's trying to make her laugh. Lasadi lets herself smile; it doesn't linger.

"He saved my life," she says. Maybe she owes him a moment of truth, too. "He had money — and people — in the CLA. After the Battle of Tannis, Nico's mercenaries pulled me out of my mangled ship. Brought me back to Dima, fixed me up. If it weren't for Nico I'd be dead or in some Alliance work camp right now." Her hand smooths over her left side, thumb tracing the ridge of scar tissue under her ribs before she catches herself. She's quiet a long moment. "I owe Nico everything."

"You owe him your life," Raj points out. "Not everything."

"What else do I have?"

He doesn't answer, and she lets the silence linger; even as it stretches on, it's not uncomfortable. Pieces Lasadi thought were fundamental to her identity have shifted, rearranged themselves into a new tableau, and it's like looking into the face of a stranger.

"I couldn't believe my crew was responsible," she finally says. "I knew them. None of them would have done it."

"Then why did you think they did?"

She doesn't want to talk about Anton, not now. Probably not ever — though she can feel the hold he'd had on her slipping, the tight band around her chest loosening. Maybe someday she'll see him on the news without having the overwhelming urge to make herself small. Maybe someday she'll be able to separate her joyful memories of Tania and Henri and Anna Mara and the others from Anton's voice in her head telling her she hadn't been strong enough to keep them alive. Maybe someday she'll trust herself again.

Raj reaches past her to touch the screen; the results of her scan appear, but the words are swimming, impossible to read. "You bruised a few ribs," Raj says. "And you've got some tissue damage that's gonna need some rest to heal, but no internal bleeding. Do you want the painkillers it's offering?"

Relief floods through her. Bruising, she can handle that on her own without a trip to Nico's doctors. "Yeah. Thank you."

"Sure." He hits another button and the autodoc system whirs, dispensing a packet of pills. Raj hands them to her and she swallows them down with coffee from the bulb he brought her. He takes the empty packet gently from her fingertips and sets it in the recycler. "You need anything else?"

"I'm fine."

"Okay. Holler if you need anything." He gives her a smile tinged with grief and exhaustion, then palms open the medbay door.

"Raj?"

He turns back.

"I believe you."

She does. His story cut a bright, gleaming path through the jagged shadows of half-truths she's spent the last three years warping her mind around in an attempt to reconcile them. She feels — not whole again. But hopeful. Hopeful that one day she might remember her way back.

"Thank you, Captain."

"Lasadi," she says. "It's just Lasadi."

This time, the smile he gives her is genuine. "Whatever you say, Captain."

When he leaves her in peace, the flicker of hope remains.

CHAPTER 29
RAJ

THE *NANSHE* IS silent when he leaves the medbay. Tora went to bed hours ago, and Jay retired, too, after sending Raj up to help Lasadi. It's not the eerie silence of Auburn Station, though — it's a comfortable quiet. It's peaceful.

Raj is going to miss it.

A quiet giggle startles him out of his thoughts — it's the kid, Lisbeth. Sounds like she and Ruby are down in the cargo bay. Raj is way too wired to sleep right now, too flush with the memory of his hands on Lasadi's back, the pale curve of her neck with her braid slipping off her shoulder and her chin tilted slightly back towards him, exposing that soft, secret place below her ear. The image is sparking a fool's dream, one he has no right to indulge, but which he won't be able to banish if he doesn't find another distraction.

Raj pushes himself down the ladder to the cargo bay to find Ruby and Lisbeth absorbed in a tablet. "Heya!" Ruby gives him what seems like a genuine smile and waves him over. "We're finding files on Lisbeth's auntie and uncle on Dima."

"Where's Alex?"

"Oh, I spaced Alex for not telling me that the ayas won't take him back."

Lisbeth stares at her in horror.

"I'm kidding," Ruby tells her with a wink. "Little brothers are the worst, though." She turns back to Raj. "He went to bed."

"He sleeps?"

"I think he got bored. Jay's not still up to teach him more bad habits about disarming security systems."

"Could come in handy."

Ruby makes a noncommittal noise. "He was supposed to become an accountant or something. Not follow in his wayward sister's footsteps."

"Yeah, but you've already got all the great underworld contacts he can use."

Ruby's side-eye is razor sharp. "I've been working these jobs so he can do whatever he wants with his life. And here he keeps asking if you have any more 'fun jobs' for us once we get home."

"You didn't have fun?"

"Yeah, getting hijacked by a rogue AI was super fun."

"Did you get anything out of it?" Raj asks.

"I got a new friend." Ruby nudges Lisbeth with her shoulder; the girl gives her a tentative grin, and Ruby hands her the tablet. "Here, run the lockpick on that database, like I taught you."

Lisbeth nods with determination and hunches over the tablet, tongue darting between her teeth. Raj follows Ruby to the exercise equipment strapped against the far wall.

"Isn't she a little young to learn how to break into a database?" he asks.

"Never too young." But the cheerfulness in Ruby's expression vanishes when she glances back at the girl. Ruby and Jay got Lisbeth cleaned up and fed, her mousy brown hair washed and combed and braided. It'll take many more good meals to erase the hollow from her cheeks; Raj isn't sure what it will take to erase the haunt from her eyes.

"They were here, Raj," Ruby says. "My parents were here."

"You found a record?"

"Kind of." Ruby clears her throat. "Rasheda showed me."

"You trust her?"

"At first she was trying to get me to help her willing-ly — I believe what she showed me was real. She had video, she said she remembered me. My mother was preg-nant, and my father — saints, Raj, he looked exactly like Alex."

"What were they doing here?"

"A resupply, seems like, but they were on the run. Someone was following them."

"Why?"

Ruby shakes her head. "I don't know. But I soaked up a lot of records of other visits to the station around the same time period. Maybe I can figure out who they were running from."

"Let me know if you need any help tracking things down."

"Will do. Hey." Ruby purses her lips. "Your court-martial file? I dug it up a while back, but I never read it. Figured if it was important, you'd tell me some day, and if you needed it for some reason, I'd have it on hand." She winces. "I probably should've wiped it from my system, but I forgot it was still there, honestly."

"You never read it?"

"Lotta people come to the Pearls for a reset. I'd already learned to trust the guy you are now, and learning who you used to be wouldn't have changed anything."

"And now that you know what's in the file?"

"It didn't change the Raj I know," she points out. "And I hope you feel the same when we learn whatever's in my missing past."

Raj frowns at her. "You were twelve when you lost your memory, Ruby. I doubt you were some kind of war criminal."

"Hey, kids can be troublemakers." She waves across the cargo bay to Lisbeth, who gives her a shy smile in return.

"I didn't do it," Raj says.

"I believe you." Ruby's gaze flicks up at the sound of the medbay door finally opening. "Did she?"

"She did." He hasn't yet let himself examine the golden splinter of hope Lasadi has lodged in his soul, but now it pulses, leaving him calm and warm in a way he hasn't felt in years. She believes him. Ruby believes him.

"How is she?" Ruby asks.

Exhausted. Hurting. Holding her own failures too harshly, and treating the help of others too suspiciously. Whatever confidence had once made her the Mercury Squadron captain, whatever fire he keeps catching glimpses of, has been fractured, and he wishes he knew who did that to her. If it's a person, he can fight them. He can't do anything about the war that gutted them both.

"I don't know," he says.

He laughs with Ruby and Lisbeth until he hears the shower finish, until the door to Lasadi's cabin closes; then he heads up to his own cabin, strangely light. He hadn't realized what a weight had been on his shoulders. How carefully he'd been dancing around the past, trying to hide this secret, sure any real relationship he cultivated was built around a black hole that would destroy him when it was inevitably unearthed.

But Ruby knew — not the truth, but that he had a secret. And she didn't care. Even Lasadi had actually believed him. *What happens next?* a small voice in the back of his mind is whispering. *If you don't have to hide who you are anymore, who do you want to be?*

CHAPTER 30
LASADI

LASADI HAD THOUGHT a silent ship would be a relief after spending the past week with strangers in her galley, in her cargo bay, edging past her in the corridors. But while it had been mildly claustrophobic at the time, part of her had welcomed it. Having people around had sparked something in her, a camaraderie she'd last felt when she was in the CLA: a group of people united around a goal. But now the *Nanshe* is achingly empty, its crew departed and only herself and Jay left on board.

He's in the cargo bay with his bags packed, having finished his final checks. His duffel sits beside the open cargo bay door; he'll be heading back to Chiara. Back home.

He grins when she slides careful down the ladder. Her ribs ache more under Ironfall gravity, but she's kept up on the meds the autodoc prescribed. In a few days she should be moving normal again.

"Hey, Las," Jay calls. "You glad to have your ship back?"

"Not my ship," she says automatically. "But, yeah." That should be true, but it feels like a lie; she can't quite put her finger on why the rooms around her own seem emptier than they did before. "Did you decide? About Chiara?"

Jay's cheek dimples and it spears through her; olds, she wants to be happy for him. "Come out with us tonight," he says.

"You two deserve a quiet meal on your own," she says. "And I need to . . ."

"You don't need to do anything around here," Jay says. "Do something for fun, Las. Enjoy a night out. Go chase down that Arquellian asshole and see if he's any good in bed."

"I don't think he wants that."

"Because you're an idiot." Jay holds up his hands to stop her from arguing. "I'm just saying it's okay to let your guard down sometimes and trust someone."

"I have you," she points out, and there's that worry washing through Jay's face again. *And you have Chiara.* She clears her throat — time to change the subject. "Hey. I know you're done working for Nico, and I get it. The last three years together have been good."

Jay shakes his head. "They've been livable. Anything good that came out of those three years was because I was working with you, and that doesn't have to end because I won't do jobs for Nico anymore." He takes a deep breath. "How much more do you need to buy the *Nanshe* from him?"

Too much more.

And there are ways to get it — selling that little mixla on her console would probably net her enough. If she could do it without the guilt.

"I'm almost there," Lasadi says. She forces a smile. "Say hey to Chiara for me."

"Tell her yourself," Jay says. "Have a celebratory drink."

"I can't."

"Are you just being a cheapskate? Because I'm buying."

Lasadi laughs. "No, go. I'm exhausted, I'm going to get some sleep."

Jay wraps her in his arms and she hugs him back, breathing in her friend's familiar warmth, the lean muscles squeezing her still-sore ribs almost to the point of pain before he steps back and claps her shoulders. "I'll see you tomorrow," he says.

She's watching him walk out when her comm buzzes with an incoming message from Tora. Need to talk. Tanzi's in one hour.

The skin on the back of her neck pricks, and she almost calls Jay back. But this is Nico Garnet business. Jay would come with her in a heartbeat if she asked, she knows that without a doubt. Just as she knows the best thing she can do for her friend right now is to respect his wishes and let him go.

Tanzi's, an elegant restaurant in Xiè's, is one of Nico's favorite places to do business. He always has a booth reserved in the back; that hasn't changed even as he got sicker, though of course he hasn't conducted his business in public for the last few months. And Lasadi has never met with Tora on her own anyplace but Nico's lair.

Will the old man be here? Did the miracle cure work — was Nico able to use Rasheda Auburn's technology already to transform his consciousness into a body that isn't failing? It seems like a procedure like that should take longer than the scant few hours they've been docked back at Ironfall, but Lasadi wouldn't know. The idea of it crawls across her skin.

Tanzi's is more than Nico's favorite meeting spot, though. It's also where Nico historically has held final meetings with people who failed him.

And tonight, Tanzi's is completely empty.

Every fiber in Lasadi's being screams at her to run.

It just means this is private business, she tells herself — and if Nico wants her dead, running won't do anything. She's already in Xiè's. He can shut down the entire place in a heartbeat and flush her out. No. The only thing to do is to talk. Even if she's in trouble, she can at least negotiate for Jay's life.

Nico's not at his usual booth. Instead, Lasadi finds Tora, sitting alongside a slim, dark man Lasadi recognizes as one of Nico's inner circle. Nico's enforcer; Colif is his name. He watches Lasadi approach with cold, dead eyes, then leans over to murmur something in Tora's ear. Lasadi hesitates, swallows past the fear wrapping a hand around her throat, forces herself to close the distance to the table. If today is the day, she'll greet death with dignity.

Colif stands and greets Lasadi with a bow, then settles himself at the empty bar directly behind her.

Lasadi forces her shoulders to relax.

"Sit," Tora commands. She pours from a bottle of amber liquid in the middle of the table. "A toast, to a successful job."

She fills her own glass and lifts it; after a moment, Lasadi lifts hers. The glass clinks quiet under the tinny music.

"How's your father?" Lasadi asks. The light catches in Tora's eyes as she sips.

"Dying," Tora answers. She twirls the glass of brandy in her fingers. "Still."

"Then the job wasn't a success?"

Tora laughs. "That's not how I see it. You know, my father didn't think I should go at first. He trusted you to deliver the goods, as you always do. I knew you'd deliver, too." Tora studies Lasadi a moment. "I volunteered because my father's organization needs a leader. Fresh blood and fresh vision, not a dying man keeping it grasped in his skeletal hand through the use of untested technology."

Slow realization dawns over Lasadi. "You don't intend to let him use the technology. So why go at all?"

Tora smiles. "Just because *he* shouldn't live forever doesn't mean it's not a bad idea to put this technology in testing." She sobers. "My father's out of the picture, Lasadi. I don't have the same soft spot for a pair of washed-up CLA fighters that my father did. But I do like you, and I appreciate your loyalty to him. Which is why I need to know if there's going to be a problem."

Lasadi almost laughs — both in relief, and at the absurdity of the question. Is she going to interfere in Tora's coup against her father? Lasadi respects Nico, she owes him her life. But is she going to put that life on the line to protect an old man from dying a natural death so his daughter can take the reins? Hardly. The fact that Nico's right-hand man, Colif, is here behind her means he's on Tora's side already. Tora probably has the loyalty of the rest of the organization buttoned up.

And anyway, whatever debt Lasadi to the old man felt she had carried over the years, she's paid it off by now.

She shakes her head.

"Good. Then I have a job for you."

Lasadi takes a long sip of the brandy to hide her nerves, her ears ringing. She hadn't been able to say it out loud to Jay back on the *Nanshe*, but she can't. She's done. It doesn't matter that this job is for Tora, it doesn't matter how close she is to buying the *Nanshe*. Hope broke free in the last few days, and Lasadi isn't going to shove it back in the prison it's lived in since she met Anton.

She meets Tora's gaze, level and unafraid of whatever comes next. "Do I have a choice?"

The twinge in Tora's cheek says she didn't expect that

answer, and she doesn't like it; she taps a gold nail against the side of her glass, thinking.

"You do," Tora says. "Take this job and continue to work with me, or take your leave with no hard feelings. I'm happy to refer you to other work. But I will be watching."

Lasadi swallows, mouth dry. "The *Nanshe*," she finally says. Tora lifts an eyebrow. "I'll take my leave. But your father and I had an agreement that I could buy the ship. Once I'd saved up enough. I want you to honor that agreement."

How the hell she's going to raise enough money not working for the Garnets — and without use of the *Nanshe* — she has no idea. But fuck it. She'll figure that out when she gets to it.

Tora takes another sip; her attention slips over Lasadi's shoulder to where Colif is standing. Lasadi can't read the expression.

"The ship is yours in lieu of your cut from this job," Tora says. "And as a symbol of the Garnet organization's generosity."

The words land like a punch in the gut. "I'm not sure what to say."

"You could say thank you."

"I — that's incredibly generous." Lasadi chooses her words carefully, aware of Nico's — *Tora's* — enforcer behind her. "But that kind of generosity comes with a debt I don't want to carry."

"It wasn't meant that way."

"You and I would both feel it."

The corner of Tora's mouth turns up. "Understood. I know the price you and my father agreed on. How much do you have saved?"

"I'm still about thirty thousand credits short." A few jobs, that's it. If she can figure out how to work them.

"Then I'll give you a thirty thousand credit discount for

loyalty," Tora says. "And you can buy the ship, free and clear of obligations to me."

Lasadi takes a sharp, dizzy breath against the feeling she's floating, suddenly untethered from a web of worries and debts and obligations she couldn't cut through. "It's a deal," she finally manages to say.

"Good." Tora glances over Lasadi's shoulder again to Colif. "Have the documents written up."

"Yes, ma'am."

Lasadi can hear his footsteps, sharp on the restaurant floor, and her shoulders relax at the relief that he's no longer standing behind her. She finishes the brandy while she signs documents on the tablet Colif brings back, the rush of the liquor barely matching the headiness of the joy of freedom.

She never keeps alcohol on the ship, but she buys a bottle of whiskey on her way back, sets the alarms, and leaves her boots kicked into the corner of the galley while she rummages for a glass. She's about to ask the computer to play some music when she realizes she hasn't stored any in the system — she'll change that. She'll change whatever she wants.

She takes the bottle and glass up to the bridge and begins searching for music, setting up preferences she'd been unwilling to formalize in the years she's been running this ship.

"Time to celebrate," she tells the little mixla on the dash, feeling a pang of guilt that she'd thought of selling it to raise the rest of the funds, even if she'd never have gone through with it. She pours a splash of whiskey from her own cup into the saucer Jay left, then tilts her head, studying it. Something else is tucked behind the mixla.

The bracelet Raj left before they boarded Auburn Station. She pulls it out, runs a fingernail over the material, trying to understand what it is. It occurs to her that it's a string from a cittern, woven around itself into a bangle.

Does Raj play? He'd never mentioned it, but when had she given him the chance?

She'll send it back to him, she decides, but for now she puts it back in the stasis field, catching herself in embarrassment when she realizes she automatically said a prayer for him.

Actually, no. Fuck it — the liquor in her blood has loosened the knot of her shoulders. Why send it to him when she could call him. Deliver it in person. Take a second chance at getting to know him, without all the secrets lurking between them.

Jay would tell her to do it — in fact he's told her to multiple times. She may not be sure how to trust herself, yet, but she trusts Jay.

And she wants this.

Her heart's pounding as she pulls up her messages to find Raj's contact info, fingers hesitant as she swipes through, searching for his name.

They still over the new message notification, her breath catching at a name she thought she'd never see again.

Las — I couldn't believe it when I heard you made it out of Tannis, and I bet you're just as surprised to hear from me. I've got a wild fucking story and I'm sure you do, too. Can't wait to hear it. First round's on me, but right now I gotta ask you a favor. I'm in a jam and need your help, Las. Bad. —Henri.

Lasadi's fingers falter over the screen only a second before she types out a reply.

CHAPTER 31
RAJ

LISBETH'S AUNT and uncle live in Timbol's Vein, a solidly working-class hub where most residents are employed in one of the several adjacent mining operations. The residents here are as suspicious as the ones in Nestor's Folly when it comes to visitors, and Raj gets more than a few cold shoulders before he finally gets a woman at a network access hub to talk with him.

Her look of suspicion when he asks for Lisbeth's aunt and uncle softens when she peers over her counter to see Lisbeth at his side. Raj thanks her for the pod number and takes Lisbeth's hand, leading her through a maze of passageways to find a cozy pod on the third level, one with a private balcony and door painted a cheerful yellow instead of left bare metal. A pair of chairs sit beside a table that might have been scavenged from a trash chute and lovingly repaired, painted green as new grass.

Raj checks the number again. Knocks.

It's a long minute before a woman in a long blue dress and orange hijab opens the door. Her nails are painted with tiny flowers, her smiling cheeks rosy, all her colors perfectly framed in the yellow of the door. This balcony is the brightest corner of Ironfall Raj has ever seen. The fragrant smell of fresh bread wafts from behind her.

"Yes?" she asks, but before Raj can answer, the woman's gaze lands on Lisbeth. She claps her hands over her mouth, eyes bright with tears, then drops to her knees with her arms wide. Lisbeth burrows herself into her aunt's embrace.

"Who is it?" a man's voice calls from behind her, and the uncle emerges from a back room to see the child in his wife's arms. "Oh, Lisbeth," he says, and the girl squirms out of her aunt's hug to jump into her uncle's.

Raj steps back, leaning against the balcony to give the family the space they need, until the uncle finally hands Lisbeth back to her aunt and turns to Raj.

"My brother?" the man asks. "His husband?"

Raj shakes his head; the grief that softens the man's features is an old one, a wound torn back open by the potential of fresh hope at seeing Lisbeth.

"My crew and I were on a salvage run to Auburn Station, and we came across Lisbeth," Raj says. "It sounds like your brother's family stopped there to resupply and were attacked by pirates. Lisbeth said she's the only one who escaped."

"And the pirates?"

"We took care of them. They won't hurt anyone else."

"Auburn Station?" Lisbeth's uncle murmurs. Raj nods. "We knew they had stopped there, and that's the last we heard from them. We put a reward on the boards in hopes that someone would go looking for them — we just wanted any news. But apparently we couldn't afford enough to catch any adventurer's attention."

"How long ago?" Raj asks. "Lisbeth wasn't sure."

"Almost five months."

"Oh, poor girl." Raj's heart breaks for Lisbeth anew. Five months among the ghosts of Auburn Station — how much courage must it have took for her to step out of the shadows and reveal herself to Raj and Ruby and Alex? "She was stealing food from the pirates," Raj says. "But she ate like a wolf once we got her back on our ship. We had the autodoc check her out and it didn't raise any red flags, but she should probably see a doctor."

The man nods. "Thank you. And here" — he reaches for his comm — "you've earned the reward."

Raj waves him away. "I got my payday," he says. "I'm sorry I don't have better news about your brother."

"You brought us Lisbeth," the man says.

"Least I could do." He catches the girl smiling shyly at him from her aunt's arms. "So long, kiddo. Take care of yourself."

"Wait, please," Lisbeth's aunt says. "Have you eaten? Join us for dinner, it's the least we can do to thank you."

"I don't want to get in the way of your reunion," Raj says, but Lisbeth has broken free of her aunt's embrace. She takes Raj's hand, and her aunt and uncle stand back as she leads him inside.

It's late by the time he gets back to his own pod; after dinner he'd found himself dreading the loneliness of it and he stopped for a couple of beers in his local haunt, seeking the ambient noise more than any conversation with strangers. But although he'd found himself sleepy by the end of the second beer, now that he's back in his own bed he's staring at the ceiling, thoughts rushing through his head.

Five fucking months.

Five months that poor girl had wrapped herself in tapestries and stolen food from pirates, with no one but a deranged, dead pirate queen trapped in an AI to keep her company.

Five months her aunt and uncle's job had been on the boards, while guys like Raj scanned through and scoffed at the tiny amount they'd been offering for a trip to a place like Auburn Station. He'd spent the better part of his time at the bar scanning the boards himself until he found the job, relieved to find the Unread tag beside it. At least he hadn't seen their plea for help and ignored it.

Though, if he's honest with himself, he probably would have. The money they'd offered was laughably small for the risk of the journey.

There are plenty of lucrative gigs on these boards — plenty of lucrative reasons to go to Auburn Station. Plenty of ways an adventurer could make a job like the one Lisbeth's aunt and uncle were offering pay off, if they were willing to do a little extra work.

Surely he's not the only one who thinks this.

He's dialing her number before he can overthink it.

"Tell me it's not headhunters again," Ruby says when she answers. No club sounds behind her this time; she's probably home in bed. In fact — he checks the time — she was probably asleep.

"Not that."

Rustling sheets and a yawn. She was definitely asleep.

"Then you wanted to wake me up to hear my voice, only? Raj we spent the last six days together."

"You said it was fun, yeah?"

"Yeah, navigating a murder labyrinth was fun."

"Don't forget fighting pirates."

"Seriously, Raj. Why are you calling."

"You want to do that again?"

"You got another gig?"

"Not yet. But hear me out. I took Lisbeth back to her aunt and uncle, and they said they'd had a job out on the boards for five months trying to figure out what happened to her and her parents. No one would take it because it doesn't pay. But combo that up with jobs that do pay — it's the sort of thing you could make a living at while actually doing something good."

She laughs. "I have real bills. And a little brother to feed, since he's not going back to the ayas."

"Let him earn his own way as part of the crew."

"Tell me a specific job first."

"I'm narrowing it down, I've been scanning at the boards. If you're interested, I can put together a pitch."

"Pitch me and I'll listen. But I'm not running a charity, am I."

"Course not."

"And Alex is unfortunately part of the package."

"I would hope so."

She laughs. "You gonna call Jay and Lasadi, too?"

"You wouldn't have a problem with that?"

"I like Jay. Alex fucking idolizes him. And Lasadi . . . she grows on you. She's quick on her feet and her heart's in the right place. I trust her."

"I'll call them."

"Tell me this isn't an elaborate plan to hook up with her, only."

A stab under his ribcage. "It's not," Raj says. "She probably won't even take my call."

"Well I can't tell you what straight girls want, but I can guess one thing about Lasadi."

"What's that?"

"She's not gonna be as nice as me if you wake her up in the middle of the night with a half-assed whiskey plan. 'Night, Raj."

✳

He gives her a few days and spends the time running numbers and searching the boards for ideal candidates. He runs ideas past a surprisingly patient Ruby, even calls Vash and Gracie, the antiquities dealers he still owes a visit to deliver the Tisare totem. And when he has a real plan, he calls Lasadi.

Leaves a message.

Calls again the next day, leaves another message.

Calls later that evening, and when the incoming request on his comm a few minutes later is Jay, he's half expecting an ultimatum to leave Lasadi be.

He sighs and answers. Can't say he didn't try.

"Hey, man," Jay says. "How you been?"

Raj frowns at the casual greeting. "Good. I've actually been meaning to get in touch."

"Yeah?"

Raj waits a beat, but Jay doesn't shut him down. He decides to take it as an invitation to elaborate.

"That kid, Lisbeth? When I took her back to her aunt and uncle, they said they'd put a job up on the boards trying to get someone to go out to Auburn Station for her. No one took it, fee was too low. She was out there five months, Jay."

Silence, then, "Shit."

"Got me thinking. There are other jobs like that one. People looking for missing relatives, asking for help. You combo that up with some other runs and you could make a difference but still make a living. I mean, we were already going out to Auburn Station. If we'd checked the boards, we would have known to keep an eye out for Lisbeth in the first place."

"So that's what you want to do."

"Yeah. But I need a like-minded crew. You in?"

Jay laughs. "Yeah, sure."

"And Lasadi?"

A long silence. "You didn't ask her already?"

"She's not taking my calls." Jay seems about to speak, but Raj is quicker — if he doesn't ask this now, he might not ever. "I need to know. Are you two together?"

"I prefer brunettes," Jay says.

"You seemed like you were closer than friends."

And Jay takes a deep breath. "We are. We fought together, which makes her my sister, and if you break her heart I'll fucking kill you, you understand?"

"Got it."

"Good. But no, we're not together. Las is all sharp edges. She hones me as a friend, but I don't want a lover who cuts that deep." Jay clears his throat. "Anyway, she isn't here, and I'm down to two possibilities. I was really hoping for option two — that she was with you."

The thrill that Jay would have thought that is tempered by the sinking worry: Lasadi's closest friend doesn't know where she is.

"She hasn't gotten in touch," Raj says, then takes a guess at option one. "Is she with Garnet?"

"Nah. You got a minute?"

"I'm free. What's up?"

"Option one means Las is in trouble. I need to go to New Manila, could use a hand."

Raj sits straighter, not believing what he heard. "New Manila?" Jay *mmm-hmm*s an affirmative. "That'll take way more than a minute."

"Fair. You in?" Now Raj can hear the tension in Jay's voice. "Or can you not go back to Indira?"

"I'm in."

Jay lets out a breath of relief. "Meet me at the docks. Slip D361, as soon as you can."

"You want me to call the others?"

"What, Ruby and Alex?"

"I'm sure they'd help."

"That would be amazing."

"Right. Hey, Jay?" He'd made his own decision in a heartbeat, but Ruby'll have questions. "What's this about?"

Jay hesitates, then sighs. "I'll tell you all about Anton on the way. Because if I'm right about where Lasadi is heading, you'll need to know."

EPILOGUE: LASADI

SHE'S NEVER BEEN to Indira. The planet was always in her childhood sky, a source of light and wonder turning to a source of anger and an object to rail against as she grew older. On Corusca, it was an inescapable oppressor: a tyrannical part of her culture's past and inevitable part of their future.

She's been watching Indira grow larger in her view over the past few days until it engulfs the entire screen, until she's swallowed up by the atmosphere. She practices breathing exercises through the panic of this entry, which she knows the *Nanshe*'s shuttle can handle. She's watched vids. She knows what to expect. But as the atmosphere blazes around the windows of the shuttle, she's becoming a shooting star — and she's been here before, flames flaring over, in, through her ship, licking at her body. The animal part of her screams this is wrong, she's making an incredible mistake.

And then it's over.

She's soaring, the sensation of flying in atmosphere subtly different but fascinating, the wispy white clouds she avoids even though she knows intellectually they're harmless. The vast greens and blues and glittering cities growing into focus as she narrows in on her coordinates on the northern continent. Beyond the cities gilding New Manila's southern coast, towards enormous diamond mountains that jut above lush emerald foliage, to where a landing strip has been cut out of the jungle.

She lands smooth, the shuttle's AI autopilot guiding her calculations of gravity and atmospheric resistance, and she's almost giddy as she comes to a shuddering stop. What an exhilarating way to make an entrance.

Lasadi sits in silence a moment with her heart beating in her throat before she realizes that giddiness has shifted to fear and she's stalling. She's here. She's come all this way, and there's no going back. Might as well get it over with.

She unclips her harness and stands, unsteady in the heavier gravity and still wincing at the residual ache in her ribs even after a week's worth of treatments. She opens the door before she can stall any longer, inviting in a wave of heat and humidity. The aroma of the jungle is incredible — verdant and rotten and clean and fertile all at once. The cacophony of birds fills her ears; something chatters high above her.

It's utterly alien.

She takes a step onto grass like a carpet, feeling fertile soil give beneath her boots. Sweat is already beginning to trickle down between her shoulder blades.

And she freezes.

Faces appear in the shrubbery, streaked with paint, bodies wrapped in camouflage, weapons at the ready. Her hand pauses at her sidearm.

"Lasadi Cazinho?" An older woman steps forward. She's dressed neat in military fatigues, black hair in a series of braids coiled into a bun at the nape of her neck, dark skin dewy with the heat of the jungle. "I'm Commander

Vasavada of the New Manila Liberation Front. Thank you for coming, comrade."

"You're welcome." Lasadi takes Vasavada's hand; it's warm. Strong. But still Lasadi is searching the group; Henri had told her he'd meet her at the landing site, but she can't make him out among the camouflaged figures.

Something rustles behind Vasavada, footsteps, and Lasadi's heart catches in her throat in hope. The beginnings of a grin die on her lips. She steps back from Vasavada and reaches for her sidearm, but a circle of guns come up around her, freezing her in place.

The man behind Vasavada gives her a dashing smile, amusement glinting in his pale blue eyes. Eyes she used to believe could see all the way to her soul; maybe they still can.

"Hello, Lasadi," says Anton. "It's good to see you again."

The adventure continues in the next book, *Blood River Blues*.

Want more of Raj and Lasadi's story? Don't miss the free Nanshe Chronicles prequel novella, *Artemis City Shuffle*.

Head to jessiekwak.com/nanshe for more.

AUTHOR'S NOTE

When I wrote the very first book set in the Durga System, *Starfall*, I had no idea the adventure I was about to set out on.

I didn't know how much readers were going to resonate with the main character, Starla Dusai — and I had no idea how much I would eventually become intrigued by the story of her parents, the notorious Raj and Lasadi.

I was worried when I began writing the Nanshe Chronicles. I'd spent years living with the characters and stories in my last series, the Bulari Saga, and meeting the crew of the *Nanshe* was odd at first. Lasadi doesn't trust that easily. Jay doesn't give up many secrets. Raj and Ruby seem like open books on the surface, but then you find out they're only showing you select pages. And Alex is still figuring himself out — let alone learning how to share himself with others.

Slowly, I began to find my way into this first book. Then the second. Then the third. Eventually, the crew started to open up to me, and I started to realize they were something special.

As I write this, I've finished the first three books in the series, along with a prequel novella (*Artemis City Shuffle*), and I feel like I know this crew pretty damn well. I sincerely hope you enjoyed this first taste of life aboard the *Nanshe*. I have a long series planned, exploring the farthest corners of the Durga System with plenty of wild adventures along the way.

A huge, huge thank you to everyone who's been reading

my books since *Starfall*. Writing can be lonely and uncertain, and every email, every text, every review, every kind word you sent has helped keep me going. Tina, Harold, Jesse, Nathanael, Tara, John, Trina, Simone, Colline, Mark, Cylia, Kate, Anja, Rita, and plenty more I'm missing — you've all been amazing.

And if you're just dipping your toe into my worlds for the first time, welcome! Thank you so much for giving *Ghost Pirate Gambit* a shot. There's plenty more in my library for to you read if you're looking for more adventure.

Thank you to the various writing Slack groups who've had my back through this process — Writer's Avalon, the Smart Fiends, the PDX Writer's Water Cooler chat. Every writer needs a safe place to melt down, and you were always there for me.

Thank you thank you thank you to my family! I'm blessed that my biggest cheerleaders are my grandma, my parents, and my sister. You guys are amazing.

Massive thanks to Kyra Freestar for her editing work and for keeping all the details of the Durga System straight for years. My hat's off to you, friend — and I apologize for not keeping better notes on my own damn world.

And, of course, the book you're holding would be one hot mess were it not for the patient and loving Machete of Critique wielded by my husband Robert Kittilson. Love you, babe. Thanks for being my first reader, my number one fan, and the biggest source of both welcome stability and chaotic adventure in my life. This writing thing would be so much harder to do without you.

See you all on the next adventure,

Jessie

Portland, OR
May 2022

ABOUT JESSIE KWAK

Jessie Kwak has always lived in imaginary lands, from Arrakis and Ankh-Morpork to Earthsea, Tatooine, and now Portland, Oregon. As a writer, she sends readers on their own journeys to immersive worlds filled with fascinating characters, gunfights, explosions, and dinner parties.

When she's not raving about her latest favorite sci-fi series to her friends, she can be found sewing, mountain biking, or out exploring new worlds both at home and abroad.

(Author photo by Robert Kittilson.)

Connect with me:
www.jessiekwak.com
jessie@jessiekwak.com

facebook.com/JessieKwak

twitter.com/jkwak

instagram.com/kwakjessie

THE BULARI SAGA

With stakes this high, humanity doesn't need a hero. They need someone who can win.

Complete 5-book series + 3 prequel novellas + bonus short stories = over 500,000 words of adventure.

Willem Jaantzen didn't ask to be a hero. He just wants to keep his family safe in the shifting sands of Bulari's underground — and to get the city's upper crust to acknowledge just how far he's come since his days as an orphaned street kid. With his businesses thriving and his dark past swept into the annals of history, it looks like he has everything he could ever ask for. Until, that is, his oldest rival turns up murdered and the blame — and champagne — begins to flow.

It turns out Thala Coeur died as she lived: sowing chaos. And when a mysterious package bearing her call sign shows up on Jaantzen's doorstep, he and his family are quickly swallowed up in a web of lies, betrayals, and interplanetary politics. It'll only take one stray spark to start another civil war in the underworld, and Jaantzen's going to have to pull out every play from his notorious past if he wants to keep his city from going up in flames.

Jaantzen never wanted to be a hero, but that might just be a good thing. Because a hero could never stop the trouble that's heading humanity's way.

The Bulari Saga is a five-book series featuring gunfights, dinner parties, explosions, motorcycle chases, underworld intrigue, and a fiercely plucky found family who have each other's backs at every step. Perfect for fans of The Expanse, Firefly, and The Godfather.

Start the adventure today at www.jessiekwak.com/bulari-saga

DID YOU LIKE THE BOOK?

As a reader, I rely on book recommendations to help me pick what to read next.

As a writer, book recommendations are the most powerful way for me to get the word out to new readers.

If you liked this book, please leave a review on the platform of your choice — or tell a friend! It's the easiest way to help authors you enjoy keep producing great work.

Cheers!

Jessie

CPSIA information can be obtained
at www.ICGtesting.com
Printed in the USA
BVHW071434010422
632670BV00002B/8